Nighthawk: THE DEACON

BY

C. Edgar North

NIGHTHAWK: THE DEACON

Nighthawk: The Deacon is the third sequel to *Nighthawk Crossing* by C. Edgar North (ISBN 9681626756632)

Special thanks to Ryan Hiebert for editing.
Cover design by Bookbaby

ISBN 978-1-54397-493-5
Contact: cedgarnorth@gmail.com

Forward

Dear Reader,

The format of *Nighthawk: The Deacon* is a series of short stories – recollections of the life and some of the antics of *Brian West, a.k.a. The Deacon*, who is active in my previous books *Nighthawk Crossing, Nighthawk: African Ice, and Nighthawk: Chief Hazel.* Many readers have commented that his espionage background would be worth exploring.

Of course, Brian is purely a fictitious character! However, some of the events mentioned did occur but names and events have been altered for fictionalization.

I selected this short story format in deference to the large number of my readers who seek audio editions and may appreciate a series of shorter stories (see Amazon.com, Amazon.ca, Amazon.uk, Audible.ca, Audiobooks.com, iTunes etc. for the audio books).

I hope you enjoy *Nighthawk: The Deacon.*

C. Edgar North

cedgarnorth@gmail.com

Chapter 1

CIA Headquarters, Langley

Sanford Crosley picked up the phone on the second ring while noting the caller ID. It was Shirley Bains, station head, CIA Bellingham, Washington. "Shirley, how're you doing?

"Just fine, Sanford. It's another dull, soggy day out here."

"Better than the cold here. I'd love to be in the Caribbean on vacation. In fact, that's where we're headed in a week or so. What's up?"

"Well, I just got a call from Bob LeMay. You know, our guy stationed in the British Columbia Interior?"

"Hot Pants! The guy you've got keeping close to the local crime guys."

"Right! He just called to say the Deacon passed away last night."

Sanford sat back in his chair. "Brian West? The Deacon? Our Deacon? Let's see, he was getting up there, into his early eighties, wasn't he?"

"Yeah. He just turned eighty-three a month ago."

"How'd he die?"

"Not sure yet. I've gone ahead and asked Bob to find out – to get a peek at the coroner's report and snoop around a bit. However, it looks like natural causes. He died overnight at his home, in bed with one of his disciples."

"Someone younger than him, no doubt." Sanford snickered.

"Yeah, a woman by the name of Joyce Ross. She's a widow in her late sixties – a former high school principal."

"Well endowed?"

"Of course! You know Brian. She's worth quite a bit." Sanford laughed and Shirley smiled at her double entendre.

Sanford sighed. "Yeah, I know Brian. He started with the agency way before my time but we crossed paths quite often."

"Did you run him when he was underground in Canada?" asked Shirley.

"No, that was before my time. But I worked now and again with Richard Duggan, who was one of the Canadians who ran him way back then. Rich is long retired now and living in Victoria, B.C. He wound up managing Brian toward the end of the Cold War. He told me a few stories about some of his escapades and I found some of it in his HR file with us – our Brian was a bit of a legend, even before we recruited him."

"How long was he underground?"

"I don't know if 'underground' is the right description. Yes, he was our man. But then, the Canadians adopted him and considered him theirs, too. They had him undercover as a diplomatic courier. He served in that role for at least twenty-five years – until the Cold War finally ended."

Shirley, a little curious, said, "He was a double agent? Recruited into the Canadian espionage service – yet also CIA?"

Sanford hesitated a bit, trying to decide how much to say. "Yes, you could say he was a double agent, but in a friendly way. We had a lot of cooperation with our Canadian friends during the Cold War. At some high level, they knew his pedigree and approved it. His Canadian passport came in handy for us from time to time. He was in on a lot of operations that were mutually beneficial. In fact, one of the intelligence departments up in Canada still has him on their part-time payroll."

Shirley stifled a snicker. "As do we. He never passes…correction, I should say he never passed any info on without getting some consideration."

"That was our boy! He'd work for you but was always out to feather his own nest. That got him into trouble more than once."

Shirley pressed. "There's a rumor that he went rogue. That he had some mafia and drug connections."

"Ah, you know our business! We deal with the devil if it's convenient. Yeah, he stepped over the line the odd time trying to line his pockets. However criminal, he was never duplicitous as far as country loyalty – he never traded in our secrets. But he got into some weird stuff, especially when he was furloughed at the end of the Cold War."

"You've got me curious."

"Yeah. Well, I'll pass this on to the HR department once you verify he's dead. I presume you asked Bob to make sure no diaries or such turn up? Nearly everything he did for us on the wild side was so long ago anyway but you never know. Someone may have a long memory and an axe to grind, or he could have penned his memoirs to pass on to his family. I'll check with the Canadians to ensure we don't trip over each other and that they aren't worried about anything surfacing. Anyway, with the Canadians, the department he worked for full-time was disbanded a long time ago. Whatever, get Bob to make sure the Deacon is quietly laid to rest."

"Got ya! I'll call back when Bob reports."

A day later, Shirley called Sanford. "Bob saw the body and assures me he died from a heart attack. Brian had open heart surgery for clogged arteries about twenty years ago, so he was a candidate for it. They did a routine autopsy because he died at home. The coroner is certain it was heart disease behind the death, maybe helped along by sexual exertion as they found Viagra and amyl nitrate in his system, and open packages of it on his nightstand. His lady friend says he died during a sexual episode."

"So, straight forward then?"

"Yeah. Nice way for an eighty-three year old to die, I guess. Bob interviewed the woman he was with, this Joyce Ross. She was understandably upset. Apparently she's organizing a memorial service with the help of some of the members his congregation. He's going to be cremated and his ashes spread in a nature preserve that he helped establish."

Sanford had Brian's personnel dossier in front of him on the computer screen. "I looked up his file. Three kids by three wives at last count. None of the marriages lasted very long, though. The kids tended to grow up without the full-time presence of a dad. Our shrinks labeled him a strong psychopath/sociopath. The wives probably discovered that and bailed out. Of the three kids, two passed away and the third is a drug addict living on the streets in Victoria. He has a brother and a couple of sisters still alive in Ontario."

"Bob managed to sneak into Brian's house late last night," Shirley added. "Everything looks as if Brian lived modestly, even down to a six-year-old Ford Taurus in the carport. He was collecting a pension from his time in the Canadian civil service, plus one from us, and had a modest bank account at a local credit union. Bob tossed the house but found nothing unusual except a bank book and a safety deposit box key for a bank in the Channel Islands. The bank account is very substantial."

"How substantial?"

"To the tune of seven hundred fifty thousand U.S. dollars."

Sanford whistled. "That's our Brian! And he has a safety deposit box there as well. Probably stuffed with gold and diamonds and, hopefully, not secrets. I trust Bob put everything back when he tossed the house?"

"Yeah, he also copied all the computer and phone files. He's sent them on to us for analysis. Apparently, Brian left a Will to be read just before the memorial service. Bob didn't find any diaries or such."

"Good. Good! Tell Bob to keep close to this until well after the heirs get their settlements. Make sure no incriminating history surfaces. Tell him to get a peek at the Will."

Shirley was a little miffed by Sanford's attempt to micro-manage and responded curtly. "Already done."

Sanford caught her emotion and moved to sooth. "Sorry, I know you have it all under control. W ith that bank account, this could get interesting. I'll talk with the Canadians and fill you in on what they've got and what they're thinking."

After being redirected from his counterpart in the Canadian Security Intelligence Service (CSIS) in Ottawa, Sanford contacted Marc DuPont at the Canadian Defense Security Agency (CDSA). DuPont acknowledged that Brian West's HR file came under his domain. "As you probably know," Marc explained, "long before CSIS we had quite a few intelligence agencies, or departments, whatever you wish to call them. We even had the Royal Canadian Mounted Police – the RCMP – heavily involved with an FBI-style thing looking for communists in every closet. We had one agency operating directly out of the Prime Minister's Office – the PMO – that handled the diplomatic level Cold War stuff internationally, usually in partnership with our NATO Alliance countries. Brian worked out of the PMO on the Latin and Romance Languages desk because he was fluent in French, Italian,

Spanish, German and Russian – quite a guy. Anyway, when the Cold war wound down and the RCMP got over their heads on a few things, there was a shake-up and CSIS was born. Some of the agencies were consolidated into CSIS. Brian didn't go over to CSIS, he took retirement yet remained on reserve. The old files wound up being handed over to Military Intelligence and there they rest. We've got the files, handle pensions and keep track of the veterans."

"Were you in touch with Brian West?" asked Sanford.

"Yeah, sometimes our veterans come in handy for periodic part-time assignments with us and the other agencies. I see in his file that he was involved in that archery weapon and that we called on him to send us intel from the Okanagan region once you guys started to take an interest. I see that was a joint operation with you."

Sanford was slightly surprised that Marc DuPont was so well informed. "Our man in the region was a little miffed that Brian was better briefed than he was," he told the Canadian. "But I understand that Brian was close to the guy who developed the archery weapon."

"That's right. They were close buddies. Brian was the one who turned him into an informer for us. He also helped get the weapon adopted by our Special Forces, way back when it was just a prototype."

"Well done!" Sanford paused for a moment, then said, "Brian was always out to feather his own nest. I bet he drew some funds from you for that project."

"Yeah, quite the talker – a strong sociopath. He kept us in the loop."

"That's our Brian!" said Sanford. "Last time we paid him was when that Indian Chief's daughter was kidnapped. He brought us into the loop on that one."

"Ah, the North Korean episode!" Marc said. "Yeah, that was fairly successful. You guys, our CSIS, the RCMP, ICE and the FBI all seemed to coordinate well on that one – and the South Koreans too, I see."

Sanford, a little surprised Marc was so willing to share, remarked, "You're going to lay this file to rest – I mean, now that he's dead?"

"Yeah, that's why I can talk to you about it. I'm about to send the file to our archives but we still have a flag on it. I'm holding it until we agree he's really dead and agency secrets are buried with him."

"You've confirmed his death?" asked Sanford.

"Yeah, but we're keeping an eye on his assets and heirs just to make sure nothing embarrassing surfaces. MI5 is also in the loop. They're poking around Guernsey in the Channel Islands looking at Brian's bank account and searching for safety deposit boxes."

"We'll keep in touch."

"You'll share?"

"As long as it's mutually advantageous to do so. You know the drill."

Chapter 2

Key Largo, Florida

The forty-four foot cruiser rode gently at anchor, tucked behind a barrier reef about thirty miles southwest of Key Largo. They had just finished anchoring and now the men had assembled on the after deck for happy hour. As they settled in on the comfortable lounge seats under the protection of an awning for the hot midafternoon sun, Pete reached into the ice chest and tossed cold beers to everyone.

Sanford was the youngest one there. Pete Reddekop, Richard Duggan, Bill Mason and Syd Richards were all in their mid-seventies or eighties.

Pete raised his beer as a salute. "Well gentlemen, here's to a beautiful day!" All clinked their bottles and said cheers before tucking into the drinks.

"Pete, it was a great idea to get together!" Sanford remarked. "What a perfect setting. I love your boat!"

"The boat gives me something to busy myself with in retirement, "a smiling Pete said. "I'm glad you looked me up when you called to say you were coming down here for some sun and fun. When you mentioned Brian's passing, I thought it would be great to get ahold of Richard, Bill and Syd since they're all snowbirds down here for the winter. We can have a little private wake for Brian since we all handled him at one time or another."

Richard raised his beer in a mock salute. "Here's to Brian whatshisname."

"That's right!" Bill said. "Brian West wasn't his real name, was it?"

Pete chipped in. "You're right! Sanford, you said you reviewed his personnel dossier before coming down here. What was his original name and where did he come from?"

Sanford smiled and took a sip. "Brian Steinson. He came from Canada."

Bill took a sip. "Ah, the Canadian connection! What part of Canada?"

"Eastern Ontario. He's the fourth son of a large religious family. His dad had a thousand acres of good farmland and was a church deacon. The area was predominately the same religion. His mom was French Canadian and his dad had German roots."

"I guess that explains how he was so fluent in Romance languages," Richard chipped in.

"Yeah, he grew up assimilating three languages. He was very bright as well. When he came to us, he tested out with an IQ over 140. They also determined he was a strong psychopath/sociopath. We also got a glimpse of that when we dug into his background during our recruitment process. The dad, a deacon in the church as I've mentioned, was heavily involved as treasurer of the congregation. The church was prosperous, owning a lot of properties and even financing business ventures for their members. Much of the church's wealth grew from inheritances – bequests – from its members, and his dad got Brian involved."

Pete, reaching for another beer, asked, "What do you mean?"

"It was routine for the dad to coddle the elderly and those in need of some form of assistance. Visiting, helping out, taking an interest and collecting tithes. He got Brian involved in that at an early age. The loyalty they built to the church often paid off in significant bequests."

"I remember him telling me a story of an elderly widow giving him a car, a three-year-old Cadillac, Richard said. "His dad was upset because it was too pretentious. It was green, big, and had huge tailfins. I remember laughing about it when he was telling the story. The widow claimed it had been her husband's car and she couldn't drive – that it was a graduation present for Brian to take to university. His dad forbade him to ever show up back home with it."

Richard smiled and chuckled. "I remember him once telling me he got his basic sex education from the widows of the congregation."

Sanford laughed, then continued. "He got basketball and academic scholarships to the church's main university in the States. They're big on languages and students doing missionary semesters to other countries. He fit right in. He was very personable. He had a unique ability to absorb languages and completed his bachelor's degree fluent in Italian, Portuguese, Russian and Spanish as well as German, English and French."

Bill reached for another beer. "Quite a guy!"

"And a psychopath to boot!" Syd remarked.

Sanford threw his empty beer bottle in the garbage bucket and reached for another. "Yeah, it proved to be a great combination for the church. He was really successful as a missionary. There's a story that in France he converted three future Catholic priests, seminarians, to his religion and arranged for them to train for leadership in the church. Apparently he convinced them to forsake celibacy for marriage and children."

That generated great laughter, and Sanford went on. "Our people verified that story. He was a golden boy in the eyes of the church elders for that coup. He was destined to go far in the church hierarchy. Brian got a Master's degree in

Sociology and started on a PhD in religious studies. That's when he got caught up in the movement against the Vietnam War and came to our attention."

Richard looked at his near empty beer bottle. "The CIA recruited him there?"

"Eventually. One of his professors was heading up an underground railroad running draft dodgers from wealthy families to Canada. Brian served as one of the guides. He got over two hundred successfully across the border and settled mainly in the Salmon Arm, Okanagan and Nelson regions of British Columbia. I guess he fell in love with the area since he settled there in retirement. Anyway, he loved the excitement and never had a problem getting his people across the border. The professor brought him to our attention and helped us recruit him. He dropped out of school and wound up in our intensive training program, where he excelled."

Richard asked, "So how did us Canadians wind up recruiting him?"

"Put it in perspective. Remember, the Cold War was in full swing and we had close working relationships with the major countries on our side – such as the NATO members, and especially Canada. Besides, he was born in Canada and had Canadian citizenship. You had your own intelligence services, and most partnered with us. He was a perfect fit."

"And he was a mole for you?"

"Yes, but apparently senior levels in both our governments approved. We considered him to be on loan to the Canadians. He was never to be placed in situations that tested his loyalty. We also borrowed him from time to time."

That comment drew some raised eyebrows and head shaking from the others.

Sanford went on. "His language skills, high intelligence and strong sociopathic tendencies made him extremely valuable. In the Cold War era Canada had an intelligence department operating out of the Prime Minister's Office – the PMO – supposedly involved in diplomatic level stuff. Brian was assigned to it in the Romance languages section which covered Europe, Central and South America. He was given the cover of a diplomatic courier. It worked well. He proved ingenious at penetrating the so-called Iron Curtain and extracting defectors."

Pete spoke for himself and the others. "Most of that was before our time. We overlapped only toward the end of the Cold War. He already had plenty of experience when I was assigned to run him. When I had him, although he was well experienced and valuable, we feared he was starting to feather his own nest."

Sanford added, "The file mentions he got wet a number of times and psych assessments indicated he had no remorse about killing if appropriate."

Chapter 3

COMING OF AGE

Key Largo, Florida

"You said he got his sex education from the widows in the congregation?" Sanford asked Richard.

"He once told me a couple of stories about it," said Richard with a laugh.

Pete took a sip of his beer and snickered. "I guess part of a deacon's job description is to keep everybody in the congregation happy."

Richard laughed again. "Right! A deacon's duty is to look after the physical – as opposed to spiritual – welfare of the congregation. He got good at it. His dad, who was one of the deacons tending to the welfare of the flock, kept him busy doing chores and minor repairs for many of the congregation. Apparently, there was more than one widow who played cougar to him."

Pete snickered again. "What a way to learn about sex!"

Millie, 1961

On a beautiful late summer day, Sam, Brian's dad, drove him over to the Brawn Farm. "Mrs. Brawn – Millie – is still grieving," Sam said. It's been three months now since her husband Lorne passed on from that massive heart attack. It's a shame as he was so young. You know, Millie's only thirty six and he was only forty five. I know at this phase of grieving, she's pretty lonely since her daughter Amy, her only child, went off to university in Kingston and the rest of her family is down in Toronto. She sees a lot of Lorne's parents and his brother and sisters, but they're all pretty busy with their own farms and harvest right now. We're trying to get her out and about and active in more of the church-related social activities and that seems to be helping.

"She's still young and attractive. I can see her getting married again sometime in the future once she gets over the grief. I told Millie you'd be pleased to wash her windows and tidy up the yard."

"No problem Dad. I hope she made some cookies again."

"Good. Take some time and talk with her. She can do with some company. Call me when you're ready to come home."

Millie was waiting on the front porch swing when they drove up. She was wearing a short-sleeved blue blouse, dark blue skirt and sandals. She had a medium build with blue eyes and freckles highlighted with bright white teeth and shoulder-length auburn hair. Brian got a whiff of fresh soap as if she had just bathed.

After a bit of small talk, Brian's dad departed. Millie turned to Brian and smiled. "I've got the window washing stuff in the kitchen. You'll find a stepladder in the barn. Can I get you anything to eat? I made some cookies."

"I love your cookies! Thank you, but not right now. I'd like to do the windows first."

It didn't take too long to do the windows and Millie invited him in for cookies and milk. As they sat at the kitchen table, Millie peppered Brian with questions about his schooling and learned that he was doing very well in grade eleven with plans to attend the church's university in Idaho. She commented on how much he had filled out and grown in the past year as he was now six feet tall and quite muscular.

Eventually, the conversation eased over to Millie, who began to open up about the transition into widowhood and the shock, the loneliness, the sad and happy memories. Brian was an empathetic and encouraging listener.

Eventually, Millie blurted out. "Brian, do you know what I miss very much?"

Brian took a bite of a cookie and shook his head. "No, what?"

She took a peppermint from the bowl on the table and offered him one too. "I don't know if you're old enough to understand this but it's a natural physical and emotional thing. I'm still young and have strong sexual urges that are hard to satisfy. I need relief as the pressure builds. It's unbearable at times."

Brian was taken aback and confused. His parents hadn't discussed sex with him and it was not covered at school. His very limited knowledge came from conversations and jokes in the boys' locker rooms and he was pretty sure none of his friends had yet "connected". He didn't know what to say when Millie asked, "Brian, have you ever had sex with a woman?"

Brian blushed beet red. He couldn't get words out. He just shook his head and looked at the table.

She asked, "Are you starting to get sexual urges yet?"

"Uh, what do you mean?"

"Well, do you have uncontrollable erections and maybe wet dreams?"

Brian blushed some more, looked down at the table, thought a moment and nodded again.

She reached over and gently lifted his face then looked him in the eyes. "Sex is a very natural thing and you need to get relief when the pressure builds but you also have to learn to give satisfaction and not just take. My husband was good at giving and sharing pleasure and I miss it very much."

Brian didn't know what to say. He was shaking a bit as he looked into her eyes. She reached across the table again and held his hands in hers. "You're old enough. Would you like me to show you how?" She squeezed his hands and he nodded. She led him into the bedroom where the blinds were drawn and a soft light was on the bedside table. She turned into him and kissed him on the lips and held the kiss as he began to kiss back. He could taste her peppermint.

She rubbed her pelvis into him and could feel his hard manhood. Then she undid his belt, fly button and zipper before pulling his pants down. She kissed him again, transitioning into a French kiss this time. "Kissing is part of foreplay along with rubbing and massaging," she said as they came up breath "Foreplay is important to build the sexual pressure. Are you feeling it?"

Shaking, tingling, Brian took a deep breath and could only nod.

"Here, your turn," she said while turning her back to him "Undress me, then kiss me."

He fumbled at first but eventually got her blouse and bra removed, and quickly took off her skirt and panties too. She then turned into him, rubbing her pelvis on his manhood. "I know you're excited. You'll probably come in seconds but don't worry."

Gasping, he came on the spot, soaking her pelvis.

"That's OK. My, that was a lot! And you're so hard too! Did you feel the relief? We'll be able to do better when you recover. OK? Come and lie down. I'll clean us up and we can do some gentle foreplay. I like massages and I'm sure you will too. Then I'll show you how to give me relief."

They spent the rest of the day in bed, where Millie brought him to life a few more times and managed to climax repeatedly herself. They had a good discussion about various positions, the feelings of relief, building to relief and mutual arousal.

"Variety is important as it helps stimulation," she explained "We both respond in a variety of ways and sex should be fun with a lot of variety in both the build-up and the act, rather than looking at it as a boring obligation. I'd love to show you some more. For example, gentling kissing the nape of my neck stimulates me. Why don't you try it?"

Brian followed directions and she began to respond.

"That's good! It's fun to gently build the stimulation. As well, you should always take pride in bringing your partner to climax. Remember, both of us must get satisfaction."

He eventually called his dad to pick him up and told him he had to return the next day after church as Millie had more for him to do.

Next day, as the congregation was exiting the church service, Brian overhead the minister, George Wyman, in conversation with his dad. "Standing in the pulpit, I couldn't help notice Millie there in the fifth row of pews. She certainly seemed happier than the last time I saw her. Perhaps she's coming out of her grieving."

"Brian's been helping her out with some of the household maintenance." Sam said. "He mentioned she seemed to be feeling a little better."

Chapter 4

Rita

A couple of months later, the Canadian winter had a firm grip on the farm belt. The day was sunny but cold with over three feet of snow on the ground after the previous day's blizzard. Church had just let out and Brian was standing outside the entrance with his mom and dad visiting with a few worshipers. Millie and another woman, Rita Downey, joined them.

Rita Downey was a new widow, having lost her husband, Ben, two months previously. Although she was bundled up for the cold, Brian noted she was reasonably proportioned – at least not overweight –- and had a pretty face. Brian's dad asked her how she was coping on her farm with the recent snowfall and she replied she had no problem plowing the road with the tractor, but was worried about too much snow on the carport roof as she was afraid to climb a ladder.

Millie suggested perhaps Brian could help and Brian's dad arranged to deliver him to Rita's farm in the afternoon. As they were walking to the parking lot, Millie took Brian aside. "Brian, Rita needs you as I have needed you."

Brian, a little embarrassed that Millie had told someone about their experiences, nodded and said, "OK."

Rita Downey may have been fifteen years older than Millie, but her sex drive was intense. After Brian had cleared the snow off the carport roof, Rita invited him in for hot chocolate and cookies. She was dressed in a fluffy-fringed red nightgown and matching slippers. When she sat at the kitchen table she opened the front of the nightgown, revealing a scanty red see-through nightie with black trim. Brian almost choked on his cookie when she revealed herself.

After some light conversation about the weather and Brian's plans for university, Rita shifted the conversation to her loneliness and reached for Brian's free hand and squeezed. "Millie said you have learned to satisfy a woman."

Brian didn't know what to say and simply squeezed Rita's hand in response.

She put two hands on his. "I haven't been satisfied since Ben got sick – and that was months ago. Oh, Brian, I hope you understand the immense physical pressure I've built up."

Brian gulped, "I think so."

Holding one of his hands, she stood and led him into her semi-darkened bedroom. They stood in front of the bed kissing long and deeply, then Rita put a hand on Brian's manhood and squeezed lightly. "Oh, that's hard!" she remarked while reaching for his belt. It wasn't long before she had helped him out of his clothes and led him to the bed. "I'm sure I can give you some satisfaction too!"

After the first go-round, while nuzzling Brian's neck, Rita said, "Let's take a shower together!"

Brian, not sure what to say, mumbled, "I've never done that."

"Yet! Come on, it can be lots of fun soaping each other down – especially rubbing and soaping."

Chapter 5

A few weeks later, Brian was at Millie's place repairing some fences. When he finished and came into the kitchen for cookies, Millie introduced him to her sister, Maggie Jefferies, who was visiting from Montreal. Maggie was a touch older than Millie but in good shape. Brian noticed she had a very firm, manly grip when they shook hands. Millie mentioned that Maggie was a registered Shiatsu massage therapist. Curious, Brian started asking Maggie a bunch of questions about the massage therapy business.

He learned Maggie had spent some time in the military as a physical therapist and had been fortunate to be posted to a hospital in Japan during the Korean War. She became intrigued with oriental massage styles as a way to help in her therapy programs. After taking classes in Japanese Shiatsu massage techniques, she was rewarded by receiving her instructor certification.

Flattered that Brian was so curious, Maggie volunteered to demonstrate some of the finer points of massage such as how to identify muscle tension and how to relieve it.

At Millie's urging, she reviewed erogenous spots and massage techniques for stimulation. Brian was enthralled to be used as a model as this was a whole new realm to him. He could see why Millie said she liked gentle massage for sexual stimulation.

He became an avid student. Maggie was impressed by his keen interest in massage and sent him some textbooks on Shiatsu which he secretly kept at Millie's place since he didn't want his dad to learn about it. Millie was a willing subject for practice and he often phoned Maggie to pepper her with questions.

Maggie took up advanced reflexology – foot massage – and soon Brian began studying it. It led him to a deep curiosity about the relationship between mind and body.

Millie couldn't keep a secret very well and word soon got around to other local widows, making him ever more popular. He found that massage was excellent foreplay.

Chapter 6

The Cadillac

During his final high school year, Brian wound up helping June Waters, a widow in her early sixties who had lost her husband Bill six months previously. Bill had been a successful farmer and had left June well provided for in both the value of the farm and a significant life insurance policy. June decided to sell the farm and move to Toronto to be closer to her two children, one a physician and the other a dentist.

Over hot chocolate and cookies one afternoon after Brian had completed repairing a clogged drain, June told him she had decided to move to Toronto. "The farm is too much work for me and I'm isolated here since I don't know how to drive. I miss my children and want to be close to them now that I have three grandchildren. I feel as if I can help them more by being nearby and being a babysitter when needed."

Brian, sipping on his hot chocolate, murmured, "I can see that. It makes good sense."

June put her hand on his arm. "You're so understanding!"

Not knowing what to say, Brian just smiled.

She squeezed his arm. "Do you think you can give me a rub? I've got a lot of tension in my right shoulder."

Brian brightened. "Sure! Sitting up here or lying down?"

"Oh Brian, it's so much better lying down."

After they were through, Brian called his dad for a ride home. "Brian, how are your driving lessons coming?" asked June.

"Oh, Dad's taking me to the driving exam next week."

"Have you been practicing much?"

"Well, Dad takes me out every day. I even drove twenty miles on the highway the other day. He'll let me drive home from here."

"Oh, that's good! Maybe when you get your license, would you mind taking me shopping? I'm pretty isolated out here and dependent on my friends and neighbors. You can drive Bill's car. It's been sitting in the carport ever since he got sick. It needs a good run and a wash."

"Sure, no problem. I'll come over and wash it for you tomorrow, after church if you'd like."

"Lovely!"

Next day, Sam delivered him to June's farm. Bill's car was only three years old, a green four-door Cadillac, huge and impressive with enormous tailfins, brushed aluminum roof and green leather upholstery. While Brian prepared to wash the car, June told his dad that the car hadn't been run for many months.

"My guess would be that the battery's dead. It may need a jump start," said Sam.

June fetched the keys and Sam tried to start it. No go.

"Brian, here's another lesson for you," Sam said "Let's get this thing started. I've got jumper cables in my trunk."

Once they had it running, June turned to Sam and asked, "Would it be OK if Brian drove me places from time to time after he gets his license? I don't drive."

"Sure, no problem. I'm sure he can use the practice."

Brian was sitting at June's kitchen table sipping an iced tea when June told him she had sold the farm. Closing would be in a month and she would be moving to a home she bought near her kids in Toronto's mid-upper scale Yonge and Eglington district. After excitedly describing the home, she said, "Brian, I'm in the middle of everything in Toronto. There's a subway station a block away so I can get around easily. Traffic is very congested on the streets so it's far better to use the subway. I can have groceries delivered or even take a taxi or the bus when I need to. As well, I've got the kids to help me get around."

"That sounds perfect for you!" commented Brian.

"I'm going to miss you though."

"Well, I'm going to be leaving for university in a couple of weeks anyway." He squeezed her hand. "But, I'm going to miss you too!"

"Oh, Brian, how nice!"

She put a hand on his forearm. "I've got some pressure building. Do you think you can help me?"

He smiled and put his drink down. "Sure!"

She led him into the bedroom.

A week later, June called Sam and arranged to meet with him and Brian to discuss a business matter. When they arrived, June had cookies and iced tea waiting at the kitchen table. Once they were seated and finished some small talk about the weather and crop predictions, June got to the point. "Sam, I've known you all your life and I've known Brian since he was born. You've been like family to me, always helping out when needed. And Sam, you and Bea were always there for me when Bill got sick.

"Brian's been a great help not only with the chores but also cheering me up – breaking me out of feeling sorry for myself. Now, I'm moving on to Toronto to be close to my kids and grandkids and, in another way, to be less isolated. It's hard living out in the country away from everything and not being able to drive."

"I can see that. I think you've made a wise decision," Sam replied "It will be nice to be closer to the kids in the big city. But, we'll miss you."

"And I'll miss you and my church family but I'll be joining the congregation the kids belong to now."

"Good! Good!"

"Sam, we've already settled the matter of the sale of this farm. At your request, it's going to a nice young couple sponsored by the church. And because of that, I've agreed to carry the mortgage at a favorable rate of interest."

Sam spoke gently. "Yes. And I thank you for that."

"However, before I sign the final papers, I want you to agree to one more thing."

"What's that, June?"

"I want you to agree to me giving Bill's Cadillac to Brian."

Surprised, Brian sat back in his chair. He didn't see it coming.

As Sam took a moment to organize his thoughts, June continued. "Brian's going off to university next week. He could use a reliable car. You know I can't drive and besides that car is a huge beast – far too big for the streets of Toronto. And, I doubt if I could get much trying to sell it. It's in great shape with hardly any mileage. I want Brian to have it."

Sam continued to think for a moment, then took a sip of his drink. After a deep sigh, he finally spoke while looking June in the eyes. "June, dear, how can I say no?"

June brightened. "Oh, good! Thank you Sam. Can you pick up some transfer papers?"

In the car on the way home from June's, Brian said, "Thanks, Dad."

"I don't like it but I had really no choice," Sam said "June's carrying the paper on the mortgage for the farm. She has me over a barrel."

"Yeah, I saw that."

"Anyway, it's a mixed blessing for you. It's a pig on gas but it's in great shape and it's so big you've got some protection if you get into an accident. It's a good highway car. You'll have fun trying to park it though."

Brian thought that over. "I guess."

"As far as I'm concerned. It's far too pretentious for a son of mine to be driving. You can take it to university but I don't want to see you flaunting it around here. Understand?"

"Yessir!"

Key Largo, Florida

Sanford finished his beer and stood up. "This Millie, what became of her?"

"Millie eventually found another man and married again," Richard said. "However, word got around among the congregation's widows and a number of them helped enrich Brian's sex education. They also ensured he got lots of care packages while away at university. I gather some of them even sent money."

Chapter 7

UNDERGROUND RAILWAY

Key Largo, Florida

Sanford stood up and stretched while admiring the sea view, then, settled into a deck chair and put his feet up on a cleat. "Does anyone know the story of his involvement in an underground railway sneaking Vietnam draft dodgers into Canada?" he asked his old colleagues. "Some of it's in his file."

"I just heard he was very successful at it," Pete said.

Bill snickered and took a swig of his beer. "Well, the church had it very well-organized on both sides of the border and the Canadians tended to turn a blind eye. The numbers were huge – something like forty thousand dodgers moved by the church alone. Brian was just a small clog in the machinery – one of many so-called 'enablers.'"

"But he thrived on it!" Sanford said.

Bill laughed, "Oh yeah!"

University of Christ, Boise, Idaho 1969

Brian knocked on Professor Bob Nash's door and entered when Bob called. "Come in! It's not locked."

Taking a puff on his pipe, Bob Nash looked up from his desk when Brian entered. Although quite fit on a five foot ten inch, two hundred pound frame, Bob was a stereotypically bearded, shaggy brown haired professor, about forty five years old. He was dressed in blue jeans and a western long sleeved shirt. His blue tweed sports jacket, complete with leather elbow patches that completed his ensemble, hung on the coat rack. Bob pointed with the tip of his pipe to a chair occupied by a stack of term papers. The office was cluttered with stacks of student papers, research notes and pages for proofing a text book he had nearly completed, which were propped up next to shelves overflowing with books. “Move that stuff and have a seat. What’s up?”

“Thanks.” Brian took a moment to find a place to put the papers before speaking. “I really enjoyed our seminar discussion today on the immorality of the war in Vietnam. I agree that the U.S. government is wasting a lot of good youth as cannon fodder for a questionable cause. I don’t want to see the lives of good people wasted. I’d like to get involved in trying to stop the war – or at least spare some lives.”

“Brian, I’m pleased to hear that!”

“I was thinking though, because I’m Canadian, I could get kicked out of the country for participating in protests on campus or in town.”

Bob looked at his pipe, noticed it wasn’t lit and reached for a wooden match from the cardboard match box beside his ashtray. As he was lighting his pipe, puffing to get it burning well, he finally spoke. “You’ve got a point. There’s always someone willing to get rid of dissenters and throwing you out of America to make a very visible example could be embarrassing for the university.”

“Sir, I’ve heard you’re involved in moving draft dodgers to Canada.”

Bob puffed on his pipe before answering. “Where did you hear that?”

“Some of the students around here noticed some of their friends are now residing in Canada. They were told our Church and members of this university are involved.”

Bob frowned and puffed on his pipe. “You heard that, huh?”

"After I heard that, I talked with my dad. You know he's a deacon in the church up in Ontario, Canada?"

"Yeah, you've mentioned."

"Dad's been involved in bringing American draft dodgers into his region of Canada as part of the church's policies. He's helping organize host families, getting students enrolled and even changing or fudging identities when appropriate."

Bob puffed some more. "Interesting."

"I think my being a Canadian could come in handy helping students to cross the border. I'd like to get involved."

Bob puffed on his pipe for a moment before speaking. "I think we can do that."

Chapter 8

Nelson, British Columbia

Brian eased the bus into a designated parking spot beside the university's gym where a slim, mature woman in corduroy slacks, winter snow boots and a colorful, heavy wool parka bearing a university crest stood waiting with a clip board. It was cold, mid-winter and dark at six o'clock. Her breath was making steam. Brian set the air brakes, opened the main door and the woman clambered aboard.

She smiled at Brian and pulled the hood of her parka back, revealing long bottle blond hair and a pretty face highlighted with dimples.

"Hi Brian, welcome back!" she said before turning toward the sea of faces seated in the bus. "Hi folks, welcome to Nelson in mid-winter," she said with another big smile. Not much different from Boise, Idaho, is it?"

That drew cheers and assorted comments. When it settled down, she continued. "Welcome to your University of Christ, Nelson, British Columbia campus. And, welcome to Canada and real freedom!"

That was met with louder cheers. When it died down, she continued. "We have arranged host families for all of you. They're waiting inside. I'm Maggie Gallant and I'm your coordinator.

"Before we go into the gym, I'll be handing around a contact card for me. Everyone take one and keep it handy. Call me if you have any problems."

She continued. "For those who are planning to remain here, you've already picked out your courses and we've already registered you. For that, you're set to go. Your registration and orientation package will be handed to you once we get inside. If you want to make changes after you've sampled your classes, you have ten days to do so and I will be your contact for that. Understand?"

Brian whispered to Maggie. "Do you want to remind them about fitting in?"

She nodded and spoke quietly. "Good point – always worth reinforcing."

"Guys and gals," shouted Maggie, "I want to remind you to make every effort to fit in now that you are here. Avoid bragging about America. That goes for everyone."

That elicited some laughter. "For those of you here for the duration, be careful to use Canadian spelling. And remember that your identity as a student has you listed as a resident in Canada at the address of your host family. Do not claim you are American citizens unless specifically asked. Under most circumstances, such as applying for a valid driver's license, bank account or credit card, we have arranged that the address of the host family will be sufficient."

As the last of the students disembarked, Maggie turned to Brian. "Great to see you again! Did you have any problems?"

Brian smiled and looked deep into Maggie's eyes. "Not at all! I crossed at the Ferry/Midway border crossing. After I explained we had a men's basketball team and a women's volleyball team aboard to challenge the Nelson U. teams, the Immigration Officer just checked student IDs. That took less than ten minutes."

"What about your return trip?"

"Our people determined there isn't too much communication between the border crossing points – especially when you only have to go through Canadian Immigration and Customs coming north and only American Immigration and

Customs going south. So far, as long as I use a different crossing point each way – like the Eastport/Kingsgate crossing on the way back – I can keep things confused. Sometimes, like this trip, I take the bus back empty the next day and claim we have to get the bus back in service, even though the team will be visiting for a week long tournament. And as you know, sometimes I take a few Canadian students down to play against Idaho just to boost the numbers for the return trip to Canada. When we do that, the American kids each get a false Canadian ID.

"Whatever works," said Maggie.

"Yeah. Anyway, I've done this enough times that I think the Canadians often turn a blind eye."

"Maybe! I know we have a lot of church members who are customs and immigration officers."

Brian smiled. "Every little bit helps."

Maggie took Brian's arm and looked in his eyes. "How about dinner at Roxanne's, then you can bed down at my place? It's prime rib night at Roxanne's and I'd love a massage and some excitement."

Brian smiled gave her a hug and kissed her left cheek. "I'll plug in the bus engine block heater and get my hand bag."

Chapter 9

Brian made it back to Boise without incident. When he walked into Bob Nash's office, Bob was on the phone and motioned to Brian to find a seat. When he hung up, he turned to Brian. "I gather everything went well?"

Smiling, Brian responded. "No problems. I even got them all singing the Canadian anthem on the way up."

Bob laughed, then turned serious. "I was just on the phone with a very rich and influential parent pleading for help for his son."

"Oh?"

"Yeah, seems there's a priority warrant out for the son's arrest for dodging the draft. On top of that, the kid's high-profile. He's been leading a number of anti-war rallies and getting his face in the news."

Brian nodded. "So the authorities want to make an example of him."

"Looks that way."

"Can we do something to help?" asked Brian.

Bob picked up his pipe from the ashtray and sat back in his chair. He reached across the desk for his tobacco pouch and began stuffing the pipe bowl. Eventually, he spoke. "He's too high profile to take across with a group. The border people will have been alerted – on both sides of the border. I'll bet they'll have a wanted poster with his photo on it. On top of that, I've learned the American Border Patrol will be running intercept roadblocks stopping traffic approaching the border."

Brian thought for a moment, then asked, "What does the dad want?"

"He's offered a substantial donation to the college building fund plus expenses if we can get him safely exiled in Canada."

"Did you agree to that?"

Bob was quiet until he got his pipe lit. "Yeah, now we've got to figure out a way. We've got no problem finding a host family but I don't think he should enroll under his own name at Nelson U."

"What about that couple over in Salmon Arm we met last month? The ones with the large cattle ranch."

"The Keatings?"

"Yeah! Remember their deacon saying they lost a son a few years back and would love to host a student? Didn't they say their son would have been draft eligible if he was still alive and they were in America?"

Bob pointed his pipe stem at Brian. "You're thinking to switch identities?"

"Yes! It's too late to register him in the local college for this semester but I'm sure they could always do with a farm hand. Besides, quietly living on the ranch for a few months until things cool down wouldn't likely draw much attention." Brian thought for a moment. "Even with a change of identity, it could be risky at the border crossings."

Bob smiled. "There are some things I haven't told you yet. We have special routes for situations like this. Leave that to me. How about you contacting this kid? Whisk him off to our research farm and prep him for a change of identity. In the meantime, I'll go up to Salmon Arm and meet the Keatings to arrange things."

Brian smiled. "You want the whole works?"

Bob smiled. "Yeah, turn him into a clean cut kid so his hippie friends – even his parents – won't recognize him. Just don't give him a military haircut. Prep him as if he was going on a church mission, white shirt and all. And don't forget Canadian branded clothing to go with the makeover."

"What's this kid's name?"

"Tim Scarlett. The dad's William Scarlett – he's big in farm machinery." Bob wrote something on a piece of paper and handed it to Brian. "Here's the dad's name, address and phone number. He's got Tim squirreled away in their ski cabin up at Tamarack and he'll bring him to you when you're ready."

Chapter 10

The night was clear, cold and crisp with no moon. Brian had checked the weather forecast which indicated a dry, clear trend for the next forty eight hours. The university's agriculture research station was on a large tract of farmland to the north of Boise. The buildings for the station were clustered on a knoll about a half mile in from the entrance gate on a ploughed and sanded road.

The guard at the gate house had alerted Brian, who was waiting at the window in the living room of the station's guest quarters when he saw the Jeep pull up. He greeted Tim and Will at the door, showed them inside and told them where to hang up their winter jackets and dry their boots. He offered hot chocolate from a thermos on the coffee table which was readily accepted. After a little small talk about the drive from Tamarack and the weather forecast (clear for 48 hours then more snow), they settled in some easy chairs and Brian got down to business. "So Tim, the feds are after you."

Tim smiled. "You can say that again! I've really been in their face organizing and leading protests. I refuse to show up for induction. I even burned my draft notice."

A frowning Will Scarlett chimed in. "Right in front of the TV cameras. He made the national news on three networks."

Brian took a moment to look at Tim. *Typical student hippie* was his first thought, as Tim's brown hair was long, shaggy and flowing down over his shoulders. He kept it out of his eyes with a large headband sporting the peace symbol. He was wearing a peace symbol medallion hung loosely around his neck on a leather thong. Tim's shirt was loose, rough cotton with no collar and a Mexican/Navajo pattern. His scruffy, faded blue jeans were held up with a brown leather belt with a peace symbol on the cast metal buckle. Brian also noticed he was not wearing a watch.

"So, you're too hot for comfort," Brian said. "What do you think of moving to Canada?"

Will looked at Tim and nodded, motioning him to answer. Tim smiled. "I've been up there skiing and once on a summer holiday. There's not much difference to our own weather. People have always been nice."

Brian laughed. "That's one way to look at it. Another is that they're not engaged in a stupid war and they do not have conscription."

Tim nodded. "Can you get me set up there?"

Brian nodded. "We can but you've got to play your part to pull it off. I took a look at your student records. I note you haven't been doing too well."

Tim looked at his feet, embarrassed. "Well, I got pretty wound up in the protest movement. I haven't been attending too many classes."

Brian went on. "It's a little late to register for this semester at our sister University in Nelson, B.C. or at the college in Salmon Arm. Besides, you'd be lucky to be admitted under probation if they let you in at all. On top of that, your high profile as a protest leader will probably attract some attention both here in Idaho and in Canada. We can't afford that because we have a lot of people successfully residing in Canada – quietly residing. You get my point?"

"Hiding out."

Brian grimaced. "Let's just say quietly residing. Most are using their own names but have local Canadian addresses. You, you're something different. You've got the law after you big time – even wanted posters up with your face on them. To be successful, we've got to change your identity – and I mean completely. Understand?"

Tim shook his head and his dad said, "I don't think I fully understand either. What do you mean?"

Brian leaned forward. "First, a cosmetic makeover. Sorry Tim, but the 'hippie'" look will have to be replaced with what I'd call a 'clean-cut' choirboy look. You'll have to get rid of the peace symbols – at least for a while. 'Clean-cut' means a haircut of course, along with a change of clothing and some coaching on how best to behave."

"Hair cut?" said Tim, looking more than a little concerned.

Brian nodded. "Just for now, until you are successfully across the border and entrenched with your host family. Then, you should go along with what the host family accepts or encourages. You've got to fit in. You've got to be accepted by the host family as part of the family."

"I can understand that," Tim replied.

Brian looked him in the eyes and nodded. "OK, now as I mentioned, you'll be away from college life – at least for a while."

Brian turned to Will. "I understand you're in farm equipment? Do you have a farm as well?"

"Yeah. I've got a thousand acres of potatoes and keep a few quarter horses for showing."

Brian looked at Tim and asked, "Do you help out around the farm?"

"Sure! I do some of the plowing, help at harvest and help muck out the stables – that is, when I'm home."

"Would you mind working and living on a cattle ranch?"

Tim smiled. "No problem with me. I love horses and cattle."

"That's what we have in mind. There's a family – members of our church – up in Salmon Arm, British Columbia that's willing to take you in. They have a large cattle ranch."

Will chimed in. "We know the area. A few summers ago, we spent a couple of weeks there on a houseboat on Shuswap Lake. Nice area!"

"Well, this family lost a son a few years ago. If he was alive, he'd be your age. They're willing to give you his identity and get you established there. They say you can either have his old bedroom or bed down in the bunk house. They say you can work with them as a ranch hand until things calm down. What do you think?"

Tim looked at his Dad, who nodded. "Sounds good."

"How can I help?" asked Will.

Brian smiled. "Thanks. You can bankroll the identity change – new clothes, Canadian identity papers, transportation costs, some spending money, etc. We're looking at about ten thousand dollars in expenses."

"No problem. Let's just get it done and done quickly."

Tim laughed. "Great! Oh, by the way, who am I going to be?"

"Jim Keating – James Alan Keating."

Brian turned to Will. "Once he's established, you can visit. I'm sure you'll like the host family."

Will said, "Great!"

Brian looked at Tim. "I've got a barber standing by so we'll get started on the physical modifications now. We should have you out of here on your way north in a few hours. After your hair cut and a change of clothes, I want to take a Polaroid for ID photos. I've got that set up in the next room. We've got some of the original Jim Keating's identification documents – birth certificate, social insurance card, school ID and such. He never had a passport, so we've got to have something with your picture on it in case we get stopped. For that, we'll make up student ID for the University in Nelson, but consider it temporary."

Tim reflected for a moment before replying. "Jim sounds close to Tim, so that's a help."

"How are you going to get him across the border?" asked Will.

"We'll let you know once he's safely in Canada. Right now, just in case you get questioned by the authorities, it's best you know nothing."

The wall phone rang and Brian got up, answering it on the fourth ring. He listened for a moment and thanked the caller before hanging up. He returned to his seat and spoke to Will. "We've got sentries on the roads around here. That was the guy coordinating them. He says it doesn't look as if you were followed. It's probably best for you to bed down here for the night – at least until Tim is moved. You can park your jeep in the first barn to get it out of sight. We don't want to take any chances of you getting apprehended. Does anyone know you're here?"

Will shook his head. "No. As instructed, I didn't tell my wife or anyone else where I was bringing Tim, or that I was going to pick him up."

"Good! Good!" Brian heard a car pull up. "Ah, that's likely the barber and the guy with the documents. We can get started."

Chapter 11

Just before first light, Brian drove the car into a parking spot beside the open, lighted hangar. Tim, carrying his duffle bag, followed Brian into the hangar. They stopped beside a small single-engine aircraft where a man was busy checking the plane's exterior. Tim was surprised. "I didn't know we're going to fly there!"

Brian smiled and looked at Tim. "It's one of the many tricks we have up our sleeve. Grab your bag and let's meet your pilot."

Brian moved toward the man at the aircraft and said, "Dan, hi! I'd like you to meet your passenger." He turned toward Tim. "Tim, this is Dan Mussalem. He's not only a bush pilot with thousands of hours flying time, he's also a fine flight instructor. You're in good hands."

In his bulky winter clothing, including a fur cap, Dan resembled a bear. He was a big man, in his forties with a weathered face and large, strong hands. He shook hands with Tim, saying, "Hey man! I've just got a few more things to check, then we'll be on our way. You can stuff your bag under the back seat. It folds up."

As Brian and Tim shook hands, Brian said, "Have a good trip. I'll drop in on you next time I'm up that way."

"What do you think of the aircraft?" asked Dan once they were airborne. "Did you like the takeoff?"

"Yeah, man! Nice and smooth."

Dan fiddled with the controls a bit, adjusting the trim before pushing a button and taking his hands off the steering yoke. He turned to Tim and smiled. "I've got it on autopilot. This baby's a real workhorse. It's a Cessna 180, only a year old. They call it a Sky Wagon but it's known as a tail dragger – that's a tail wheel for steering on land. It's got lots of power with easy STOL – that's Short Takeoff and Landing capabilities. It'll do one hundred seventy miles per hour max with a cruising speed of one hundred sixty-three. It's big enough for six adults or about a thousand pounds of cargo.

"We've got a range of one thousand and twenty-four miles at fifty-five percent throttle. And, you noticed we're ski equipped with wheels for land and skis for snow and ice. Tail draggers work best on skis – far better than tricycle gear with a nose wheel like the Cessna 172. A nose wheel with skis can get stuck in wet or unpacked snow. In this weather, we can land on lakes, roads and even fields.

"I've filed a flight plan to Deer Park airport just outside Spokane. It's about three hundred miles away and caters to small aircraft. We'll stop there for a pee break and breakfast. If anyone gets nosy here, I've simply gone to Spokane. There, I'll file a flight plan to Kamloops, BC but I'll route through Salmon Arm. It's roughly three hundred fifty miles. If I fly low between the mountains, there's no radar coverage in the Salmon Arm area so I can land to drop you off, then carry on to Kamloops where I deliver this plane to the customer and clear Canadian Customs and Immigration. Then I'm on my way home.

"Right now, the weather's good all the way – clear and crisp. By the way, you won't be listed as a passenger on the flight plan from Spokane."

"Where are you going to drop me off?" asked Tim.

"Right at the ranch. They've got a nice lake for landing this baby. They say the ice is three feet thick. I've been there before."

A few days later, Brian knocked, entered and took a seat across from Bob in his office. Bob smiled when he looked up. "Good news?"

"Yeah, I was just talking to Will Scarlett. He's one happy daddy. Tim called home yesterday and told his folks he's really excited about his placement. He introduced his parents over the phone to the Keatings, his host family, and both got along well. The Keatings took him to church and introduced him around as a distant cousin. Tim – now Jim – is happy as he's met a number of girls in the congregation. He's already got a driver's license and the Keatings have said he can drive one of their pickups. He's been given his own horse and loves riding it and working the cattle."

Bob nodded. "Mr. Scarlett dropped in with a check for all expenses, well over ten thousand, and he pledged a million to the university's building fund."

Chapter 12

SHEPARD

Key Largo, Florida

Richard looked at his beer and took a small sip. "I remember the first action he had when he was with me."

Bill said, "The one we relabeled Operation Shepard?"

"Well, you did," Richard replied. "It was our operation, a Canadian operation, and we called it something else. Brian impressed us and showed great initiative. He made it all look simple."

Moscow, USSR, 1975

After delivering his diplomatic pouch to the mail room supervisor, Brian made his way to the office of Peter Reddekop, the 3rd Secretary of Cultural Affairs. After accepting a glass of sweet tea and settling in a chair in front of Peter's desk, Brian stated, "I was told in Ottawa to report to you immediately upon my arrival."

Peter had a file folder on the desk in front of him and casually opened it while he responded. "That's right. We've got you in mind for a little project."

Brian, looking upside down at the opened file, noted a photo of a man on the top of the papers.

Peter continued. "We've got a Russian senior metallurgical engineer in the Ministry of Defense who wishes to defect. Your task will be to get him safely to London."

Brian kept a blank expression. "And how am I supposed to do that?"

"We'll get him to the Soviet-Finnish border. How we do that and who is involved you don't need to know. You're to help get him across and on to London."

Brian nodded. "Interesting. What have I got to work with?"

"For one thing, you have some diplomatic cover, plus a little help from the Finns and the Brits. On top of that, we have an excellent team that will get him to the border."

Brian asked, "I guess you've looked for the best border crossing spots?"

"Yeah, there're quite a few good choices. But that will be up to you in the end."

"The Finns are in on this?" Brian asked.

"Up to a point. They've helped before. They've got people in Border Security who'll turn a blind eye and not push things on their side. You know, for some consideration, and as long as they're assured the guy is just passing through and not planning to stay in Finland. You'll be paymaster and make all the arrangements. One of their officers will work with you to make the arrangements including transport. He's an old hand at this."

"Sounds simple enough."

Peter went on. "I've gotten you assigned to a series of diplomatic courier runs from Ottawa to Moscow, then on to Helsinki, Finland, London U.K. and back to Ottawa. That way, the Soviets will not likely trigger that you'll be going off the grid a bit. You'll overnight in Helsinki, then fly out to London the next morning. That'll leave plenty of time to pick up your man and get to the airport when the time comes and plenty of time to set things up overnight on your earlier trips."

"OK. When do I start?"

"Right now." Peter took an airline ticket out of the folder and slid it across the desk. "Here's a ticket to Helsinki.

You'll take the diplomatic bag to our embassy, where my counterpart will introduce you to the Finns and get you a tour of the possible transfer sites. For security reasons, there's no need to learn about the defector until the last minute. You should be on your way to London tomorrow."

"How many trips before the transfer?"

"Not for you to know yet. You know how fluid things can be."

"OK, but I have one request. I need a car and driver to take me to one of the black markets here to pick up some jars of caviar. I want to build up a stockpile in Finland. They're great for bribing."

"You've got it!"

Three weeks later, Brian walked back into Peter's office and handed a map over the desk. "All set on my end," Brian told him. "Here's a map and co-ordinates for three best crossing points. I've labeled them A, B, and C. I recommend point A."

Peter took a close look at the map before commenting. "All farmland? All fairly open? I thought you'd pick wooded areas."

"That's likely what the Soviets think. They have greater security in the wooded areas. You can see we're fairly close to a Finnish guard post as well."

"Interesting. I presume you have this well thought out and I should not want to know the details."

Brian smiled. "Correct! I also need authorization to draw down fifty thousand Finnish markka in small and medium used bills. I'll need that with me on the night of the transfer."

"I'll see to it right now. I presume you're ready to go anytime?"

"Anytime, the sooner the better. With this plan, we've got to do it now, before the weather gets cold."

"OK. Set your end up for next week then. I'll get things moving here."

Chapter 12

Finland

Brian was in a guard shack on the Finnish side of the border. He was introduced to the ten border guards present by Lars Holmgren, the superintendent of the guards for the sector. In Finnish, Lars was explaining their presence to the men. "We're going to have a little action here tonight." He gestured toward Brian. "This gentleman has no name as far as you're concerned. But he's a friend. He's here to pick up a Russian defector who will be crossing in your sector. You are not to apprehend the defector, nor are you to assist him. However, you are to be part of a diversion."

He moved over to the large, detailed map of the sector and pointed out an area. "This is open country. Farmland. The Soviets have cultivated it right up to the border fence, including the area between the fence and the dirt road running along their side of the border. We've done the same on our side."

He pointed to paths about thirty feet wide running along both sides of the fence. "You see our road. The farmer has an electric wire fence, a small one, running alongside. But, across the border, there is the Soviet dirt road and no fence on their field – probably because it's planted with wheat.

"Our Finnish farmer, for the past few weeks, has been grazing sheep in his field." He pointed. "Here."

Most heads nodded. They could see what was coming. One of the men beamed. "So, there's going to be a break in the fences and the sheep are going to wander across the border."

"Right! And you're going to sound the alarm. Eventually, that is. You'll advise your counterparts on the other side and help round up the sheep that have not crossed the border."

Another guard spoke up. "What about the sheep crossing the border? Do we demand the Soviets return them?"

Lars smiled. "Yes, but don't protest too much. No shooting. You know your counterparts will be delighted to take the sheep home for their families."

Lars gestured toward Brian. "This man has bought the whole flock of sheep from our farmer. If some don't make it across, you're welcome to keep them for yourselves." That elicited smiles all around. "But we'll make sure a lot get across. We want to create a round-up frenzy on the other side."

That generated some frowns. "Don't worry, our friend here has something special for each of you." He nodded again to Brian.

Brian had a packsack with him. He picked it up off the floor and placed it on a table with a noticeable "thunk". When all eyes were on the packsack, he spoke in Russian. "Gentlemen, I'm sorry I do not know too many words in Finnish but I am told you all are fluent in Russian." Everyone nodded assent.

"No need to know who I am or where I'm from but I come bearing gifts." He reached into an outside pocket on the packsack and pulled out a packet of Finnish markkas and flourished them in front of the men. "Some cash consideration for your participation – by the way, your government has approved this, so there's no worry about retribution."

All eyes were on the currency "A thousand markkas for each of you – when this is over, that is."

He handed the currency to Lars. "Until the job is done, Superintendent Lars is entrusted with the money. OK?" That got the men cautiously nodding agreement. Brian had also made a deal with Lars that he would receive twice that amount when Brian and the defector were safely boarding their flight to London.

He left some time for the thought to sink in before speaking again. "As a deposit on your sincere participation, I brought this along." He reached into the packsack and brought out ten quarter-kilo cans of Russian caviar. He could see and almost hear the jaws drop – a real luxury! And so much of it! That was worth a thousand Finnish markkas each alone! He handed them out and waited a moment for all to carefully examine the tins.

"There are over seventy sheep that will be loose," Brian explained "Please make sure at least two-thirds of them cross over the border." That drew laughs. "Seriously, we need everyone busy over there chasing sheep and we need to have their tracks confuse footprints."

One of the corporals spoke up. "How soon does this happen?"

Lars looked at his watch. "Now. The fences have already been breached. You should wander over in about half an hour, notice the breech and alert your counterparts. In the meantime, no need to send patrols in either direction for, say, half an hour. Our man will be crossing at the breech shortly, if not already. We're leaving now to pick him up. We should be gone by the time you get there. Oh, and don't shoot the farmer."

The action went like clockwork. The defector and his contact from Moscow rode an old farm truck filled with bales of hay to within a kilometer of the border. Stefan, the contact, said, "I'm afraid this is as far as we're allowed to go by vehicle." He pointed to a ditch. "Follow the ditches due west toward the border." They shook hands and embraced. "Good luck, my friend."

With a map and compass, the defector made his way in the cover of ditches, then crawled the last two hundred yards on his belly through the wheat field. He was aided by some sheep wearing bells grazing near the breach in the fence. He ran the last few yards across the dirt road and through the breech, not stopping until he made it to the cover of the ditch on the Finnish side where he ducked down and waited. A few minutes later, Lars drove up in a jeep with Brian in the front passenger seat. Lars had the jeep's headlights on as he wanted the Soviets to think they were just another Finnish patrol.

After a moment to confirm the defector's identity, they corralled more sheep into the breach to help cover footprints. Wasting no time, they picked up the man and drove off down a side road from the border toward town. Lars radioed the nearest guard shack to advise the Soviets of the sheep breaching the fence.

Lars dropped Brian and the defector off at the main gate of the Canadian embassy, saying he and his people would be shadowing them the next day on their way to the airport and until they were airborne.

Two of the embassy's security men escorted Brian and the defector to a windowless room in the basement where a photographer had set up a screen and a stool.

Brian, in Russian, turned to the defector and said, "Boris, we've got to make you look and act Canadian and we've only got a few hours to do so. We're going to change your appearance and identity, fit you out in new clothes etc."

Boris smiled, revealing some stainless steel teeth. "Thank you! I'll do whatever you want."

Brian closed his eyes and shook his head. "This is going to be a little harder than I thought. We're going to have to change the appearance of your teeth. You'll also have to avoid smiling, the caps on your teeth are a dead give-away."

Boris frowned. "A dentist? Will it hurt?"

"No, no. A makeup artist will change the color of your steel teeth – maybe use a prosthesis."

"Oh."

"First, after you shower we change your hair and get rid of your mustache. We have Canadian-made clothes and new identity papers for you. We'll photograph you for a passport and we'll have to rehearse the details of your new identity. The flight's in the morning. We'll be going First Class. In the meantime, we've got a lot of work to do. You can sleep on the plane. Have you ever worn contact lenses? We're going to change the color of your eyes."

An embassy car and driver took them to the airport where they checked in without incident. At the boarding call, Lars met them in the hallway leading to the aircraft, exchanging handshakes and hugs as Brian slipped him an envelope, Lars said, "Thank you Brian. Have a great flight. I've got you covered until the plane departs."

"Thank you, my friend."

They deplaned in London where an embassy car and driver took them to the Canadian Embassy High Commission. Brian's part in the operation was finished.

Next day, as he was picking up a diplomatic bag for Ottawa, he asked the 3rd Secretary, Nigel Holmes, what became of Boris. Nigel looked at the wall clock. "Right about now, he's an hour out of Langley Eustis Air Base on a U.S. Air Force transport. We turned him over to the Americans. They'll debrief him at some safe house near Langley then integrate him into American society."

Chapter 13

SKAVAL

Key Largo, Florida

Taking a sip of his beer, Richard said, "I remember the time he wound up deep in the Soviet Union…"

Sid jumped in. "You referring to the Kyrgyzstan project?"

"Yeah…"

Ottawa, Canada, 1979

Brian walked up to the reception desk for the diplomatic courier's office in the sub-basement of the Prime Minister's Office. He was greeted with a smile from Marie DeLaval, the rather plump and nearing retirement receptionist and gatekeeper. In French, she said, "Bon jour Brian! Richard's waiting for you in his office. Go on back."

He responded in French. "Merci, Marie. I love that blouse on you."

She blushed and mumbled a thank-you as he went past her desk. Brian passed a few offices until he reached Richard's, then knocked on the closed door and entered when Richard called.

After greetings, Richard motioned for Brian to sit in a comfortable chair facing him across the desk and took his seat opposite. He looked at Brian. "You're looking fit. Did you enjoy your vacation?"

"Thank you, yeah, took two weeks for scuba diving in the Florida Keys. It was great!"

"Good! Good! We need you fit for your next assignment."

"Uh huh, what've you got in mind?"

"You're to take a diplomatic bag to Moscow. Then, we want you to leg on a bit from there."

"Inside the Soviet?"

"Yeah, it'll give you a chance to use your Russian language skills."

Brian grimaced. "Oh boy! You want me to go deep into the Soviet?"

"You've got the idea. Most of the time you'll have diplomatic courier cover. But there's a little bit of off-the-cover work at the destination."

"So, the interesting part is at the destination? What's up?"

"You're to go deep into Soviet territory to a remote part of Kyrgyzstan to the Lake Issyk-Kul area.

"Issyk-Kul?"

"Yeah. I'll show you on a map later. As you know, the Soviet Cosmonaut program is based in Kazakhstan, which is on the plains next door to Kyrgyzstan.

"Kyrgyzstan is mountainous with the north side of the Himalayas bordering onto China and Tibet in the south and China's Tian Shan Mountains to the east. Anyway, there's a health spa up in the mountains near the city of Karakol where the Soviets take their cosmonauts when they return from space."

A little fidgety with the slow speed of the briefing, Brian said, "OK, so what am I to do?"

"You're going to the spa as a diplomatic courier. Reason for that is Canada has a joint space research program with the Soviets and we've got a medical team posted at the spa. One of our astronauts is on their space station and will soon be returning to earth after six months in orbit. You'll courier in documents and bring out reports, and such. You'll do this once a week for at least three months. "

"No problem with that," Brian replied. "So what's the add-on?"

"First, a little background. Lake Issyk-Kul is a huge deep lake, the tenth largest in the world. It's also a salt lake but doesn't have as much salinity as the major oceans."

Brian leaned forward in anticipation. "OK…?"

"It's home to the Dastan Engineering Works, which is a Soviet Navy torpedo factory and testing range for designing, building and perfecting torpedoes."

"Ah!"

"Western spy satellites have picked up tests of a new torpedo that's superfast. We think it's based on using air bubbles for cavitation and we're not sure how they power it. Anyway, our satellites have observed it reach speeds in excess of three hundred miles an hour."

"We want a closer look?"

"More than that, we want the blueprints."

"And, how are WE going to accomplish that?"

Smiling, Richard said, "WE, that's you, by the way, are going to pick them up from a disgruntled engineer who works on the project. You can bring the micro-fiche out in the diplomatic bag."

"This is getting interesting! Of course, it's not going to be simple. Richard, what's the rest of this?"

A smiling Richard countered. "I'm afraid you're getting to know me too well. In exchange for the blueprints, you've got to get the engineer out. He wants to come over to our side. He's been promised money along with a new identity and career, so you don't have to negotiate that. You just have to get him out."

"Has he been vetted? He's not a bait or counter spy?"

"He checks out. He has a German background – his father was one of the many Third Reich scientists captured by the Soviets. He has no children. His wife recently passed away and he has lots of relatives in West Germany, America and Canada. He wants a new life."

"Seems reasonable. But I can't take him out in a diplomatic bag."

"Nope! Nice thing is that the Chinese border and a checkpoint is only ninety-three miles away. It would be great if we could take him out there. Except it's been sealed since the Soviets and the Chinese broke off relations in 1969."

"So, this guy's out in the middle of nowhere, effectively in a sealed country surrounded by some of the highest mountains in the world thousands of miles from friendly territory," Brian said. "Even if we got to China, its hostile to the West and I bet they'd love to pick this guy's brains for their own military research." Brian stewed in thought for a moment. "Oh, and IF, just IF we managed to go west and south, we get to Afghanistan, a country which happens to have a war going on with Soviet occupation at the moment. Man, you picked a good one!"

Richard nodded. "You've got it!"

"So, I somehow get him out of the country then I come back under diplomatic cover?"

"Precisely. Let's go into the board room and I'll fill you in on some of the details. Then, you're off to the farm for a planning session and to get a little more fit."

Chapter 14

Canadian Embassy, Moscow

Brian was checked through security and escorted into the Canadian Embassy's mailroom where he was met by Simone Barchuck, a fifty-something stocky and chubby bottle blond serving as 3rd Secretary of Cultural Affairs. After Brian unlocked the diplomatic bag and left it with the mail room supervisor, Simone escorted him to her office on the third floor. He declined a glass of instant coffee and settled into a sofa opposite to Simone, who had taken an easy chair. After some pleasantries and catching up on the usual politics at home, she eased into the assignment. "I've been in the loop for this project from the start. There's been no problem getting you clearance and a flight to Frunze, Kyrgyzstan. But you'll be going overland the rest of the way to the space sanatorium just outside Karakol. It's almost 250 miles from the Frunze airport. That's a good day's drive but the roads are good and it's spring. There's a military airport near the torpedo factory but it's strictly off limits for you."

"We've hired a car and driver for you. No problem. But you can be sure the driver will be a KGB loyalist."

Brian passed that off. "That's normal."

"Yeah. You'll stay at the spa in quarters that have been set aside for our space health team. It's a bunch of cottages. There's no obvious security and the team has been free to let off a little steam in Karakol."

"Where do I meet the defecting scientist? What's his name? And what does he look like?"

"He and others from the torpedo factory tend to have a favorite bar in Karakol. That's where you'll meet.

Conveniently, that's where our space science team likes to hang out. I'll fill you in more a little later."

"Good. Good."

"When you're ready, you'll take in a change of identity and travel permits for the guy."

"OK, any ideas how I get him out?"

"That's your problem. You're a very creative person – or at least that's what I've been told. You'll have time to reconnoiter and plan." Simone looked him square in the eyes, holding his attention. "It's occurred to us he may be better off dead once we get what we want from him."

Brian, assessing her intensity, thought for a moment. "It would save some work, wouldn't it?"

"Consider it a last resort. We would rather have this person's brains and dedication to help follow-through on developing a similar weapon, and maybe future weapons, for our side. We'd look rather dimly on losing him – unless it was completely unavoidable."

Brian nodded. "I understand. What about the Canadian space medical team?"

"Good question. Most won't know anything about this operation, but there's a senior officer working with us who can't be compromised, of course. All members have been vetted for loyalty and they've all been given the usual lecture about not getting too close to their counterparts in case someone wants to recruit them. They all are fluent in Russian, though. Most are from our prairie provinces."

"Makes sense, lots of Russian-speaking Ukrainians on the prairies. If we can do it, I'd like to get the blueprints out first and then go back for the guy."

"Good idea!"

"What about contingency plans?"

"Let's look into that after you've made one or two trips in your courier role and had some time to reconnoiter."

Chapter 15

Frunze, Kyrgyzstan, 1979

It had been an overnight flight for Brian from Moscow to Frunze. He had learned flying with Aeroflot tended to be a bit nerve-wracking as the aircraft interior was Spartan and the flight attendants surly. The aircraft on the run was an Ilyushin Il-86, a four engine jet considered reliable but with old (1960s) technology jet engines. Brian had managed to get a few hours' sleep but was still groggy when he disembarked.

As Brian exited the terminal, he spotted a tall thin man holding up a sign with Brian's name on it spelled in Russian Cyrillic. He introduced himself as Ivan Rosanoff and said he would be Brian's driver. Ivan was about thirty five years old, a thin one hundred thirty pounds on a six foot frame. Brian noted his oval face, blue eyes and natural blond hair on a very small head. "Pinhead," Brian thought. They shook hands and Ivan led him to their vehicle, a rusty and mud-caked four-door Lada of dubious vintage. While Ivan was stowing Brian's luggage in the trunk, Brian remarked on the car in Russian. "A Lada. Is it reliable?"

Ivan smiled. "It doesn't ride any better than it looks. However, it's mechanically sound and easy to repair. It comes with a good tool kit. Our major problem is avoiding potholes. But I carry a spare tire and a couple of extra inner tubes."

Brian joined Ivan in the front seat. "Comrade, that's reassuring."

Ivan laughed.

Brian gagged as he closed the door. "God! What's that awful smell in here?"

A sheepish Ivan said, "I'm sorry comrade. I spilled a bottle of kumis. It's impossible to get rid of the smell unless I throw out the back seat and floor mats. I've tried washing and scrubbing but it hasn't worked. It'll fade eventually unless we have a hot day."

As Brian was rolling down his window, he said, "Kumis? What's kumis?"

"Fermented mare's milk. It's our national drink."

"No doubt an acquired taste."

"One grows up with it here. It also is claimed to have some medicinal properties. We'll be heading east. We've got a mountain pass before we reach Lake Issyk-Kul. We'll stop for lunch and refuel at Balykchy. It's a railhead on the west end of the lake. We've got over four hundred kilometers to go to get to Karakol. It's just fifteen kilometers from the south-east end of the lake."

Brian was impressed by the quality of the highway from Frunze, over a mountain pass and descending toward Lake Issyk-Kul. It was a wide road, four lanes of good pavement. On each side, it was lined with tall Elm trees. It seemed every twenty kilometers there was a distance marker with a unique piece of bronze art of various wildlife from eagles to deer in action poses. Ivan commented that the distance markers were a make-work project by the government to encourage artisans.

Brian also noticed marijuana growing wild alongside the road and remarked on it. Ivan said it was low-grade wild hemp.

The road was dotted with security check-points every one hundred kilometers, or so it seemed. Brian had both his diplomatic passport with him, as well as Soviet-provided travel orders, which were always quickly accepted. After a few checkpoints, Brian commented on this and Ivan laughed. "That's their job, yes, but they're more interested in making money by shaking down merchants trying to move goods – especially black market stuff."

After lunch, Brian was impressed when he saw the size of Lake Issyk-Kul and noted it was encircled by the Tian Shan mountain range. Ivan quickly turned into a tour guide. "Yes, it's over sixty kilometers wide and one hundred eighty long. Due to the mountains surrounding it, there is no surface outlet. It's salty but only point six percent salinity compared to the average three point five percent for seawater. The name Issyk-Kul means 'warm lake' in Kyrgyz."

"Does it ever freeze?"

"No."

They arrived at the front gate of the sanatorium, where a guard checked their credentials and directed them to a tree-lined road leading to a cul-de-sac street of cottages. The grounds seemed spacious and were well treed with tall grass. Off in the distance behind their cottage, Brian could see a large six-story building. Noticing Brian looking at it, Ivan said, "That's the main building, a combination hotel, hospital, laboratories and offices. Behind it there's an attached building housing a fifty-meter swimming pool, mineral tubs and therapeutic pools."

Feeling a bit hungry, Brian asked, "What about food? Where's the cafeteria?"

Ivan pointed. "Across the street. It's underground in the air raid shelter."

As they began to walk up the path to the cottage a woman came out. "You must be Brian West. Welcome! I'm Sonja Romakoff, Head of the Canada Space Medicine team."

Brian managed a mumbled response but was enamored with Sonja's beauty. She was a blonde, blue-eyed forty-something with short cut spiky hair, standing tall at five ten in flat shoes. Brian quickly noticed no wedding ring.

Ivan asked when he'd be needed next. "Tomorrow," Sonya replied before turning her attention to Brian. "We've got a guest room in my cottage here. You can have it. I gather you're turning around in the morning for a flight out tomorrow night? If we go out for dinner or to the pub in Karakol, we'll use my car and driver. There's a group of us heading for the pub tonight."

Ivan handed Brian his carry-on bag and departed, mentioning that there was a building for drivers and spa staff, and its phone number was in the cottage telephone directory.

Sonja led Brian into the cottage, closed the door, and silently circled her hand around the room and made a signal for silence. Brian caught on. The walls were bugged. She pointed to a door, saying, "Here, this is the guest bedroom. There's a washroom adjoining. After you freshen up, let's go for a walk around the grounds. They're quite lovely this time of the year and there are some nice walking paths. Later, if you feel up to it, we'll join some of our people for dinner and drinks at a pub in Karakol. We've got a favorite haunt there."

"Sure."

On the stroll, well away from the buildings, Sonja said, "It's safe to talk now. The people here are great – especially the Soviet space medicine people. However, we're out of here after our man returns from space and we've had some time to conduct our post flight analysis. That should be five months from now."

"So, who is this guy who wants to defect?"

"I met him at the pub. A lot of the engineers from the torpedo factory, you know, Dastan Engineering Works, hang out at the same pub we like. We're pretty friendly. He's a good dancer. He also speaks German and so do I. He's lonely after his wife died and I'm recently divorced. We became friends and he asked for help to get a new life. I reported this to our embassy in Moscow and they suggested that I encourage him. And here we are. We want to get engaged."

"What's his name?"

"Karl Schultz. As you were probably told, he's a mechanical engineer and a rocket propulsion physicist. He's one of the team that developed a high speed torpedo which flies through the water using bubbles channeled through the tip to minimize resistance. It basically creates an air pocket – he calls it a cavitation effect, like riding through air. He claims the torpedoes they're putting into production are capable of three hundred miles an hour. He also says they've been designing nuclear payloads for them. In fact, one section of Lake Issyk-Kul has been declared off limits because they had a nuclear spill.

"Wow! Serious stuff."

"Yeah. His team has been told they're ten to twenty years ahead of the West on this."

"This isn't going to be easy. We're right in the middle of the USSR, with no friendly neighbors. Tell me, are any others from your team aware of this?"

"Well everyone is in on the romance part – they call it an affair as we all know we're here for a short time – but nobody knows that he wants to defect."

"What about his comrades? Do they suspect anything?"

"The romance part, yes, but nothing else."

"Are you sure?"

"No. They're a suspicious lot. This whole region is a strategic area for weapons production and research. Because of that, travel is highly restricted with permits required even for relatively short distances and everyone is monitored."

"Things are getting more complicated."

"I've been told that you, of all people, can figure out a way."

Brian laughed. “First, let’s meet your Karl Schultz.”

Sonja looked at her watch. “Let’s head back to the cottage. My car and driver will be here in half an hour. I want to freshen up before we go into town. It’s Friday night and our people have the weekend free, so probably everyone will show up. The torpedo factory also takes the same weekends, so we’ll meet a lot of their personnel. I hope you like to dance.”

“I do! How’s the food?”

“Far better than the cafeteria here. The owner has good roots in the local markets including the black one, so pretty good choices. The band is very good, lots of danceable music.”

Chapter 16

Sonja's car and driver arrived promptly at six-thirty. "My driver is Sasha Yomtoff," Sonja said on the way to car. "He says he's originally from Leningrad. I'm sure he's KGB assigned to keep an eye on us."

"That's normal."

"Yeah. We live with it. He's a nice guy with a wife and a couple of kids. We follow the Soviet custom that everyone's equal so he becomes part of our entourage, dining, drinking and dancing with us. He'll join us at our table so be careful what you say and do."

"How's his capacity for alcohol?"

"Better than mine. But I still worry about him driving me home after a party. Lucky there's not much traffic on the roads and it's not a great distance. Sometimes, I've driven us home."

"So, how will I get to meet with Karl Schultz?"

"Everyone's friendly. He and some of his friends are part of our social set now that we've been here so long. We'll probably wind up sharing a table with a mix from the space med center and the torpedo factory plus some others. Anyway, Sasha's a good dancer too and I'll pull him onto the dance floor from time to time, as will some of the other women – to give you a chance to talk with Karl."

Brian wasn't surprised to find his driver, Ivan, sitting in the front seat with Sasha. He said Sasha had invited him along as he had the night off. Brian patted him on the shoulder and said, "Great! Welcome comrade, your first drinks are on me."

Sonja introduced Brian to Sasha and they exchanged comrade greetings. On the way to the restaurant, Brian was able to get Sasha to talk about himself and his family and quickly determined Sasha's accent was indeed from Leningrad.

The restaurant turned out to be in a single-story building on a side street in the outskirts of Karakol. Upon entering, Brian noted the restaurant/pub/nightclub was larger than it looked from the outside, with a spacious dance floor and stage where a seven-piece band was setting up. There were many assorted sized tables scattered around the perimeter of the room, some in bench style that could accommodate twenty to thirty people. One of the large bench tables had two men and a woman seated who waved for Brian and Sonja to join them. Sonja introduced them as Steve Lind and Marjorie Smith, part of the Canadian space med team, and Lars, their driver. Brian introduced Ivan.

After introductions and seating, Lars joined a woman at another table. Sasha and Ivan took seats at the table that were closest to the dance floor and away from the others, "We got here early to get a good table," Steve said to Brian while motioning to the waitress. "What are you drinking?"

"Beer for me." With a wink, he looked at Steve. "I'm buying for the drivers and I'll buy this round for us."

Steve smiled. "Gotcha!"

Brian ordered a pitcher of beer and a bottle of good quality vodka for the drivers, who were very appreciative.

The table soon filled with more members of the Canadian space med team, Soviet space medicine staff and others. Karl Schultz arrived with two friends from the engineering works and Sonja did the introductions. Karl had sandy blonde hair, blue eyes and a rugged face. He was about six feet tall, slim but muscular and about one hundred eighty pounds, Brian guessed. Sonja had told him earlier that he was fifty-six years old.

Karl recommended the barbequed lamb on skewers – "shashlik" – as it was a local favorite. Casual conversation over dinner established Karl was an outdoors man who liked hiking in the mountains, cross-country skiing and sailing. He belonged to clubs for each, and was on the directorship of the torpedo factory's sailing club, which boasted a fleet of a hundred sailboats of various racing classes including some larger boats equipped for long distance travel and camping. He mentioned he loved single-handed sailing and had won a number of trophies.

Brian kept an eye on the drivers, ensuring their drinks were quickly refilled and making sure they weren't spilling anything or pretending to consume. Well into the evening Sonja pulled Sasha onto the dance floor and Marjorie coaxed Ivan up to dance. Seizing the opportunity, Brian headed to the restroom. A few moments later, Karl joined him at the next urinal. He spoke quietly in German. "You can help?"

"Yes, but I need a token of your sincerity. I'll be back next week." He zipped up and quickly left. Karl stayed for a few moments before returning to the table. By that point of the evening, the drivers were well intoxicated. They took turns toasting their marvelous host who kept them in food and drink.

The evening ended at midnight with Brian and Sonja helping the drivers to the car. Sonja managed to convince Sasha to let her drive. He took the front passenger seat and quickly passed out. Brian helped Ivan into the back seat and got in as Sonja started the car. He said, "You've done this before!"

"Oh, yeah! No problem. We'll drop them and the car off at the drivers' dorm and walk to my place. This has become routine."

Ivan quickly fell asleep.

Chapter 17

Karakol Bazar

On the way back to Frunze in the morning, Brian asked Ivan to take a slight detour so that he could buy some caviar in the Karakol Bazar. "No problem," Ivan responded. "I can help you find the best."

The bazar seemed to be well organized, occupying about a square block of semi-permanent and permanent small structures built on a shallow hillside leading to a large building that Ivan said was the soccer stadium.

Ivan led Brian down a couple of inside aisles to a booth in what seemed to be the seafood and meat section and introduced him to the proprietor, a grizzled, tall, slim sixty-something man with black eyes and long gray hair in a braid . "This is Hozak, he keeps the best caviar out of sight under the table." With Ivan's help, Brian selected a high grade of caviar and bought six half-pound tins.

Back in the car, Brian asked, "Is Hozak a smuggler?"

"You know he's black market. Apparently, he's well connected with the local smugglers. He's got family in Kazakhstan and sources his caviar there."

"What about China? I saw a lot of goods from China in the bazar. I thought the border was closed."

"It is, but smuggling is well-organized. Guards are bribed. Most of the smugglers are Muslim of the Uyghur sect which overlaps into Western China next door – lots of family ties across the border. On top of that, there's discrimination both in China and here, which alienates them. Smuggling is a way of life – has been for centuries. It's also a way of life for people of Karakol to shop at the bazar as there's not much available in the government stores."

Chapter 18

Karakol, Kyrgyzstan, USSR

Brian returned a week later, once again being met at the Frunze airport by Ivan and driven to the recovery sanatorium near Karakol.

"Will you be going to the nightclub again this trip?" asked Ivan.

"Sure, you want to come along?"

"You bet!"

That evening at the club, Sonja and Brian were surrounded by familiar faces. Ivan and Sasha were once again included and Brian made a point of supplying them with drinks.

When both Sasha and Ivan were occupied on the dance floor, Karl made his way to the washroom and Brian followed a minute later. Karl slipped something into Brian's jacket side pocket and whispered, "You'll find I'm sincere. More next week."

When Brian got back to the cottage, he pulled the object out of his pocket. It was a small piece of 35mm film wrapped in tissue paper. He placed it in the diplomatic bag.

Upon departure, Brian asked Ivan to take him back to the bazar where, he once again purchased six tins of caviar and had a casual conversation with Hozak.

Back at the embassy in Moscow, Brian presented the negative to Simone Barchuck, who quickly handed it off to a technician to enlarge and print. She returned in twenty minutes with the print and they examined it.

"It's the head end of a torpedo." Simone said. "The heading says 'Final Production Version.'"

"I was told their new torpedo makes bubbles and flies through them to cut resistance," Brian said. "It's called cavitation. That's how they get their speed."

Looking closer, Simone asked, "What produces the bubbles? Compressed air? Gas? Rocket fuel? We've got part of the solution here. These nozzles are great, but we need more."

"Well, he's shown his sincerity."

"Yeah. I'll pass this on. In the meantime, have you come up with any ideas on how to extract this guy?"

"It's going to be tough. Karakol is certainly buried deep in the Soviet Union. You just can't walk across the border into China – and the Chinese aren't friendly to us either. The closest 'friendly'" area is Pakistan and that's over seven hundred miles away across the Tibetan mountains or through Afghanistan. Road, rail or hiking is out. There's no water route either."

"The original slide is on its way to Ottawa in tonight's diplomatic bag. You're to take a diplomatic bag to Ottawa tomorrow and discuss this with Richard when you get there. He says he's got someone who's willing to put a little thought into the problem."

Chapter 19

Ottawa

Brian was warmly greeted by Richard when he arrived at his office in Ottawa. "Great work, Brian! That fiche of the torpedo head got a lot of people excited."

"Good! Good! Simone and I were wondering what they use to provide the air bubbles."

"That will come. In the meantime, I've got a guy coming in to help brainstorm the extraction." A few minutes later, Marie Laval escorted a visitor to Richard's office. After a quick greeting, Richard introduced him. "Brian, this is Ron White from Langley. He specializes in covert extractions." Ron was an African-American in his mid-thirties, six feet and two hundred fifty non-flab pounds who looked as if he had been a pro football linebacker and even had a broken nose to hint at it.

After a handshake, Ron spoke. "I hear you've got quite a problem. Someone deep in the Soviet Union with no friendly neighbors."

"That's it." said Brian. "Way out by Lake Issyk-Kul close to Karakol."

"Since Richard called, we've been studying the area. Too bad the Chinese aren't friendly as you're only ninety or so miles from their border on a good mountain pass."

"I was told the crossing is sealed," Brian said. "No traffic at all allowed."

"But there's some smuggling, I gather."

"Yeah," said Brian. "You see that in the local bazar. Lots of consumer goods showing up."

"We've conducted intensive satellite recon and spotted some caravans – horses or pack mules crossing."

"Interesting!" said Richard. "But China's still hostile territory to us and the location is thousands of kilometers from the Chinese coast. It's no good for our needs."

"I agree," Ron said. "Shortest path is through Pakistan. At least we've got friendly relations there. Straight line is under six hundred miles but that's high altitude over the Himalayas and then into the Tian Shan mountains."

"You've explored other routes?" Richard asked.

"We could skirt along the mountains and contour run the foothills bordering Tibet and Afghanistan, then follow the old Silk Road in Kyrgyzstan's high mountain valleys to Karakol. There's guaranteed to be good radar surveillance by the Soviets along the Kyrgyz-China border. However, it's a possibility that detection can be evaded, especially if an aircraft stays low between mountains. Mind you, there's very little radar coverage in Afghanistan along its border with Tibet in the Himalayas. That's desolate territory, almost solid mountains."

"You know that for a fact?" asked Richard.

"Well, we've been tweaking the Soviet occupation of Afghanistan a bit by supplying the Taliban. We have some experience in the region. Plus our satellites have the technology to register ground-based and aircraft radar emissions."

"Would you have a suitable aircraft with the range to get to Karakol and back?" Brian asked.

"You need a craft capable of high-altitude STOL, low radar signature, terrain-hugging capabilities at night, and long range. Yeah, we've got something. I'll get my people to examine the satellite maps to select potential landing sites. I presume you want something close to Karakol, say near the sanatorium?"

"No, not too near the sanatorium. We can't compromise our people there."

"OK. Can you scout out some sites if we give you a few to choose from?"

"Can do."

Chapter 20

Karakol, Kyrgyzstan, USSR

On the next trip to Karakol, Brian asked Ivan if they could take an hour to do a little sightseeing. "I guess so," Ivan answered. "At least near Karakol there are a couple of sites tourists seem to like."

"Like what?" asked Brian.

"Well, the ski hill is very popular in the winter but it's closed now. It's about twenty km on the other side of town anyway."

"Someone said there was a waterfall and a pretty warm lake nearby."

"Oh, yeah! It's just before the sanatorium. Not very far. We can go there, if you want."

"Sure!"

When Ivan turned off the highway, they followed a good, wide paved road for about five miles before turning south into a box canyon with a poor gravel road beside a creek, which they followed for less than a kilometer before reaching the lake. It was a small but majestic lake with powder blue milky water closely surrounded by tall mountains. Immediately across from them, a waterfall well over a hundred meters high cascaded onto rocks at the base. They stopped and got out of the car to get a better view. "It's beautiful!" Brian exclaimed.

"The lake is glacial fed," said Ivan, playing the tourist guide. "That gives it the milky blue look." He pointed. "Over there's a hot springs feeding a few man-made pools. The water's very therapeutic. The hot springs seem to drain into the lake and it can be quite warm."

On their way back to the highway, Brian casually asked, "This road we're on, it's well maintained and quite wide. Does it lead anywhere?"

"Yeah, the Chinese border is only about sixty kilometers away but the crossing is closed. The road isn't used much right now except for people wanting to hike in the mountains and for supplying the soldiers manning the frontier."

"Oh, so there must be a mountain pass to China?"

"Yeah, the road winds through the valleys almost to the border before it becomes hilly up to the pass. It's a popular road for cycling clubs on weekends when the weather's good."

That evening, Brian, Sonja and crew returned to the nightclub. Again, Brian and Karl found the opportunity to meet in the restroom for a quick word.

"You're sincere," Brian said. "Thank you."

Karl whispered. "You'll get me out?"

"Yes, we're working on it. How about another installment of sincerity?"

"Like?"

"What is the propellant used to make the cavitation?"

"Oh, rocket fuel, of course. Same for propulsion. I suppose you'd like the formula?"

"Yes, that would be nice."

"Get me out then."

Prior to his departure for his flight back to Moscow the next morning, Brian walked with Sonja to the cafeteria for breakfast. "A delicate question," he asked, "but are you bedding Karl?"

"We're adults. We have needs."

"Here, at the cottage?"

"Sometimes. Sometimes at his apartment, other times at a hotel. He belongs to the sailing club at the factory, and sometimes we take a boat out for a picnic or an overnight campout."

"OK, if I bring you a letter for him, can you get him to read it here and then destroy the letter?"

"I can do that."

Chapter 21

Ottawa, Canada

Back in Ottawa, Brian was again in a meeting with Richard and Ron White. “Rocket fuel!” exclaimed Ron. “Interesting! Probably solid state stuff. And they’re using it for the main thrust as well? Interesting and simple!”

“As an inducement, he says he’ll bring the formula for the rocket fuel with him when he’s extracted.” Brian said,

“That would be valuable! All we have to do is get him out,” replied Ron.

Richard spoke up. “Yeah, Ron, I gather you’ve got things worked out from your end?”

“All set up. We’ve stationed two aircraft and their ground support in Islamabad. One is for backup. Crews are training. All we need now is to confirm a time and place.”

“OK,” Brian said. “I’ve scouted out a few of the locations you recommended and narrowed it to two, as you suggested. Both seem good to me. Best time would be about half an hour after midnight.”

“How are you going to get this guy to the rendezvous?” asked Richard.

Brian smiled. “Smoke and mirrors, man! Smoke and mirrors.”

Chapter 22

Karakol, Kyrgyzstan, USSR

Back in Karakol, Brian suggested he and Sonja take a walk in the woods. “We’re set up, ready to move,” Brian said once they were well out of sight. “You mentioned the torpedo factory was going to close for summer holidays next week? I think we can take advantage of that.”

He handed her a letter and asked her to read it, which she did. Sonya didn’t hesitate after she’d finished reading, and her response was right to the point. “I can do that.”

“Good,” said Brian as he produced a lighter and proceeded to torch the letter.

Back in the cottage, Brian pulled an envelope out of his diplomatic bag and handed it to Sonja as he pointed to the name on the envelope and used an index finger to motion silence. She took the letter, nodding to indicate she knew what to do.

The evening was becoming routine, meeting with their friends for dinner and dancing at the nightclub, with Brian generously buying dinner and drinks for Sasha and Ivan to ensure they were both very drunk and not fit to drive. Again, Sonja drove them home. When they stopped at the guard gate of the sanatorium, they were waved straight through. Sonja driving was getting to be routine.

In the morning, Brian, with Ivan, once again visited the bazar and bought six jars of caviar from Hozak. By this time Hozak viewed Brian as a steady and valuable customer, greeting him as an old friend and taking a few minutes for small talk, where Brian would learn about his extended family and their mercantile ventures.

Chapter 23

Ottawa, Canada

Brian was once again meeting with Richard and Ron in Ottawa. "We've got the logistics hammered out and the crews are constantly practicing," Ron explained. "We've done runs duplicating the terrain and conditions and we've worked with our Taliban friends. As you know, we have our Special Forces advising in Afghanistan and have set up two refueling stops there just in case they are needed. We've got three contingency plans and have been practicing them as well."

"Great! Our man is all set," Brian replied. "If everything works right, he won't be missed until he's safely out of the Soviet."

"Then the main worry will be the weather," said Richard. "So far, it looks as if we'll have a good weather window."

Chapter 24

Karakol

When Brian returned and stepped inside the cottage at the sanatorium, Sonja was waiting for him. "It's holiday time at the torpedo factory," she said. "Everyone gets two weeks off starting tonight. Not sure how many will turn up at the nightclub tonight."

"Oh?"

"Karl's not coming. He's booked one of the club's sailboats and is going camping along Lake Issyk-Kul for two weeks."

"By himself?"

"He said he'd be meeting up with some of the others in the club at some of the anchorages. He likes single-handed sailing."

They once again went to the pub/nightclub and Sonja drove home. Again, on his way out of town the next day, Brian picked up caviar in the bazar and had a long, friendly conversation with Hozak about his family and their business ventures.

The next Friday saw Brian make the now-familiar run from Moscow to Karakol. At the nightclub, one of Karl's friends from the factory, Stephan Minsk, joined them at their table. "Any word from Karl?" asked Sonja.

"Last I heard, he had made it halfway down the lake to a campsite just before Barskoon. One couple from the sailing club spent the night with him there. They came back for a wedding – that's where I saw them –- but said he was planning to go north across the lake."

"Isn't that over a hundred kilometers to the north shore?"

"About that. We had a squall last night. I hope he made it across before that."

Toward the end of the evening, Brian had a slow dance with Sonja. He murmured in her ear. "Set?"

She squeezed him. "All set." They returned to their table, and Brian ordered another round of drinks for Sasha and Ivan. When the drinks arrived, they joined the drivers at their end of the table and Brian proposed a toast to international comradeship. This was returned by Sasha who, slurring his words, managed to blurt something about Soviet-Canadian friendship. Ivan, who appeared to be even drunker than Sasha, managed to mumble something about comradeship across nations.

It was obvious to everyone that Ivan and Sasha wouldn't last the evening. About a half hour before closing, Brian and Sonja helped their drivers to the car before they passed out. As Sonja drove out of town, she asked, "Time?"

Brian looked at his watch. "We're slightly ahead. They're both out of it."

Brian gave directions heading east out of town. Sonja drove along a deserted, flat wide road for a few kilometers before Brian said, "This road leads to the Chinese border and isn't well used. Good road, though. Good thing we have a half-moon tonight, I can pick out landmarks. We've been lucky with the weather – the weather gods are with us. Pull over here, there's a gravel road and a good place to turn around."

She parked, turned off the lights and they both got out. Sonja opened the trunk and helped Karl get out. They embraced. "Good luck, Karl. I'll miss you!"

Karl hugged her tight. "I'll miss you too!"

Brian looked at his watch. “Ten minutes. Karl, can you give me a hand here?”

Sonja pulled out a small flashlight and the men proceeded to find the car jack and wrench, taking off a rear wheel and replacing it with the spare tire.

Just as Brian was putting the tire and tools back in the trunk, they heard an aircraft landing. In what seemed like a few minutes but was probably shorter, it pulled up close to their position. As the engines began to idle down, a side door opened and a man jumped out and ran toward them. He was wearing night vision goggles, black coveralls, boots, gloves and helmet. He shook hands with Brian after they exchanged code words.

The aircraft was hard to discern as Brian could barely make it out in the darkness. It blended into the night with what seemed to be a matte black paint job. Brian had been told it was a special paint to absorb radar. He couldn’t make out the engines but noted they were very quiet – probably fan jets. He couldn’t even get a good handle on how big it was but presumed it was twin-engine. He did note as part of its profile that the main wing was overhead the fuselage which was in keeping with STOL capabilities.

Brian pulled Karl over to the airman and said, “Here’s your passenger. Treat him well.”

The airman helped Karl into the aircraft, jumped in himself, and closed the door as the plane started rolling. Seconds later, it took off in in less than a thousand feet and went into steep climb.

Brian put his hand on Sonja’s shoulder. “So far, so good! Now, we’ve got to get back to the sanatorium before the Mickey Finns wear off.”

Sonja, laughing as if trying to relieve stress, said, “It’ll be difficult to keep a straight face in the morning when we give Sasha a hard time for sleeping right through our tire change.”

“Yeah, I managed to put a nail in the tire we took off and let most of the air out. That should work.”

When they drove up to the gate of the sanatorium, Brian held up his dirty hands for the guard to see. “We had a flat tire,” Sonja explained as she pointed to the two passed out in the back seat. “They weren’t any help at all.”

The guard laughed. “That happens!”

As was routine, Brian and Ivan headed back to the airport the next day after breakfast and stopped at the bazar for more caviar. “What do you do with all that caviar?” Ivan asked.

“Gifts, my friend. Gifts.”

Chapter 25

Karakol, Kyrgyzstan, USSR

Brian returned to Karakol the next Friday. Sonja greeted him at the cottage with the news Brian was expecting. "There's been a bit of excitement. Karl Schultz's sailboat was found adrift on the lake and he's missing. I'm quite upset about it." That evening at the nightclub, Sonja was visibly upset. Many of her and Karl's mutual friends spent time comforting her.

Stephan Minsk joined their table and updated them on what he had learned at the sailing club. "They're still searching. They're even using military aircraft and patrol boats. His sailboat washed up on shore with the mainsail still up. His wallet and documents were on board. Apparently, there was trace of blood and hair on the boom and the deck where he may have been hit if it swung quickly."

"It makes sense," Brian said. Single-handed sailing, hit by the boom and knocked overboard. Perhaps when a squall came down on him quickly. Ouch!"

Sonja broke into tears and was comforted by some of the ladies at the table.

On their walk to the cafeteria for breakfast, Brian said to Sonja in a low voice, "You deserve an Emmy. You're great as a grieving lover."

"Well, he was great to know. I was coming off a divorce and he was a great listener and dancer. And, we satisfied each other's needs. But, life must go on."

Brian stuck to his routine on his way back to Frunze, stopping at the bazar in Karakol for six jars of caviar and a long chat with Hozak.

Moscow

Back in Moscow a week later, Brian asked Simone, "Have we heard anything about Karl?"

"They made it out safely. Apparently, he's being debriefed in Diego Garcia. I gather he's proven to be very valuable."

"Great!"

"You're not to pass that along to Sonja. She's best off staying put and playing the grieving lover."

"Will they ever reunite?"

"Best for everyone that they don't."

On the next Friday's run to Karakol, Brian found Sonja in slightly better spirits. "Our astronaut lands tomorrow. We're all really excited."

"How much longer will you be here?'

"We figure, if our guy's healthy, that the readjustment to earth will take a month. We may be going home in five or six weeks."

"Great!"

Key Largo, Florida

"That's quite a story!" Pete commented. "Did the Soviets ever figure out what happened to Schultz?"

Richard looked at his empty beer bottle and stood up to fetch another. "Not that we were ever aware of. However, the KGB was thorough and interviewed all Schultz's friends and acquaintances. Sonja played it pretty cool. I guess she was resigned to never seeing him again. They also grilled the caviar vendor heavily but it soon became evident he knew nothing.

They eventually concluded it was a boating accident and that the lake was so deep, his body might not ever be recovered."

"Schultz proved valuable," Bill stated "He was given a new life in another country."

Chapter 26

NICARAGUA

<u>Key Largo, Florida</u>

Bill got up to put his bottle in the trash bucket and went below to the head. When he returned, he reached in the ice chest for another beer. “Syd, didn’t you use Brian’s services when you were on the Central American desk?”

“Yeah. 1980. The Canadians officially didn’t want to be involved but they lent him to us as their contribution to the cause.”

“Was that the Somoza thing?” asked Bill.

“Yeah, he earned his keep. He was instrumental in recovering over one point two billion dollars in funds the Somoza family had stashed in offshore accounts.”

“His file mentioned it was a black op and that he killed.” Sanford said.

“Yeah, and he had no problem with that. He killed – let’s say executed – ex-President Somoza’s number one son and a couple of his bodyguards. That son was a real bastard, just like his dad. He was sanctioned. Brian got rid of him once he felt he had wrung all they could out of him.”

Sanford said. “And there was the son’s wife.”

“Apparently she was killed in self-defense when she took a shot at him.”

Syd said, “We figured that was when he started to go rogue. The team leader feels a large packet of investment grade unset diamonds, some bearer bonds and hundred-dollar bills disappeared. He couldn’t verify it though and no one approached Brian about it. Small change when well over a billion dollars was recovered.”

CIA Headquarters, Langley, 1980

Brian was led into Syd Richards' office and introduced by the receptionist. Welcoming him, Syd shook hands with Brian and offered him a seat in front of the desk. "Brian, we've got an op planned for Central America and could do with you on the team."

Brian smiled. "Will it be interesting?"

"Yes, and you may even get to use some of the skills you picked up through our training program. We've got two weeks to get you in shape so I'm sending you back to camp."

Two weeks later, Brian was back in the same office sitting across from Syd in comfortable armchairs separated by a coffee table. Syd was sipping his coffee and Brian was munching on a cinnamon bun. "Did you enjoy your tune-up?" asked Syd. "You look as if you dropped a few pounds."

"I feel great! I shed at least five pounds and toned up some unused muscles. That was a pretty good orientation on Nicaraguan and Honduran current affairs, too."

"The instructors said you liked the diving."

"Yeah! I'd love to do a clandestine underwater approach sometime."

"Well, you never know when that training may come in handy. But let's get down to business."

"Sure! What's up?"

"As you know, Nicaragua has been a problem child," Syd said. "We booted Anastasio Somoza DeBayle out of a very corrupt presidency with the help of the Sandinistas. We financed and trained them even though we had helped Somoza come to power in the 60s. What got us most upset with Somoza – and his whole corrupt family, for that matter – was when they stole the earthquake relief funds in 1972 and got worldwide notoriety because of it. That was really the turning point in our diplomatic relations. He and his family had to go."

"Well, you got what you wanted."

"It's still a mess. Mind you, that can be said for most of Central America. We try to push things and Cuba's always interfering. We're often dealing with dictators and near-dictators who quickly become corrupt, if they aren't already. It's always a mess."

"And Somoza?"

"Right now, he's fled to Paraguay with his mistress and half-brother after he wasn't granted exile in America, and he's taken some of the family millions with him."

"Some of the family millions?"

"Yeah. The family controls most of the industry – hell, ninety percent of the economy – of Nicaragua. They made fortunes supplying the allies in WWII and seizing the properties of expat Germans. Now, they own almost everything from textile factories to the cement monopoly, plantations, oil and gas – you name it.

"We know they have big money stashed in banks in various offshore tax havens. The key to that is Anastasio's first son, Carlos. He's the hub of the finances. As far as we can tell, there's more than a billion U.S. dollars stuffed in offshore bank accounts."

"Ah! I'm beginning to see where this may be leading."

"Like we want to strip the family of much of their offshore money? Our revenge for absconding with the hurricane disaster relief funds? That's part of it."

Brian leaned forward. "And you want me to do what?"

"First, get into Nicaragua and Honduras and scout things out. Find out where the son, Carlos Somoza DeBayle, is hiding out. Rumor has it that he's somewhere in Honduras trying to manage the family empire from there. Locate him and recon the location for a raid. We feel your Canadian passport will come in handy."

"Can I expect some local help?" asked Brian.

"We've sort of burned our bridges with the Sandinistas and they're currently pulling the strings of power in Nicaragua. I'd be careful there. Right now, Honduran politics are, let's say, uncertain at best. Not much help there. Mind you, we still have some contacts. Just don't draw attention."

"Hence, the use of me and my Canadian passport. Deniability?"

"That and your fluency in the language and your great ability to schmooze your way around. Yeah. It'd be a bonus if you could also pinpoint the location of Poppa Somoza and find out which offshore banks he's accessing. We know he's in Paraguay."

"I guess you have others following through on that."

"Yeah, but bear in mind any intel you can contribute to that exercise will help."

Chapter 27

Managua, Nicaragua

Brian arrived in Managua late in the afternoon. Once he settled in at his hotel, he went down to the lobby and sought out the concierge. He presented himself as a Canadian looking for a warm place to get away from cold, long Canadian winters and was thinking of building a villa in Managua. Brian asked him to compile a list of businesses that specialized in selling and installing security alarms, then went out to get some fresh air and take in the some of the sites. When he returned, the concierge presented him with a list of five names, and Brian requested that he make appointments for the next day and reserve a hotel car and driver to take him around. Brian tipped him well, then had dinner at the hotel's five-star restaurant before settling in to get some sleep.

The following morning, Brian was third down on the list of security companies when he struck pay dirt. He explained to the salesman that he was planning on buying a villa on a large piece of property and wanted a very good security system. The salesman let it slip that his company even made installations across the border in Honduras. He said one contract, for 'a special client,' was probably the most elaborate and expensive installation they had ever done.

Brian casually probed. "I'll have over three hundred meters of beach frontage. What can you suggest for that?"

Bragging a bit, the salesman replied. "Well, for that special client I mentioned, we did over two thousand meters of waterfront ranging from beach to mangrove swamp. It was very elaborate, with infrared and vibration sensors."

"That must have been expensive!" exclaimed Brian, pretending to be a bit cost conscious.

"Overall, the installation came in at just over two million U.S. dollars."

"Did that cost include back-up electricity sources?'

"Oh, yes. They specified triple redundancy and made sure the generators were placed in different locations around the property."

"Wow! I'm afraid my needs aren't that fancy but it's good to know you have the expertise."

"Thank you! We'll be most pleased to give you a bid when you are ready with your project."

That night, Brian returned to the shop and easily circumvented its security system and locks, which he noted on his first visit. After finding the installation drawings for the homes of major customers, he copied ones that fit what he was searching for. He was sure a project located on the Pacific coast of Honduras, just across the border from Nicaragua and close to the Inter-American Highway, was the likely target and worth first review. The property included a mansion, outbuildings for staff quarters, a ten-vehicle garage, three enclosed power generators and a combination workshop/boat house. The owner was listed as a company in Panama called Santiago Holdings.

He needed verification. Next day, Brian went to church. Rather, he sought out a Catholic priest, a CIA cooperator who Brian had been briefed on. Priests had begun assisting CIA operatives in the years when the church found it convenient to be supportive.

He found Father Sebastian waiting for him on the near-deserted square in front of the Cathedral de Santiago – the old cathedral of Managua which had been condemned after the 1972 earthquake. After introducing himself, Father Sebastian said, "Let's play tourist and guide, I'll point out some architectural features as we walk around the perimeter."

"Think we're being followed?" Brian asked.

"You never can tell. Best to be cautious."

As they slowly walked, Brian spoke first. "I understand the cathedral didn't survive the earthquake."

"Correct. Right now, it's proving to be cheaper to build a new one. It has a very original name, the New Cathedral de Managua. Someday, the Old Cathedral de Managua may be restored. The architecture is unique."

"Inspired by Belgium?"

"Yes. Belgian iron frame from the turn of the last century. Magnificent!"

"Our mutual friends said you might be able to help me," Brian said.

Father Sebastian took a moment to point at a carved cornice on the cathedral, then casually looked around the entire square. "You know, your people created a retirement plan for some of us. We're grateful. I'm looking forward to retiring in Vancouver, Canada."

Brian responded. "Yes, and your help today will go to supplement it."

"How much?"

"Ten thousand U.S. dollars has been authorized. We wish to learn more about where Carlos Somoza DeBayle is residing."

"I see. You're aware that the wife of Carlos, Juanita Maria DeBayle, is a patron of our church?"

"Yes, Father."

"She is a regular in confessional when she is in Managua."

"Has she relocated?"

"She has. They have established a new residence over the border along the coast of Honduras. It has water frontage near Gallifenero on the Gulfo De Franseca and faces Ile de Tigre – Tiger Island."

Brian shook hands and took his leave. "Thank you, Father. You've been very helpful."

Back at the hotel, Brian asked the concierge where he could rent a car as he wanted to drive into Honduras. "I'm afraid that's impossible, sir," the concierge answered. "No rental cars are allowed to cross the border."

Of course, the concierge had a cousin who would sell him a car and maybe buy it back if Brian returned to Managua. Brian wound up buying a ten-year-old American-made Ford Falcon – four-door, basic, but mechanically sound. "Perfect cover!" Brian thought.

Chapter 28

San Lorenzo, Honduras

After clearing the border crossing with no difficulty once he produced ownership papers for the car and purchased local insurance, Brian drove to San Lorenzo and settled in to a four-star hotel jutting out on piles over the water in the tourist district of La Cabana. He introduced himself to the concierge, mentioning he was a Canadian looking for a place to escape from the long Canadian winters. The concierge was eager to promote San Lorenzo, quickly pulling out a map, pointing out significant points of interest and suggesting the best locations for selecting property and building a home.

Brian was already briefed but listened encouragingly, looking for nuances. He was aware the government had developed a deep sea port when they dredged the harbor in 1978 and it was the only one for major shipping on the Honduran Pacific coast. He was all ears when he casually asked about the airfield northwest of the city and the concierge let it slip that it was officially deactivated but still occasionally used.

"Is it a government sanctioned airfield or do people using it have uncertain purposes?" asked Brian.

The concierge answered in a conspiratorial tone. "Let's say some types of people and cargos pass through mainly at night. The runway is quite long, over twelve hundred meters. Hopefully, one day it will become a real airport again. Right now, it is officially abandoned and the police are encouraged to ignore the traffic. I've been told a very wealthy person has built a hangar and stores a jet aircraft there. He has made some repairs to the runway. It's rumored he wants to buy the whole airport to use as his personal field."

"Interesting!" Brian pointed to a spot on the coast closer to the Nicaraguan border. "This looks like a promising area for property. I'd like a beach front home."

"It has good beaches and some mangrove. But there's not much for sale. A rich guy bought up a huge portion in the Gallinero Beach area right down to Punta Bravik, about three thousand hectares." He pointed to the map and circled the area with a pen.

"Wow!"

"Si, he's the guy with the jet plane in a hangar at the airfield."

"Wow! If he likes it so much, it must be a great spot! I'd love to see it from the water and see if there's any available land worthwhile nearby."

"I have a cousin, Ezra, who owns a shrimp boat. You can charter him by the day. I also have a cousin, Nicholas, who sold that land to the patron. He would be a good one to deal with for your property search."

"Excellent!"

Brian went through the process of getting the concierge to line him up with Nicholas, the realtor. They set up a trip the next day on the other cousin's shrimp boat to look at the waterfront around the Gallinero beach area down to Punta Bravik and beyond. In the meantime, the realtor took him by road to show him available properties in the area.

They passed a fenced compound that had a huge iron gate and a guard house which the realtor pointed out as the estate belonging to the rich Nicaraguan. Brian noticed the electrified chain-link fence surrounding the property was interspersed with numerous CCTV cameras. "That guy sure likes his security!" Brian commented.

"Si! He even has round-the-clock patrols with dogs. Nick replied. He even has people in small fast boats guarding the waterfront."

"Who is he?"

"We have not been told, my friend. Lawyers purchased the property in the name of a corporation. But we know all the guards and other workers come from Nicaragua and they don't associate with us."

"Under whose name did they buy the land and do the construction?"

"It's a company registered in Panama called Santiago Holdings."

"Have you met this guy?"

"Si, he has a Managua accent and a very pretty wife who is quite a bit younger than him. I met her also."

"Do you know his first name?"

"His wife calls him Carlos. He calls her Maria. He must be very rich as they always have bodyguards with them."

Chapter 29

Brian felt the shrimp boat was perfect cover since the area had no yachts or fast boats to speak of and flying over would equally attract attention. As Nick had mentioned the previous day, a fast inflatable boat came up to them as they neared the compound. Brian noted the boat was equipped with radar and big twin outboards. It had two well-armed men aboard with one driving and the other carrying an automatic rifle. The shrimp boat captain just waved and carried on course. The fast boat pulled away with the driver and his partner waving.

"Do they ever board you?" Brian asked Ezra, the shrimp boat captain.

"They did the first couple of times but they know me now. We just wave. I have shrimp pots past Punta Bravik and pass through to tend them every other day."

Ezra's course allowed Brian to get a pretty good view of the shoreline. Through binoculars, Brian noted the compound had a wharf jutting out which had two additional fast boats tied to it. He focused past the beach and got a great view of the main house which seemed to be quite large, in excess of six thousand square feet if Brian correctly remembered the drawing he copied from the alarm installer.

As they drew near Punta Bravik, Nicholas spoke as he pointed. "The property goes right around Punta Bravik."

Brian focused his binoculars on a small building right on the point and noted it had a large radar mast on top. Brian muttered to himself. "He's worried about being approached from the sea."

Next day, Brian decided to take a look at the airfield. He followed the gravel road toward the airport and was approaching what seemed to be the gate leading to the airfield when two armed men jumped out of the bush and flagged him to stop. One came up to the driver's window which Brian had rolled down earlier. "What do you want here?"

Showing them the map he was using, Brian pointed to the airfield. "I'm a tourist from Canada. I'm just exploring. Someone told me there was an abandoned airfield and I thought I'd check it out."

"Not a good idea. You'd best turn around."

Brian did as he was told and left. That evening he returned, hiding his car and walking in through bush well away from the road. He was aided by night vision goggles, which helped him spot two guards smoking in front of the hangar in addition to two more huddled near the entrance gate where he had been turned away earlier. He waited. Twenty minutes later, his patience was rewarded. The main door of the hangar opened and lights went on. He could make out the shape of an aircraft.

At first glance, he thought it was a twin engine Learjet but then thought better of it as it was bigger – maybe a Gulfstream. He managed to get a couple of telephoto shots of it before he heard the sound of an aircraft approaching. In a moment, runway lights came on. A minute later, an aircraft landed, then turned and taxied up to the hangar. Brian watched as the twin turboprop plane, which he thought may have been a Beechcraft, refueled and was soon airborne. The runway lights were extinguished and the hangar door closed.

Chapter 30

Brian drove back to Managua and sold his car back to the vendor at a huge discount. He demanded a receipt but rationalized that he could have tried selling to someone else for a better price but that would have taken time – better to make a quick sale at a huge discount. Besides, it was on the expense account.

Back in Langley CIA HQ, he was warmly received by Syd. They sat around the coffee table in Syd's office and were soon joined by two others whom Syd introduced as Brett Marks and Ron Field, both from the black ops division of the Central America Desk.

"So, you think you may have pinpointed where Carlos Somoza is hiding out?" Brett asked Brian.

"Probably. We need more verification. That's why I'm back here."

"How can we help?'

"Can you get satellite photo surveillance of the property I outlined and also the airfield?" asked Brian.

"Sure, day and night. We can also compile a timeline going back a few years."

"That would be great! Do you also have infrared thermal imaging?"

"No problem. Our people have already reviewed a few recent satellite imagery passes. They've picked out some likely guard posts, guards on patrol, etc. The Big Bird satellite also picked up radar in use and its antenna location. Looks like a radar with a fifty-mile range."

Brian winced. "Ouch! An interesting challenge for an air or seaborne assault."

Brett smiled. "We're examining multiple tactics. Not to worry. We've done this sort of thing before."

"The airfield is being used at night," Brian said. "Apparently this 'Carlos' keeps a jet there in a hanger. It looks bigger than a Leer jet. I took photos for your people to examine."

Brian continued. "There's a rumor that this 'Carlos' renovated the airfield and keeps a jet there. That got me curious. I was stopped while trying to explore the airfield. That really aroused my interest so I went back at night and observed a fueling stop for a twin-engine Beechcraft."

"It's probably a refueling spot for drugs going north and cash going south," Ron said.

"Could be," Brian said. "But rumor down there is that this 'Carlos' controls it."

"Nevertheless, we'd have to neutralize it, just as insurance, if we raided the compound," Syd said. "The jet is interesting. The photos you took reveal it to be a Grumman Gulfstream II. It has a good range, over four thousand miles, for fourteen passengers plus two crew and a forty-five thousand foot ceiling – pretty nice. I have someone researching its ownership background."

"The airfield could be a point of entry and/or egress for some or all of the assault team," Brett mused.

"After we review the satellite images, we'll insert a recon team to scout it out," said Ron. "That shouldn't be too hard for Special Ops."

Syd and Brett nodded.

"Can you get someone to check the records in Panama to see who actually owns this Santiago Holdings?" asked Brian.

"Already done," Syd replied. "You're right, it's Carlos Somoza DeBayle."

Brian sat back in his chair and smiled. "Bingo!"

"The schematic and site plan you sent of the security system is excellent!" Brett said to Brian. "We're working on plans to breach it."

"In fact, we're narrowing down on a multi-pronged assault," Ron said. "First, we'll go in covertly from the sea with a diversion and a main thrust. We'll secure the airfield as well, of course."

Brian perked up. "An underwater assault? I'd love to participate in that!"

"Well, we thought so!" Syd said. "We've also got a role planned for you to access the offshore bank accounts and drain them. It's back to the farm for you to do some more training and much, much more planning."

"We have some problems to iron out," Ron said. "Right now, the biggest hurdle for an underwater assault is the shallowness of the Gulf of Fonseca. It's a bit shallow for a sub. Those guys have radar with fifty-mile range that could possibly spot a sub surfacing or running on the surface to drop off a waterborne assault force. The radar is likely good enough to pick out small inflatable boats as well. They'd have to be launched well out of range and that's too far to swim in underwater and too far even for our midget subs. We could launch the assault force by using an underwater lock-out hatch on a sub, though. But the shallowness of the Gulf makes it difficult for a sub to manoeuver underwater – lots of rocks and shoals to contend with."

"Anyone passing by, like local shrimp boats, are always checked over by guards in fast boats," Brett commented. "A drop-off from a local vessel would have to be timed just right. However, it can be done."

Brian interjected. "There aren't too many local boats in that area and very few visitors. The local boat operators are a very tight community. It could be hard to get a local boat but you could imitate one by going slow. I've been scouting things out pretending to be looking for land to buy. Why not buy up some waterfront property nearby and launch the seaside underwater assault from there? Uncle Sam can afford it."

"Good idea!" said Syd. "We can sneak in our team as specialist contractors. Great cover with that!"

Chapter 31

Honduras

On his way back to San Lorenzo, Brian flew in to Tegucigalpa, the capital of Honduras, even though he was a bit reticent about landing at Toncontin International Airport, which held the dubious reputation of being the worst, most dangerous international airport in the world. Fortunately, the weather was clear and calm when he landed in the early evening. He spent a few days in the capital checking on land title regulations for foreigners and creating a list of contractors and building suppliers. He also elected to buy an unpretentious but reliable car. The hotel's concierge came through with a cousin in the car business who had just the right vehicle. It was a seven-year-old Volkswagen Beetle – common, economical and reliable. The cousin managed to get the car registration and license completed in half a day. Brian found the foreign trade department at the Canadian Embassy helpful in securing a reliable lawyer who specialized in land transfers.

Three days later he was rolling along Highway CA5 to San Lorenzo. The highway turned out to be a very good road. Brian had been assured that the reputation Honduras had earned as fraught with car-jacking and highway murders, although real, applied mostly to richer prey than Brian portrayed in his VW Bug. He arrived safely in San Lorenzo with no incidents, although he had a hard time trying to find a clean washroom.

Back in San Lorenzo, he contacted Nicholas, the realtor, and told him he was ready to make a purchase. Nicholas was delighted. He was even more delighted to learn that Brian had already arranged financing and wanted a quick closing on a prime beachfront property about a mile north of

Punta Bravik. He rushed to the hotel with papers for Brian to sign for the offer. Back and forth negotiation over the purchase price took only a few hours and the acceptance was completed by the following afternoon.

Brian demanded an early title transfer and all the furnishings in the small three bedroom house on the property. He contacted a local lawyer who was an associate of the one Brian had retained in the capital and arranged that the two lawyers would work closely to push the paperwork through. Brian offered both lawyers an incentive for quick closure, which they readily accepted. Latin American banks are often quirky but Brian's lawyer in the capital assured him there would be no problems with a wire transfer of funds and a quick registration of the deed.

While waiting for the title transfer, Brett and Ron arrived and checked in to the same hotel as Brian. Brett would play the role of prime contractor and Ron would be the architect. They brought some drawings for a new, much larger home to be built on the property. The existing house would remain, doubling during construction as a base for the men and intended to be eventually used as guest quarters. They quickly began seeking out local building trades and meeting the bureaucrats responsible for building permits. They had no problem lining up a quality workforce as they were willing to pay well in cash.

Construction on the foundation of the new house began immediately after the title passed and the building permit had been approved. Brett and Brian moved into the old house and Ron departed. Two large shipping containers arrived, ostensibly with building materials but also containing their assault tools. Two of the Special Forces, a lieutenant and a sergeant, arrived under the guise of sub-trade contractors.

Once the ground was dug for the foundation and forms for concrete completed, construction was stopped and the local crew paid off in cash. They were told there was a delay on approval for amendments to the design drawings. Over the next few days eight Special Forces members trickled in, dressed in civilian clothes and ostensibly posing as sub-trades.

Brett was the operation's overall leader. He detailed a team to reconnoiter the airfield and gather intel on the jet stored there. It didn't take long for them to observe one of the clandestine night-time refueling stops and begin to assess the routine. After two week's observation, they concluded there were two flights each week, and duffel bags would be taken once a week from the aircraft and driven to the Somoza compound. Brett and the others concluded it was most likely the bags contained U.S. dollars flowing down from America.

One question they eventually answered, almost by fluke, was the identity and location of the pilots for Somoza's jet. Quite by accident, two of the team met them in a hotel bar, struck up a conversation, and learned they were pilots housed in the hotel and flying a private jet aircraft. Over a couple of beers, they admitted they hadn't been very busy lately as the owner tended to run his business affairs from his home office. Talk got around to aircraft maintenance and they learned the aircraft was in excellent shape, always ready to go on short notice.

That gave Brett an idea. They would take over the airfield and steal Somoza's jet.

Chapter 32

The assault on the Somoza's compound was a joint effort between the CIA operatives and a Special Forces team based in Key West as part of Joint Interagency Task Force South.

Under a quarter moon, the underwater assault team entered the water at eleven p.m. Weeks of observation suggested this was an optimal time since the people in the house would be getting ready for dinner, which tended to be served around midnight. Intelligence profiling the Somozas reflected a habit to have drinks before dinner from eleven to midnight followed by a leisurely dinner. Satellite observation showed the security crew also took turns having dinner in the main building kitchen over that period.

Regardless, Somoza's security operation was very professional with at least four men and two dogs constantly patrolling the property and a full-time gate guard. It was assumed that security systems and radar were monitored from an office in the dorm where it was likely six or more guards were resting in separate rooms. The dogs had a kennel compound under shade trees twenty yards behind the office/dorm and it was estimated it housed at least six dogs.

Three fast boats were moored to a jetty close to the guards' dorm/office – a single-story concrete building set back a hundred feet inland at the south side of the beach. It had been observed that the boats seldom patrolled at night, tending to come out only when a vessel was passing by.

Getting to the Somoza's beach underwater was an easy task. Brian's property was only a mile away, which was quickly and easily traversed with the assistance of underwater personal scooters called Sea Tows. These were fifty-five pounds of battery, electric motor and propeller in a bullet-like carbon fiber housing with a silent twelve-mile range and maximum speed of seven miles per hour. The team didn't have to dive deep but had to be silent and show no bubbles. For that, they used rebreather sets with up to a six-hour supply of oxygen. They had timed the dive to take advantage of the tide, giving them a three knot current pushing them toward their landing zone.

Their real problem was getting out of the water and across the beach to neutralize the guards, dogs and other workers before entering the house. It was uncertain how many guards might be in the house but it was assumed Carlos Somoza would put up resistance.

Thankfully, the schematics of the security system showed a lack of sensor coverage of the dock and the entire area from the dock down to the guards' dorm and dog kennel. They assumed this blind spot was intentional, because the path from kennel to dorm building to dock was so well-travelled that sensors would be a nuisance. However, there was a CCTV camera mounted on a light pole that covered the beach. The security schematics also showed that the alarm system, including CCTVs, were monitored not only in the dorm office but also at two other stations located in the main house and in the guardhouse at the main gate.

They had decided on a three-pronged attack: six assailants from the water at the pier; two on the main gate guard house; and two men on a diversion to draw off some of the guards to a distant corner of the property abutting the main road. The assault's timing was based on the underwater swim team getting into position, then silently attacking the guard's dorm and neutralizing the dogs in their kennel. Brian would be part of the second wave of the underwater team tasked with attacking and entering the main house once the personnel in the dorm and the kenneled dogs were neutralized. Once the house was secured, it was his task to access Somoza's bank account records.

The water was murky, though it was a moderate temperature and their thin wetsuits sufficed to keep the swimmers warm. Each diver also wore a multi-pocked cotton jumpsuit over their wetsuit filled with tools of the trade. Each had a waterproofed pistol with attached silencer and a waterproofed and silenced combat rifle. Each diver had a compass and GPS which aided their navigation, bringing them spot on to the pier. The Sea Tows also had sonars which provided a picture of depths, obstacles and bottom conditions.

Brian and Fred, his Special Forces team dive buddy, were the last of the waterborne assailants. They surfaced under the wharf just as the lead team was going into action. Two were in position on either side of the wharf, using the bank for a little cover. They trained their weapons on the door and facing windows of the bunkhouse. First objective was the light pole, with its bright yard light and CCTV camera, at the shore end of the dock. One of the team shot out the CCTV camera with a silenced round. Another shot two seconds later took out the yard light. In a moment, the bunkhouse door opened and a man was silhouetted in the doorway from the backlight in the dorm. He fell to a silenced shot when he stepped out. Another followed hurriedly and was also taken out.

Under cover from their buddies, three SEALs rushed up to the dorm walls and worked their way down to the side windows. One continued ducking low to the rear of the building and covered the windows and door on that end. A guard tried to run out the back door but was shot down. Given an all clear signal by the guys covering the windows, two of the team entered the building. The office was empty, presumably because its occupants ran out to see what happened to the light and CCTV and were mowed down. Cautiously, the two team members advanced into the dorm rooms, methodically checking each and silently shooting two asleep in their bunks.

Brian and Fred were tasked with keeping an eye on the main house. It remained quiet. Brian knew the dining room and kitchen were on the other side of the house and he assumed the house's occupants may not have noticed the missing yard light.

Once the bunkhouse and office were cleared, Brett gave the signal for the other teams to move. Two men moved on the kennel and tranquilized the dogs with darts.

A few minutes later, the team at the airfield reported they had it secured.

The diversionary team crashed a pickup truck into the fence at the extreme end of the Somoza property, which diverted the three guards and their dogs patrolling the perimeter as well as drawing the gate guard out to the road to investigate what had happened. Thirty seconds after the diversionary leader reported, the main switch for the security systems was shut down.

As they rushed toward the accident, the guards and their dogs were ambushed by two of the team lying in wait at the crash site. Another two team members took out the gate guard when he came out of his gatehouse to look down the road.

As the pickup was only lightly damaged, the assailants loaded the bodies of the guards and dogs in the truck bed, then drove up to the gate where they were let in by the two members who had secured it. They would remain at the gate to ensure no one entered.

The body of the gate guard was also loaded in the bed of the truck and the assailants drove to the main house to report in.

Concurrently, Brian and Fred were joined by four others at the main house. As practiced, they spread out and approached the house from four sides. This time, they used stun grenades and rushed in. Brian and his partner took the back door to the kitchen, which instantly turned problematic. The cook and maid were quickly killed but a table was occupied by three security guards and a woman having dinner. One managed to pull his handgun but Brian shot him in the chest before he fired. A second got a shot off but it went wild as he was hit with a shot from Brian. The third and fourth were felled by Fred. It was later learned the woman was Carlos' secretary.

Others breached the front door and surprised Carlos and Juanita, who were sitting at the dining room table eating their main course. They were both quickly subdued, but not before Carlos dove for a pistol lying on a nearby credenza. He was tripped up before he could get to it, then clubbed for good measure. With one man guarding Carlos and Juanita, two others cleared the remaining front rooms and found no one. When they returned, they manacled Carlos and Juanita with plastic wrist ties.

Chapter 33

After Brian and Fred finished clearing the back rooms of the house they joined Brett, the team leader, in the dining room. He radioed the others that the house was secure and received responses that all guards and compound personnel had been killed.

Brett turned to Brian and said, "Looks like Carlos here is not badly hurt, just roughed up. He's all yours. The boys will set up a perimeter and get rid of the bodies."

Brian gave Carlos a shove toward the master bedroom, saying in Spanish, "Carlos, you'll be much more comfortable in the bedroom."

"Why? What's going on?" asked Carlos.

"Nothing you'll remember," Brian said.

Brian shoved him face down on to the bed and bound his ankles with a plastic slip tie. Keeping Carlos on his stomach, Brian took a small kit out of one of his pockets containing a hypodermic needle and a vial of liquid. He filled and tested the syringe, then administered the hypo to one of Carlos' thighs. In seconds, Carlos was under.

Brett walked in just as Brian was putting the syringe in. "What's that?"

"Call it truth serum, if you will. Technically, it's SP-117-A – sort of a variant of the old WWII scopolamine. This stuff gets them talking truthfully but leaves no memory. It's something the CIA borrowed from the Soviets and enhanced. There's no taste, color or immediate side effects. He'll have no recall of talking to us. I'll let him rest for a half hour and then get to work. We're going to have a long chat."

"What do you want to do with Juanita?"

"Let's talk to her first. I want to size her up. I'll give her the same treatment once I've finished with Carlos. Maybe she can verify some of the accounts."

Juanita was brought into the bedroom and made to sit on a sofa. "I know you've got a safe in here, what's the combination?" asked Brian.

She sneered at him with contempt. "You, you want our valuables? My jewelry?"

"Not really. You can have them. We want some information."

"Information?"

"Yes, access to your offshore bank accounts."

"No! Never!"

Brian slapped her hard across the face. She slumped back. Brian asked again – even though he knew the answer, he wanted her compliant. "Where's the safe?"

Tearfully, she pointed to a mirror on the wall. "Behind that." As Brian glanced at the mirror, she reached down into the folds of the sofa with two hands because of the manacles. Fumbling a bit, she produced a small .38-caliber revolver. She hastily aimed and fired at Brian, grazing his left arm as he ducked aside.

Brian got off a quick shot, hitting Juanita in the heart, and was followed a half-second later by a three shot burst from Brett, who had been just a little slower bringing his assault weapon to bear.

Brian spoke first. "Well, that leaves Carlos. Let's see what he says."

"You OK? Brett asked. "Looks like a bullet took a piece of your sleeve."

Brian gave his arm a glance. "Just a graze. Shit! Never trust a woman!"

After Brett slapped a battle dressing on Brian's arm, they got back to work. Carlos readily gave up the combination to the wall safe behind the ornate mirror Juanita had pointed out. Brian opened it and fished around with one hand as he examined the contents. He pulled out a cloth-bound notebook and examined it. "Ah, numbers for bank accounts and access instructions. Looks like six banks, each in a different country. Mauritius, Switzerland, Nassau, Channel Islands, Antigua. Lots of accounts – some seem to be personal and others seem related to corporations they own. I think that's pay dirt!"

Brian tossed the notebook to Brett. "Look for a journal or ledger or both," the team leader told him. "You'd expect that he's keeping records of what's in each account."

Brian went back into the safe and fished around some more. He pulled out a black velvet bag and palmed it. Next he brought out a ledger book and passed it to Brett to examine and went back to the safe while slipping the black bag into one of his pockets. "There's a lot of cash in here," he exclaimed. Brian started pulling out wads of bills and stacking them on a nearby dresser. "Some local currencies but mainly U.S. dollars. Whoa, lots of U.S.-denominated bearer bonds – some with million dollar face values! Plenty of Juanita's jewelry too." Deeper in the safe Brian found bars of gold. "We've got gold here too! Man!" He pulled out twenty gold bars, each weighing a kilo.

Once the contents of the safe were piled on the dresser and examined, Brian and Brett got back to Carlos. With careful questioning and coaxing, and a tape recorder running, Carlos managed to verify each account and the process for accessing them. Once they were satisfied they had identified everything, the next step was to access and drain the accounts.

Carlos had a large and magnificently decorated office/den down the hall from the master bedroom. Its central feature was an ornately carved rosewood desk and credenza. The walls behind and to one side of the desk featured Pablo Picasso paintings. A carved rosewood secretarial table on another sidewall held an IBM Selectric typewriter and a telephone. A teletype machine perched on its own stand a few feet away.

Brian looked at a row of four telephones on the credenza behind the main desk. “Looks as if Carlos has his own telecom system. Here’s a satellite phone.”

“Makes sense,” Brett said. “I saw a satellite dish on our way in.”

“Makes our work easier,” Brian mused. He picked up the sat phone and dialed the first bank on his list, which Carlos had said would be open at this hour. Brian gave the appropriate account number and coded answers to verify he was the account holder, then gave instructions to transfer the funds to an account he designated in Grand Cayman. This was acknowledged and Brian was given a transaction completion number. “Well, it worked,” said Brian after he’d hung up. "I didn’t want to get the bank suspicious by empting the account so I left a few million in it. We can hit it again later.”

A half hour later, he contacted the destination bank in Grand Cayman and spoke with his contact who confirmed the money had been transferred in. Brian arranged for it to be transferred to an account in St. Louis, Missouri, then phoned Ron Field in Langley and gave him the transaction number. He then went back to transferring funds from the other accounts, following the same routine of sending the funds to an intermediate bank, then on to St. Louis, all the while keeping Ron in Langley informed.

After several transfers had gone through, Brian confided to Ron that he was a little worried Papa Somoza might get suspicious if he were to do some banking and notice the money movement. "Don't worry about that," Ron replied. "He's in Paraguay. Of course, he's probably had access to the accounts. But, he was assassinated a few minutes ago."

"Oh, by our guys?"

"Let's say he seems to have incurred the wrath of a local paramilitary group. They even burned his house down. You've got a few hours before the news gets out so move the rest of the funds ASAP."

Chapter 34

While Brian was busy, Brett photographed the contents of the safe and made an inventory list. He then rummaged around the closets, coming up with some duffle bags and packed them with the valuables. He figured the haul was over two hundred million, considering the large stack of U.S. dollar bearer bonds.

Brian finished up in an hour. "Time to go," said Brett.

They departed in the early morning. Brian and two of the team took the fast boats back to Brian's property where they sank them offshore. Two men took one of Somoza's trucks over to Brian's property to pick them up. Brett and the others, with the unconscious Carlos and Juanita's body, took Somoza's Mercedes, another pickup truck and a Jeep to the airfield and met up with the team that had taken over the field.

An hour before dawn, a twin-engine Beechcraft touched down and taxied up to the Somoza hangar. Brett was standing in front of the open and lighted hangar and greeted the two men who got out of the plane. "Hi Jim, Whitey." They shook hands and Brett pointed to the Somoza jet in the hangar. "There's your baby. We fueled it. Just awaiting your preflight check."

"Great! I love the Gulfstream II," Whitey said. "It'll probably take us less than half an hour for the preflight check, then we'll fly it out of here. Bobby Green and Sam Norden are flying the Beechcraft."

"Good! We've got the rest of the team shutting down our staging house and should be here in less than half an hour. Our two guests and four of us will come with you. The others will follow in the Beechcraft."

It wasn't long before Brian and the remainder of the team arrived in two more of Somoza's vehicles. Brett and Brian split the duffle bags full of valuables between the two aircraft, just in case one plane was lost. Brian and Carson, one of the Special Forces team, carried the unconscious Somoza onto the Gulfstream II, while Duke and Mack carried the blanket-wrapped body of Juanita aboard.

Chapter 35

Key West, Florida, Naval Air Station (NQX)

The Gulfstream II touched down at Key West Naval Air Station and was escorted to a hangar. Once its engines shut down, the jet was towed inside and the hangar doors were closed before the passenger door opened. Brian was the first off, carrying duffel bags in each hand. Ron Field was waiting and greeted him warmly.

"It went smoothly?" asked Ron.

Brian was all smiles and still high on adrenalin. "Oh, yeah! Have you got an ETA on Brett and the rest of the team?"

"The Beechcraft's slower, of course. They should be landing in an hour."

"O.K.! Here's half the bags of valuables. Brett's got the other half. We thought it best to split it up just in case of mechanical problems."

"Fine! What about Carlos and Juanita?"

"They left the aircraft at five thousand feet when we were well out to sea. Juanita was pretty stiff by then but Carlos may have felt the impact."

"O.K., we'll debrief fully later."

"Tell me, what about the bank transfers?"

"Everything's sitting in a CIA-controlled bank account in St. Louis. A very nice operation, man!"

"What are you going to do with the jet?"

"That's a nice bonus! It'll get a new identity and be added to our clandestine aircraft inventory."

Chapter 36

BANKING AND COCAINE FOR USSR

Key Largo, Florida

"How did Brian get into money laundering and dealing with drug lords?" asked Sanford.

"I guess that started back in his days as a diplomatic courier in Canada," Pete responded. "There was more than one instance during the Cold War where our people got cozy with some of the criminal elements."

Ottawa, Canada, Prime Minister's Office (PMO), 1979

Marc DuPlese, director of the Romance Languages Division in the Intelligence Unit, had Brian's full attention. He was speaking in rapid French. "Brian, we need you to make some close friends in the Soviet."

"Friendships. Like develop some moles?"

"Oui. As you know, the black market – call it an underground economy, if you will – is thriving in the Soviet Union. To us in the West, it's a sign that their controlled economy system has serious flaws. It has resulted in a very large criminal element that is becoming extremely powerful."

"Let me guess. You want to exploit this somehow?"

"Oui. I understand you have made some friends at one of the black markets in Moscow?"

"Yeah, I often buy caviar. It's good for bribes. Sometimes I'll trade Danish canned hams for caviar. I've gotten to know a couple of favorite vendors."

"By the way, thank you again for the jar of caviar! Do you feel the vendors are tied in to the underworld?"

"They'd have to be to get their goods – and probably the right to sell them – without hassle."

"Of course. Our NATO friends, especially the Americans and British, want to establish greater relationships with the Soviet underworld networks, as they could be helpful in many instances."

"I understand. Like what we do in Latin America."

"We'd like you to build on your relationships and try to gain enough confidence to be introduced to the leadership. You may use the cover of your diplomatic bag to help smuggle for them in order to get ingratiated. Others are doing this as well and we may use you to make payoffs."

"I see."

Over many visits to the largest of Moscow's black markets, Brian's developed a vendor contact. Ilya Trepkie became quite friendly with him – especially when Brian traded a dozen small tins of Canadian maple syrup and six jars of Cheese-Whiz for some caviar. Confidence built over many visits, with Brian trading goods Ilya requested like Tylenol C and other hard-to-find near-prescription drugs that Brian could easily conceal in a diplomatic bag.

Ilya also liked Brian paying in U.S. dollars. When it came to black market currency exchanges, Brian was quick to negotiate a premium rate that was far better than the official government exchange. This was due to the significant demand for hard currency especially U.S. dollars.

After a dozen trades, Ilya broached the subject. "Brian, would you be interested in making some good money?"

Brian sized Ilya up, then looked him squarely in the eyes. "That depends. Try me, I can keep a secret."

"You say you often make a run between Moscow and Geneva?"

"Yes, I have one run coming up in two weeks. From here to Geneva then on to Ottawa. Why?"

"Could you take something for me to a friend in Geneva – something small that will fit easily in your diplomatic bag?"

Brian hesitated, pretending to contemplate. "It depends. I'd be taking a risk. What's in it for me?"

"How about a thousand U.S. dollars?"

"Something small?"

"Yes, just a few grams – say, 100 grams."

"I can't unlock and open my bag until I'm in the Canadian Embassy. Delivery to your person would have to be after that."

"It's something I want to deposit in a bank. I will give you the person to see at the bank upon arrival."

"Well, that's possible. I often make deposits to Government of Canada accounts at one of the Geneva banks."

"Excellent!"

Two weeks later, Brian paid Ilya another visit. Along with a half dozen tins of caviar, Ilya gave him an envelope with the name of a Geneva bank written on it along with a contact person and phone number. The number 182 was also written beside the name of the bank. "I've cleared this with the bank. They will be expecting you, but phone first," Ilya said.

When Brian returned to the Canadian Embassy, he showed the envelope to Marie Beauchamp, 3rd Secretary, who was running the operation. She took the envelope out for examination, and not long afterward called Brian back into her office. "That's a packet of well-cut high clarity one carat diamonds. We can't tell if they're Soviet man-made or natural – either way, quite valuable. Looks as if you're being tested."

Brian smiled. "No problem. I'm looking forward to the delivery in Geneva."

"We'll be covering your back but we won't step in if someone attacks you – that'd blow your cover."

Brian frowned. "Thanks."

Marie smiled. "Brian, I know you can talk your way out of anything."

Chapter 37

Geneva, Switzerland

Brian took a taxi to the bank, where the doorman ushered him across the lobby to a receptionist who confirmed Brian had an appointment with Monsieur Pierre Marks. She called M. Mark's office to inform him of Brian's arrival, then looked up at Brian and smiled. "Monsieur Marks will be here directly."

In a few minutes an older gentleman in a navy blue pinstripe suit, white shirt, black shoes and expensive dark blue tie tastefully bearing the bank's logo arrived. He introduced himself to Brian as Pierre Marks and motioned him to follow. They took an elevator to the third floor and Brian was led into a small meeting room. "Please have a seat," Monsieur Marks said, "I understand you have an envelope for me."

"Yes." Brian took the envelope out of his pocket and pushed it gently across the table to Monsieur Marks.

Marks picked it up and carefully examined it. "I have been instructed to receive this from you if it appears intact and to give you a receipt for it." He pressed a button that was hidden under the table. "My assistant has prepared a receipt and will bring it."

In seconds, the assistant brought in two pages of paper on official letterhead stating the bank had received a sealed envelope bearing the number 182. Brian signed off that he had delivered it and Monsieur Marks signed for the bank. Brian then asked, "May I open an account with you?"

"Of course!" M. Marks had his assistant bring the papers to create a new account. When Brian finished signing and determining a password, M. Marks carefully reviewed how to access the account by phone and in person. Brian handed M.

Marks one thousand U.S. dollars as the first deposit and received a pass book in return.

They shook hands and the assistant escorted Brian out of the building.

Chapter 38

When Brian next returned to Moscow, he brought Ilya two thousand bubble-wrapped pain-killer tablets of which cocaine was a key ingredient. Ilya was delighted as he shook Brian's hand and palmed U.S hundred-dollar bills into it. "You've earned a lot of caviar with those pills!"

"Are you and your friend in Geneva happy with my first visit?" asked Brian.

"Everyone is happy. Your delivery went well. Are you prepared to do some more?"

Pocketing the money, Brian smiled. "Absolutely!"

"When is your next run to Geneva?"

"Next week. I'm doing Moscow to Geneva and back."

"I'll have another envelope for you to take to Geneva. Can you bring a package back?"

"How big is the package?"

"Two kilos. It will easily fit into your diplomatic bag."

"A thousand U.S. dollars each way then."

"Agreed."

Marie DeLaval was waiting for Brian in the embassy's mail room when he returned from Geneva. "How did it go?"

"No problems. I delivered the envelope to the same banker and picked up a package weighing about a kilo. It's in the bag here. My bet it's either heroin or cocaine."

"Let's get our guys to take a quick look before you deliver it to Ilya."

"It seems sealed very well."

"We have our ways. No one will know we looked at it."

Ilya took a quick look at the package Brian handed him before putting it under the counter. He beckoned to someone behind Brian, who reached into his pocket and palmed a wad of U.S. hundred-dollar bills to Brian while shaking hands. In a moment, a teenage boy came up to the booth. "You want me Dad?"

Ilya handed him the parcel and said, "Take it to Uncle Ivan." Ilya turned to Brian and asked him to wait with him until the boy came back. They chatted for a few minutes until Ilya's son returned. "Uncle Ivan wants to meet your friend."

"Brian, my brother would like to meet you," Ilya said. "Mikhale here will take you to him now, if you don't mind."

Brian followed Mikhale through the maze of stalls on the bazar's ground floor, eventually making their way to a loading platform that led to an office tucked above the shipping floor. The boy knocked and they entered when someone inside called.

Brian found himself face to face with a tall, large man with an unkempt black beard and black curly hair in a shaggy cut. He was dressed like a workman in rough clothes. They shook hands and Brian noted that the man was strong, with large hands that had seen hard labor. He motioned for Brian to take a wooden chair facing a big well-worn wooden desk, then seated himself behind it.

He took a long appraising look at Brian and said in Russian, "I'm told your Russian is good."

"Your accent sounds Georgian, but not from Tbilisi," Brian replied.

He laughed and slapped a hand on the table. "Very good! I'm from a coastal city but I've been here for twenty years."

"What can I do for you Mr....Mr.?"

"Kasteroff. Ivan Kasteroff – but you may call me Ivan. Have you enjoyed working for me?"

"For you? What do you mean?"

"You have a pocket full of U.S. hundred-dollar bills. They came from me. I control this market and half the black market activities in Moscow."

"The money is much appreciated. I am pleased to be of service. I trust we may do more with our relationship?"

"Yes, let's discuss the routes you have and frequency, then I can do some planning."

Chapter 39

Marie and Brian were in her office sipping typically hot Russian tea in glass mugs. “So the two kilo package was heroin,” Marie said.

Brian was a little surprised. “You’d think they’d have a more direct route for that – it likely originated in Afghanistan, which of course the Russians occupy right now.”

“Maybe it came from the Golden Triangle of Burma, Thailand and Yunnan, or perhaps the Guangxi region in China. That route is usually between Macau and Portugal, or through Thailand to America.”

“Ah!”

“We were half-thinking, what if you made yourself more valuable to Ivan by introducing him to a source of cocaine?”

“Interesting! I could easily sound him out – maybe bring him a sample?”

“Our American friends like the idea and can set you up.”

“You got this all planned already?”

Marie smiled. “Not without your input to finalize it.”

The next run was more of the same. Brian returned from Geneva with another two kilos of heroin for Ilya and was paid well. As he pocketed his money, he told Ilya, “I’d like to see Ivan.”

When Mikhale returned from running the parcel to Uncle Ivan, Ilya left him to mind the stall and escorted Brian to Ivan’s office. Ivan was a little surprised but friendly. “Brian! Comrade! I understand everything went well?”

"It did. I'll bet the packages I'm moving for you are heroin and I don't mind couriering in drugs for you. But I have something that may interest you as it's really big in America." He handed Ivan a small plastic baggie of cocaine.

Ivan held the bag up to the light and looked carefully. He then inserted a penknife blade and extracted a bit of the white crystalline powder. He wet a finger, poked the material, and placed a sample of it on his tongue. "Cocaine. Quite pure. You have a source?"

"As you know, my job also takes me to Latin America. I can get you good prices."

"And a way of getting it to us."

"Unless you get into moving big quantities, then you'll have to get creative."

Ivan thought for a moment. "If it works, then I would want to meet your source."

"That can be arranged if you can meet me in another country, say Switzerland?"

He sighed. "That is difficult. Can you bring your source here?"

Brian thought for a moment. "One of them. Maybe."

Ivan looked at the packet again. "Best we start small. How much do you want for a kilo delivered here?"

"I'll deliver here but I want full payment in either a hard currency or gold to my Swiss bank account before I deliver."

Ivan smiled. "One third. Balance in U.S. dollars when I see and test it."

The bargaining had begun.

Chapter 40

After successful trips once a month over the next six months, Ivan approached Brian. “I would like to meet your source and see if we can move bigger quantities of your cocaine. It is becoming popular here.”

Brian relayed the request to Marie at the embassy, who was pleased. “Good job Brian! We were waiting for this. You’re to meet with Marc DuPlesse and a couple of CIA types in Ottawa to set it up.”

Brian was able to get a good night’s sleep in Ottawa before the scheduled meeting in Marc’s office. When he arrived, he was shown to a small conference room where Marc and two other men were waiting. Marc introduced Peter Swift and Reg Mendoza – both CIA. Peter took the lead. “So, this guy, Ivan Kasterof took the bait?”

Brian, helping himself to a cup of coffee, nodded. “Yeah. Do you guys have a line on him?”

Reg Mendoza spoke up first. “Our people in Moscow say he’s quite high up in the local mafia. If he told you he controlled half the black market in Moscow, he may not be bragging. He’s certainly well-entrenched in the underworld.”

“OK, so what do we do now?” Marc said. “I doubt if he’s powerful enough to get permission to leave the USSR. Add to that, it’s hard to get a visa to enter the USSR.”

Reg looked at Brian. “We’ll have to meet him on his own ground somehow.”

“What have you got in mind?” asked Brian.

“We present someone from a country friendly to the USSR – say part of a trade delegation or a student on a study visa," Marc suggested. "Brian, you could arrange a meeting in Moscow."

"That could work," said Ron. "I'll talk to my contacts at the Central and South American Desk and see what we can come up with."

A week later, Brian was back in the same conference room with Marc, Reg and Peter. Ron opened the conversation. "We connected with the right people on our Central and South American Desk and they were most helpful. I think we've got a pretty good solution. One of the people they've been cultivating is a big cocaine producer who has a son in graduate school in Moscow."

"Moscow?" said Marc, a bit surprised.

"Yeah. The dad's not only a big cocaine producer, but the local communists there have been helping the producers to fight the government – and us, by the way. Our government has been financing and assisting the Bolivian government to combat cocaine production, so Moscow and Havana have been playing the other side."

"So the US is supporting the government to try to wipe out cocaine production yet this guy, a big producer, has the communists on his side fighting the government?" Marc asked.

Peter smiled. "You got it! But our agency feels it best to cultivate all sides – especially those who may rise to power. We can win some brownie points by helping our producer get set up with a new buyer."

Brian snickered. "And we're also contributing to the Soviet government's drug problem."

Marc frowned at Brian. "It pays to have friends in the underworld."

Reg looked at Brian. "Our guy in the field will introduce you to the producer and you can run liaison between him and the son in Moscow."

"OK. When do I start?"

"We'll brief you on the dad and what we have in mind today. Then, you're off to meet him tomorrow."

"And just where is he?"

"Bolivia. You're to make a diplomatic bag run to La Paz and we'll have a meeting arranged there."

Chapter 41

La Paz, Bolivia

After dropping off his diplomatic bag at the embassy, Brian was able to get six hours sleep before he was due to meet his contact. He had just finished showering when the contact, Hector Munoz, called to announce he was waiting in the hotel's lobby.

Hector was Mr. Average – average build and Spanish looks, modest clothes and about fifty years old. They shook hands when they met in the lobby and Hector directed Brian to a car he had parked down the block – a non-descript sedan, about five years old, and a model quite common on the streets of La Paz.

Once they'd got into the car, Hector spoke. "We'll be meeting papa Miguel Garcia for lunch. He's in town on business, so we don't have to go out to his ranch. He's one of the cocaine kingpins in the region north of here. He went socialist when the government started a campaign to stop cocaine production. You see, cocaine is an ancient drug here in Bolivia. It's entrenched and a good portion of the population does not support the current government attempts to stop production. That's been an opportunity for Cuban and Soviet-sponsored socialists to get a significant foothold here. They're threatening to take over the government. My bet is they will in a few years as the current government is rapidly losing popularity."

"And Uncle Sam's been financing the current government to stop cocaine production?" asked Brian.

"Yeah, the government takes the money and the leaders grab much of it. But they have had to show some progress, so they've been heavy-handed with the producers at times."

"What's Miguel like?"

"Miguel's a great guy – very personable and a leader in the Movement for Socialism," Hector said. "But with him socialism is a tool – business comes first."

"Do you know anything about the son in Moscow?"

"Yeah, I've met him. He's a chip off the old block – pragmatic like his dad. Working on a graduate degree in chemistry courtesy of a Soviet scholarship."

"Chemistry," Brian noted "That'll come in handy for their business.

"So, how come the CIA is close to Miguel Garcia if he's a socialist?"

"We do business," replied Hector. "He has reliable quality. Besides, it's not obvious we're from Uncle Sam."

"So, I'm here as a Canadian to create a little distance."

"It helps a bit. But he knows I'm CIA – and a good customer. Plus we do each other favors from time to time."

They met at a Chinese restaurant where Miguel had reserved one of the private rooms at the back near the kitchen. As they were led by a hostess through the main part of the restaurant, Brian noticed a couple of guys positioned at a table just outside the door to the private room. It was obvious they were wearing shoulder holsters under their jackets. One recognized Hector and nodded. Before he entered the room, Brian looked back and spotted two more near the front door.

Miguel was standing by a round table talking with a waiter when they entered. He was in his early fifties, about five-ten and two hundred muscular pounds with a swarthy complexion, handsome smiling Latino face and curly black hair. Hector introduced Brian. As they shook hands Brian received a strong grip while noting Miguel's large work-hardened hands. He sized Brian up. "Pleased to meet you

Brian. I understand you're a Canadian courier with their Diplomatic Corps."

Brian spoke in Spanish. "Yes, Sir. My runs take me to the Americas, Europe and the USSR."

"Your Spanish is good! Please, sit down, I've ordered a seven-course meal. I hope you like Chinese food."

After they were seated, mineral water and green tea were served before Hector broached the subject. "As I mentioned, Brian has an interesting opportunity that may interest you. Brian has a friend in the Moscow mafia's black market for whom he has been doing some favors. Brian's been buying cocaine in Trinidad and Nassau and taking it to Moscow in his diplomatic bag. As you know, no one is allowed to inspect a diplomatic bag, and it's been working well."

Miguel reached for a plate of sweet and sour chicken. "Interesting. Go on."

Brian interjected. "I've also been doing some banking for him in Switzerland."

"For a fee, of course?" asked Miguel.

Brian took a sip of his green tea. "Yes. I am paid well."

Miguel looked at Brian. "I presume in hard currency like U.S. dollars?"

"Yes. Sometimes Swiss francs."

Miguel smiled. "So, you are looking for a better and cheaper source of cocaine?"

"My friend in Moscow wants more than I can carry and I want to opt out as the risk of discovery grows with every trip."

"How much can you safely carry?"

"A kilo or two at a time and I can only make a trip once every couple of months."

Miguel thought for a moment. “What volume does this man want?”

“At least one hundred kilos at a time. He has begun to develop a significant demand for the product.”

“For me, getting product into the Soviet Union is quite possible – especially through Cuba. But getting paid in hard currency may be a problem.”

“As I mentioned, I want to back away from this,” Brian said. “I don’t have the time to organize it.”

The next three dishes arrived and they busied themselves sampling. As they were eating, Miguel spoke. “I have heard about the Swiss banks and their secrecy. Brian, have you experience with them?”

“I have some contacts there, yes. I even have an account there – both safety deposit and banking. They offer a lot of services with absolute discretion.”

“Do you think the Swiss are better than the Caymans, the Bahamas or even Antigua?”

“Maybe Antigua is a runner up but I’d be worried about the Bahamas and the Caimans right now as they’re concerned about the Americans putting on pressure to release information. As it is, the Americans now have a large clearinghouse in St. Louis through which every offshore transfer of funds to and from the USA must be reviewed. It is starting to worry many people.”

Miguel nodded. “Yes. I’m aware of that.”

When they were finishing their meal, Miguel spoke. “If you give me the name of your Moscow black market contact, I will check him out and get back to you. If this looks reasonable, I have a son studying in Moscow whom I would want you to introduce to your contact.”

Chapter 42

Two weeks later, after another two-kilo cocaine run, Brian met with Ivan in his office. "The son of one of my sources is studying in Moscow at one of the engineering institutes. He's here on a scholarship taking chemical engineering. His father says the son is empowered to make arrangements for larger quantities."

Ivan smiled. "Interesting. What is his name and where is he from?"

"He's from Bolivia. He's here working on a Master's degree. He did his undergraduate degree in chemical engineering in Cuba – that's also where he studied Russian."

"Is he fluent in Russian?"

"Not the best but he's OK. I've met him."

"And what is his name? What institute is he attending?

"His name is Juan Garcia and he attends the Tomsk Polytechnic Institute."

Ivan nodded his head. "His level of Russian must be good to get into that school. I'll check him out and get back to you."

Brian met with Ivan a week later. "This guy, this Juan Garcia checks out as a grad student," Ivan said. "I'm willing to meet him."

They met in Gorky Park on a sunny warm Sunday. Ivan came up behind Brian and Juan as they were strolling toward the largest roller coaster. As he passed them, Ivan said, "Take the roller coaster. I'll be waiting at the exit. Follow me then."

As they got off the ride, they saw Ivan in the crowd. They followed at a distance while he led them on a path behind the attractions and eventually into a service alley leading to an office behind the boat rental concession. After they followed him in he shut the door and motioned to them to be quiet. He waited a few minutes until someone knocked on the door – two taps, then three, then another two quick taps. Ivan didn't bother to open the door. "Good! My friends have been watching and say you were not followed."

Brian introduced Juan to Ivan. They shook hands with Ivan looking Juan squarely in the eyes. Then Ivan said, "You are from Bolivia?"

"Yes, my family has a plantation north-east of La Paz in the Chapare region of Chochabamba."

"Your father is Miguel Garcia? One of the leaders in the Cocalero Movement?"

"That's right. That's how I got to study in Cuba and here. He's active in the Movement for Socialism. He's also one of the founders of the Sovereignty of the People Party."

"Third in command right now."

Juan smiled. "Yes. You are well-informed."

Ivan laughed. "As you can see, we like to know who we are dealing with."

"Brian says you want cocaine in quantity. My father has authorized me to work with you."

"So be it. We need to work out quantities, transport, delivery points, prices and payment."

"Can you take delivery in Cuba or Colombia?" suggested Juan.

"No problem, but Havana is preferred. We can ship from Cuba either by air or sea. Colombia is uncertain, too many prying American eyes."

"How and where will you pay? Soviet rubles are worthless to us. We want hard currency – preferably U.S. dollars – or gold, maybe diamonds. Payment must be in a safe location, such as Switzerland, Mauritius, Belize, Macau or Antigua."

"We need to settle on a price FOB Cuba."

"$16,500 U.S. dollars a kilo for 90% pure product. You will get the opportunity to inspect and approve the quality and quantity in Cuba."

Ivan was surprised. "That's a lot better than I've been paying Brian!"

Brian interceded. "I've been charging you European prices. They're far higher than prices closer to the source in Central America and a few Caribbean countries. Besides, we're not talking just one or two kilos at a time through Cuba. You said you wanted quantity."

They eventually settled on $12,500 U.S. per kilogram with a minimum quantity of one hundred kilos per shipment. Payment was a problem. Brian volunteered, for a fee, to courier hard currency, gold or diamonds to Geneva where the funds could be put in trust with a law firm or bank, and then transferred with a phone call. Juan balked at the idea of diamonds unless there was a premium on the price per kilo to cover the risk of re-selling the diamonds on the trading market.

Ivan, feeling the transfer of funds to Geneva was a bit tedious, had a different plan. "Why don't we just pay you in U.S. dollars or Swiss francs at point of transfer? I have good people in Havana. I'd expect a discount for that."

Key Largo, Florida

Pete threw his empty beer can in the trash and reached for another as Bill spoke. "Brian was able to gracefully back away from the cocaine deal. Ivan was very successful with it. He grew to be one of the major cocaine suppliers in the Western Soviet. He made millions which he later used to snap up some very large and profitable companies when the Soviet Union collapsed."

Pete added, "Brian kept up his relationship with Ivan, which provided a font of intel and services."

"Do you think he benefited personally?" asked Sanford.

Bill laughed. "Of course! He had started to get sticky fingers by then. We allowed him to keep his delivery commissions and we know he took the cocaine we sourced direct from Colombia and marked it up to European price levels. His visits to Geneva also offered him the opportunity to stash some of it away."

"This Juan Garcia – was he real?" asked Stanford.

Pete commented. "Oh yeah! We didn't front anyone. We were cultivating both sides in Bolivia. Daddy Miguel Garcia was one of the country's biggest cocaine producers, and the socialist movement was and still is pro-cocaine. He was a leader in the movement. We just turned him on to a good business opportunity."

Chapter 43

PANAMA

Key Largo, Florida

Richard Duggan got up, stretched, and helped himself to another beer. "Brian retired from the diplomatic courier job when his intelligence service was disbanded at the end of the Cold War. I gather he was seconded to you for a while before that."

Bill Mason put his feet on a cleat and leaned back. "Yeah, we kept him busy in Central America for a spell."

"Like Panama," said Pete.

"Yeah. We sent him into Panama in advance of the invasion back in '89. His Canadian passport came in handy."

"Deniability?" Richard asked.

"No, not really. Just that most of our people were well known to President Nachos. He used to be head of Panamanian Intelligence and he worked closely with us most of the time he was president."

"But he had his own agenda," Pete said. "While he was helping us move arms to groups we supported in Nicaragua, Colombia, El Salvador and Guatemala, he was also moving cocaine for the cartel and selling them protection in Panama. He took a fee for drug flights that refueled in Panama and was heavily involved in laundering drug money through the Panamanian banks. He made big money when he sold citizenships and really pissed us off when we learned he had supplied Cuban Intelligence with over five thousand Panamanian passports."

"He was also tied into the Iran-Contra fiasco that muddied our President," Pete said.

Sanford waved a finger. "Hush, we still can't talk about that!"

"Anyway, we inserted Brian into Panama with orders to keep an eye on President Nachos and his family's movements," Bill said. "When the invasion started, Brian was tasked with accessing some of the offshore bank accounts of President Nachos. He was successful to some extent."

Pete looked at his near-empty beer bottle. "I hear he got wet in Panama. He killed again."

"Yeah!" confirmed Sanford. "That's in his file."

Panama City, 1989

Brian took a taxi from the airport to the Marriott Hotel in downtown Panama City and checked into an executive suite. He told the receptionist he was a businessman and would need the suite for about a month. After negotiating a monthly rate including breakfasts and laundry service with the front desk duty manager, he used a Platinum credit card which seemed to impress the manager.

Once Brian had settled in he pulled out his satellite phone and touched base with Bill Mason at CIA HQ in Langley, Virginia. I've got word that Steve Charleston's in Panama," Bill said.

"I know him well," Brian replied. "We've worked together before on some laundry deals, like when I helped start the trust companies in Nassau and Antigua. He brought in a lot of business. You got a number for him here in Panama?"

"Better than that, he's also staying at the Marriott. You know it's a favorite haunt for Americans. I bet you'll run into some others you know there. He's in room 1212."

"I remember he was very tight with President Nachos and brought some of his business to the Nassau trust company."

"Right!"

"Thanks, I'll find him." Brian managed to catch Steve in his room in the early evening and they met in the main bar.

Steve was a tall, slightly flabby fully blond Texan with blue eyes, still fairly handsome at about sixty years old. He was wearing designer blue jeans, western boots, and a designer jean shirt with jeweled bolo tie under a tan ultra-suede sport coat. He greeted Brian warmly with a fist bump and a bear hug. "Brian, I haven't seen you since Nassau! It's been a while. Thanks again for getting me appointed to the board of directors of Antigua Trust."

"No problem. I assured them you'd bring in a lot of business."

"Yeah! They even arranged citizenship for me – very useful! How'd you know I was here?"

"Oh, Bill Mason mentioned it."

Steve did a bit of a double take. "Bill Mason? I haven't seen him for a few months. He's keeping tabs on me?"

"I'm to relay a message relating to your health."

"Uh, oh!"

"Yeah. Seems the French and others are ganging up on President Manuel Nachos. They're planning jail time for money laundering. You may not want to be within a thousand miles of Panama when the axe falls as there could well be spillover. You and Jesus Cruz have been named."

Steve took a large swig of his drink. "Oh shit! Any word how soon this will take place?"

"I was told it may be as early as next week, and that they've been building a case that's ironclad. This info is a gift from Bill Mason. Please don't share it with anyone."

Steve nodded his head, took another sip, and thought for a minute. “OK, thanks for the tip. But I know Bill Mason. He likes quid pro quo. You looking for something?”

“Other than a thank-you drink and fancy dinner next time I see you in another country? Yeah, you know the game. Brief me on this mistress of Manuel Nachos and his wife and kids?”

“Well, he plays around and his wife Lucy is pissed about it. After three kids, the marriage is sterile. To top it off, her parents and siblings hate him. She’s threatened divorce – but this is a Catholic country so you know she’s stuck. He’s very tight with the Cardinal of Panama. He’s flatly told her he won’t entertain a divorce.

“He and Lucy have separate bedrooms – that is, when he sleeps at home. If you meet her, watch out, she likes sex and doesn’t get it as much as she would like.” Steve smiled. “She’s very grateful though when she does.”

“Been there?” asked Brian.

Steve smiled broadly and nodded slightly. Brian fell silent for a moment and sipped his drink while looking Steve in the eyes. “Can I get an introduction?”

Steve roared laughing. “Aw, you’re a desperate old man?” His joking faded and his face got serious. “Business?” Brian nodded. “Bill Mason’s type of business?”

Brian nodded again. “Also, what can you tell me about his Number One mistress?”

“That’s Vivien Mays, a bit of a blonde bombshell about twenty years younger than Manuel. She’s also pretty bright. He treats her with respect and uses her as a confidant. He’s got her settled into a fancy apartment close to the palace. He’s even got a car and driver/bodyguard assigned to her.”

Brian let that comment settle for a moment. “I bet she’s got some secrets.”

Steve smiled. "You're right on that! She's sat in on some of our meetings. She's no dummy!"

"How about I buy you that fancy dinner now and you can fill me in a little more?"

"Sure! Grub's decent here at the Marriott. What more can I tell you?"

"Well, phone numbers would be a start. I'd like to get close to the two of them."

"The missus *and* the mistress?" Steve laughed. "You're living dangerously!"

Brian replied with a half-serious tone. "I want to convert them to my religion I've started my own church." Then he smiled and laughed.

Steve roared with laughter. "Bedroom conversions?" He laughed again and choked on his drink.

Brian smiled. "Don't knock it until you've tried it. It's a great way to get some sex. I'm more of a deacon than a minister as I give both physical and spiritual enlightenment."

Steve roared with laughter. "It works?"

Brian smiled and sipped his drink. "It works."

Over dinner that evening, Steve asked, "Seriously, you think I should get out of Panama ASAP?"

"It's real, man. Something big is coming down."

"OK, I'll take the hint."

"That's wise, man. Before you go, could you show me this apartment where Vivien Mays lives and maybe point out the bodyguards?'

"No. But knowing Bill Mason, you have a photo of her and you've already got good intel. Besides, you've got eyes and ears, brains and patience."

Brian nodded. Steve rattled off her address and apartment number, which Brian wrote down before posing another question. "What about Mrs. Nachos, she ever leave the palace?"

"Best place to find her is at the main cathedral – the basilica in the Old Quarter. She goes there almost daily at nine a.m. for all of five minutes, then across the street to a small café where she has breakfast. She's got a bodyguard but usually only one, who doubles as a driver. She's got a love nest in a penthouse about a mile from the palace. That's where she lets loose. I'll call her tonight and give you an introduction. You can always meet her casually in the café. Her bodyguard usually stays outside in the car. But watch out, she loves an affair and is very demanding."

"Thanks! What about Manuel? Does he have a set routine?"

"He's most often found in his office in the palace except for Siesta. He's generally in Vivien's apartment for that – usually between twelve-thirty and three. Sometimes he lingers longer. I've had to meet him there a few times for business."

"What about dinner? Does he eat in the palace with his wife?"

"Sometimes. She has to be present when he's entertaining. Sometimes he has dinner at Vivien's. He's also been known to take Vivien out to dinner to a fancy restaurant outside of town with a private room. He often does business there – you know, our kind of business. Occasionally, he takes Mrs. Nachos out – but only for public appearances at special events."

Brian thought for a moment. "How does Vivien stay in shape?"

"She goes to an upscale fitness center almost daily. It's on the second floor of her building."

"Ah!"

"Does Mrs. Nachos stay in shape?"

"She has a personal trainer who goes to the palace three mornings a week."

"What about the Nachos children?"

"The three girls – Lena, Susan and Tuti – are now ladies. All are enrolled in universities stateside."

Steve put his napkin down and pushed back his chair. "Well, Brian thanks for dinner and the hot news. I'm going to take a flight out in the morning. Anyway, I've finished my business here. Good luck 'converting' the ladies!"

Brian laughed as he shook Steve's hand. "I need the practice."

Chapter 44

Brian met Lucy Nachos in the 3233 café across from the Basilica of St. Mary in the Old Quarter near the palace. Steve was good to his word and had told Lucy about him. She entered the café and took a seat at a small table in a corner. Brian had been sitting nearby at a separate small table in the middle of the room. He walked over with his coffee and introduced himself in Spanish as the friend of Steve's.

She looked him over and smiled, then invited Brian to sit at her table. Brian made a quick appraisal. She was of fair beauty, in her mid-fifties, of medium height and well-proportioned. Lucy's facial skin was tight, giving her eyelids a slanted look which led Brian to notice the surgery scars on her neck from a facelift. He also noticed no grey hair and assumed she had it colored. "So, Mr. West, Steve told me you were in a similar line of business as him and that you were old friends. Are you a banker?"

Brian smiled. "You can say that. I'm associated with an offshore bank and trust company. I'm here in Panama developing business with some of your banks."

"How boring!"

Brian smiled again. "You might say that!"

"Steve told me you also were a deacon in your own church. Now, that has me very curious. You know, I'm a Catholic – but may we say the religion has some restrictions?'

"Yes, they frown on divorce," Brian replied.

"Touché, Mr. West! It can leave one very unhappy. Did Steve tell you I've been wanting a divorce for years?"

"He did! I'm so sorry to learn you're unhappy."

"Your Spanish is excellent, Mr. West."

"Thank you! I seem to have a facility for languages – Italian, French, Russian, Latin, German and English. You know, the Romance languages."

She smiled and switched to French. "I studied French in Paris when I was in college. I spent three semesters at the Sorbonne. France was interesting because of all the different dialects when you travel around the country."

Brian answered in French. "Yet there is a national movement to shame everyone into speaking Parisian French."

"Yes, I noticed! I've been there many times since with my husband when he went over on business."

Brian complemented her. "You indeed have a very fine Parisian accent."

She smiled broadly. "Please call me Lucy. May I call you Brian?"

Brian nodded.

"I welcome the opportunity to speak French," Lucy said. "Perhaps you can tell me more about your religion."

"I would be delighted! I'm sure you will find it very spiritual and enlightening."

She laughed and looked at her watch. "But not here, not now. I have a hair appointment. Perhaps we may continue at my apartment. Here, let me write down the address. I'll clear you with the doorman. May I see you around three this afternoon?"

Brian was cleared by the doorman and directed to the fifteenth floor. When he asked what apartment number to ring, the doorman said, "Sir, there is only one apartment on that floor."

Lucy answered the knock on her door dressed only in a see-through shorty nighty, red and sheer, with no panties. Brian took a deep breath and managed to say, "I love the nighty."

She smiled and took his hand as she closed the door and spoke in French. "I've just finished Siesta," she purred provocatively. "The bed is still warm, voulez-vous coucher avec moi (won't you come to bed with me)?" She led him through a spacious living room to a bedroom. She turned into him, raised up on her toes and planted a kiss squarely on his lips.

He responded with a hug and tentative French kiss and Lucy rubbed her pelvis into him while deepening her kiss. Brian had enough presence of mind to notice her perfume, a light amount of Chanel Number 5, which helped stimulate his mood.

Before he knew it, she was expertly undoing his belt and shucking his pants off, rubbing her face into his crotch as she knelt. In seconds they were writhing on the bed, both naked.

Brian discovered she was almost insatiable. He was a master at giving satisfaction, carefully pacing himself while providing sensuous stimulation and building her to multiple breathtaking orgasms. When she finally slowed down for a rest, she exclaimed, "It's wonderful! If all the priests in your religion are like you, how do I sign up?"

Brian laughed. "I'm not a priest. I'm not sworn to celibacy. They call me a deacon. A deacon is someone who looks after the physical welfare of the members, but I am also a spiritual guide. I can help you find enlightenment."

"That's obvious! Physical delight and maybe spiritual! I want to learn more. Pour us a drink of that champagne chilling on the night table and tell me about your religion. It's New Age, isn't it? Our cardinal says it's based on the occult and should be shunned."

Brian laughed and reached for the champagne and glasses. "I've heard that before," he said while pouring. "In fact, 'New Age' may be too broad. It's a term loosely used to define alternative views – still believing in a creator, mind you – but adopting the good from many religions in the world, including pagan beliefs and even science." She accepted a glass of the champagne. They jointly said cheers and sipped as Brian continued. "It's more spiritual than the business of selling a religion based on guilt and enforcing strict yet questionable views."

"Like forbidding divorce or abortion and marriage outside the faith – like a church I'm familiar with."

"Yes. And there's also intolerance of people with differences, like gays and lesbians."

"Sounds like my church. We have a very restrictive cardinal who hates lesbians."

"This so-called New Age concept started in the U.K. during the 1950s and spread quickly to North America and Australia. It's best described as a more holistic approach that selects good things from various religions. You know, the ancient Mayans, Navajo and Pueblo Indians have passed down a profound spirituality which should be adopted by others.

"The movement really took off in America just a couple of years ago in 1987, when there was a planetary alignment in mid-August and a so-called 'Harmonic Congruence' festival took place in Arizona. It drew a huge crowd. I was there. Some claim it was a prelude to the dawning of the Age of Aquarius – you know, peace and harmony that begins within you."

"Is it one common movement?" asked Lucy.

"No, that's why I said it's such a broad term. There are many spin-off concepts and beliefs. I feel there is much to admire in indigenous American beliefs and many of them fit with our traditional Christian/Buddhist/Muslim/Jewish concepts. I've studied various philosophies and compared them to my own religious upbringing. My father was a church deacon and I grew up with the Bible. I've sort of reached my own interpretation of spirituality and I've found many others who share the same values and beliefs."

She began to fondle him while gazing at his growing erection. "Does your religious philosophy believe in variety in sex?"

He began rubbing her and found she was wet already. "Yes, but only with consent and tenderness."

"You'll find me very knowledgeable."

That evening Brian was on the satellite phone with Bill Mason. "Steve Charleston is in Antigua," Bill told him. "He called and thanked me for the advice to get out of Panama. Are you making any progress?"

"I've met and entertained Lucy Nachos. She has a private love nest and invited me there. We're getting along fine. She likes a good massage."

"What about the mistress?"

"I scouted out her apartment. There's a commercial fitness center in her building and I was told she goes there frequently. I took out a membership and will give it a whirl tomorrow morning."

"Did Mrs. Nachos say much about the president?"

"Not much except she wants a divorce and the cardinal has forbidden it, and that her husband and the cardinal are best buddies. She's very unhappy but has to put on a false front. She's forced to attend state dinners and be the congenial hostess. Otherwise, they have separate lives. She knows about the main mistress and says he has many others. Tonight she's playing dinner hostess at the palace to a delegation from Argentina."

Chapter 45

The fitness club was an American franchise with all the standard equipment and an upscale atmosphere. In contrast to some Latin American countries, it was a co-ed facility where men and women shared the same equipment in one large room. Brian easily spotted Vivien Mays using a treadmill. She was the only blonde in the room and was quite attractive. She was wearing a sweat-stained tee shirt, loose grey sweat pants, and designer Nikes with pink laces. Brian took the treadmill beside her after asking if she minded. She gave him a look, smiled and said, "Go ahead."

He quickly struck up a conversation after asking what setting her machine was on. He established that he was a Canadian in Panama on business for a month and enquired about jogging paths.

Brian noticed her accent and asked about it. "I'm originally from Texas but I've been here a while," she said with a smile. "Not many notice my accent. If you're a Canadian, how come your Spanish is so good?"

"Oh, I took it at university and I've had lots of practice."

They met again in the fitness club a few times and Brian struck up conversations while working out side-by-side. He felt she was enjoying their discussions as he was getting her to talk about herself. After the fourth workout, he asked if she would like to join him afterward for coffee at the adjoining café. She agreed and Brian continued to get her to open up about her life and her ambitions.

Over coffee she began to rub her left foot and Brian asked what the problem was. "I think I need new shoes, my feet start to hurt after only a few miles on the treadmill."

"Maybe it's an arch problem," Brian commiserated.

"Maybe. It really just started."

"I took lessons on reflexology – you know, foot massage. I could massage that if you'd like?"

Skeptical, she asked, "Where did you learn that?"

"Well, when I was a teenager, I was introduced to Shiatsu – that's a Japanese massage technique. I found it really neat, so I took some time to study it and learned to administer it. Did you know a full massage in some traditional oriental styles takes at least two hours?"

"No? Really? That could be neat! Does it hurt?"

"Not if time is taken to relax all the muscles. But there's one routine that twists the back and snaps the neck. You've got to be good to do it right. Part of the routine is great for improving your balance, which stems from the inner ear."

"Oh!"

"Anyway, that also got me interested in reflexology. The Chinese claim to have been doing it for eons. I took some time off to regenerate and wound up studying it at the Evergreen Holistic Institute in Oregon. It was probably one of the best two weeks I've ever spent."

She sized him up for a few moments. "I have an apartment upstairs. We could give it a try if you've got some time."

"Now's OK."

Chapter 46

Once again, Brian was giving Bill Mason an update on the satellite phone. "I think I've established a good friendship with Ms. Mays. I haven't made it to her bed yet but the relationship is building. She likes a good foot massage."

"Good! Things are going to pop tonight," Bill said. "If you can, I want you to fill us in on where President Nachos will be."

"I'll be with Mrs. Nachos this evening. I've been invited to spend the night. Apparently, the president has nothing going on with affairs of state and is taking Vivien Mays to a restaurant out of town for dinner."

"Nuts! We were hoping he'd be in the palace. Try to pinpoint the address of the restaurant President Nachos will be at. Our people will tail him anyway but try to verify."

"Is it time for me to get some account numbers?"

"Well, we're so close to zero hour, if she's not planning to be with him, do your thing. You're authorized to use chemical interrogation on her if you need to."

Chapter 47

Lucy had quite a menu for sexual approaches that evening but she ran out of steam near midnight. "Oh, Brian, that was fun! I'm sore but I will remember this lovely evening every step I take tomorrow!"

Brian leaned over and gave her a gentle kiss on the lips then moved to her breasts. "Don't worry. I'll relax you later on with a good massage."

He noticed her getting aroused and paused to reach for the glasses of champagne. He handed her a glass. She drank it quickly then lay on her back saying, "Ravish me again, before we break for dinner, if you please."

Brian obliged but ten minutes afterwards she fell asleep and didn't really notice the prick of the hypodermic needle he used on her thigh to inject the truth serum. The knockout drops he put in her champagne had worked. He let her sleep while he searched the apartment, finding a wall safe and some relevant papers in a desk in a bedroom that seemed to have been converted into an office. He found a diary in her bedside night stand, glanced through it and discovered some good reading – including a list on the inside cover page of safety deposit box numbers for various banks in Panama and five other countries. He searched the diary more thoroughly and came across combinations to two safes, which turned out to open the one in the apartment and another in the palace.

He used a mini-camera to photograph all pages of the diary and the papers.

Brian then switched his attention to Lucy, rousing her awake with another injection that kept her in the drug stupor and talking. He probed for more information which he made sure to record on his micro-cassette recorder.

Using the combination found in the diary, he opened the safe and rifled through the contents. In addition to a silk pouch of jewelry, about one hundred thousand dollars in U.S. currency and some documents, he found a Colt .38 Police Detective Special – a small snub nosed revolver – and saw that it was fully loaded. He also found a package of bullets for the gun. He put both back and was going through the papers when someone knocked, then banged, on the front door. After a few seconds, two men walked in, and one of them shouted, "Security!" Brian grabbed the revolver and tried to hide behind a tall curtain.

One of the men called out. "Mrs. Nachos, Mrs. Nachos it's security, it's security. The palace is being attacked. We're here to remove you to safety. Mrs. Nachos?" The other pointed to the bedroom/office. "Light's on. Also a little light in her bedroom."

One stood just inside the front door with his hand on his holstered pistol while the other went to the bedroom door, knocked and called again. "Mrs. Nachos?" He waited a few seconds before entering the bedroom. When he returned, he was drawing his gun, whispering," "She's sound asleep. There's an open bottle of champagne and two glasses on the nightstand and a man's clothes on the chair. There's no one in the bathroom."

The other pointed to the bedroom/office. "Light's on in there."

One kept his gun on the doorway to the office/bedroom while the other, gun in a two-fisted grip, searched the other rooms and returned. "Other rooms clear."

They carefully approached the bedroom/office. With one covering the other they rushed in and spread out. One noticed the opened wall safe and pointed. As he was bringing his attention to the safe, the other noticed a curtain puffed out a bit. He pointed his gun at it and shouted. "You in the curtain. Come out slow and hands up."

Brian stuck his left arm out and raised it upwards. "Don't shoot! I'm coming. I'm naked. I'm not armed." He began to slowly ease out to his left. The men's eyes were fixed on his emerging naked body. As he was easing out, he managed to get off two quick shots through the curtain with the gun in his hidden hand. He caught one guard in the chest and the other in his gun arm shoulder. Both fell and Brian was quick to grab their weapons. After quickly checking each man and determining one was dead, he tended to the one with the shoulder wound. As Brian was applying a makeshift dressing from pillow cases and a towel, he asked the man, "Who are you and what are you doing here?" He decided to bluff a bit and said, "You've never violated her privacy before."

"Presidential Guard," the man said through clenched teach. "My ID's in my wallet."

"I'll accept that. But why are you here? Did you say something about the palace being attacked?"

"The Americans are invading to overthrow the government. United States Marines have landed on our beaches and parachute troops have taken the airports. The palace has been attacked by helicopters. I have orders to escort Mrs. Nachos to safety."

"Just the two of you?"

"We have a car parked downstairs. We're to get her to the Vatican Embassy. The cardinal has assured sanctuary."

"What about President Nachos?"

"Another team has taken him there."

"What about Ms. Vivien Mays?"

"She refuses to go to the Vatican Embassy. She says she will remain where she is. We are to guard her building as long as we can."

"I'll get dressed and help get you to a hospital, "Brian said. "I'm sorry about your partner but I didn't know what was going on. I thought you were going to rob us." Brian could see the man was borderline conscious. He went into the bedroom, refilled his serum syringe, and returned to the guard. "I'm a doctor. I'm going to give you something for the pain before I try to move you." He gave him an injection and got dressed while waiting for him to fully pass out, then plucked the car keys from his pocket.

Brian once again did a thorough search of the apartment before reloading the gun, wiping prints off it, and pocketing the two spent casings. He went through the safe's documents and noted a paper listing some bank accounts and passwords, taking time to photograph it before he pocketed it. After carefully wiping down the safe and its contents, Brian closed the safe and rehung the covering picture. He took the guards' guns with him.

Lucy was sleeping comfortably when he took the elevator to the building's lobby. The doorman had disappeared and Brian could hear gunfire, many helicopters overhead and occasionally artillery in the distance. The streets were deserted. He found the gunmen's car, drove it to the hotel, and left it in the parking lot after dumping the guns and spent cartridges down separate storm drains a few blocks apart.

Back in his room he called Bill Mason on the satellite phone. "I can hear the attack underway," Brian said.

"Yeah. Our troops have landed on a number of beaches and some have taken the main airport. Helicopter gunships have already strafed the palace. What progress have you made?"

"First of all, can you contact our troops nearest Lucy's apartment? I need a mess cleaned up. I got jumped by two of the President's Guards who had come to the apartment to take Lucy to the Vatican Embassy. One of them is dead and the other is unconscious from a dose of truth serum, but he was shot in the shoulder. The wound's not bad. He'll live. Lucy is also out from the truth serum and won't wake for a good six hours. I think the unconscious guard won't remember anything but I don't want the two guards found in the apartment. I don't want Lucy to know they were there. I cleaned up some of the blood though maybe the people you send will do a better job – but make sure they get in and out before Lucy wakes up. If all goes well, she'll have no memory. If so, I can see her again if needed."

"I've got some of our own people nearby. Should be no problem. Hang up and I'll call you back after I get it moving."

Fifteen minutes later Bill called back. "OK, that's underway. When they're done, I've got a squad of soldiers standing by to go in and arrest Lucy. That way, she'll never know you were the one to grab her diary and papers. Now, catch me up on what you learned."

He filled Bill in on what had transpired in Lucy's apartment. Bill was pleased. Brian went on. "The diary is a goldmine! I'll give it a good read again and photocopy it at the business services office in the hotel. Then I'll pass the roll of film I took of it, and the diary itself, on to your people here. With the attack going on, things could get lost – best to have a copy."

"Agreed. But I've got a pen and I'm recording this anyway. Give me the salient accounts and passwords now so we can move on some accounts immediately."

"Yeah, OK. There's also the combination to a safe in the palace."

"OK, I'll pass that along to the powers that be. I've just got word the Vatican has announced President Nachos has been given sanctuary in their Panama Embassy. That really complicates things."

"You'll have to talk him out,"

"Yeah. What do you want to do about Vivien Mays?" asked Bill.

"Well, according to the bodyguard I shot, she's elected to stay in place at her apartment. They've got a security detail guarding her but that can evaporate when things fall apart. I think she's safe enough till then. I'll be watching her and will move in when appropriate. Then I'll interrogate her chemically."

Chapter 48

Brian managed to convince the hotel night manager to open the business services office and allow him to privately copy the diary and some other papers. He tipped well.

Next morning, he walked through the lobby to the hotel's restaurant. The lobby and all the meeting rooms had been taken over by various international media. Brian noted NBC News had taken over a large space near the entrance where lights and cameras were set up in a makeshift studio. As he passed by, the lights and cameras were focused on a news anchorman interviewing a man dressed in a blue suit.

Brian was just about to step into the restaurant when some masked and well-armed gunmen burst through the front doors into the lobby. He watched as two NBC TV anchormen standing close to the entrance, dressed in their company logo blazers, were executed at point-blank range.

He ducked for cover behind a large potted plant when the gunmen turned on a production crew, shooting down the camera and sound men, the anchorman, and his interviewee. They grabbed three more TV news people Brian knew were American broadcasters and hustled them out to a waiting van while two of the gunmen sprayed the ceiling with bursts from their automatic rifles.

Brian eventually made his way with difficulty to Vivien's apartment building and spent much of the day staking out the fitness club and adjacent café. Although they were in plain clothes, he managed to identify and avoid the Presidential Guards assigned to keep an eye on Vivien. The streets of the Old Quarter bristled with Panamanian troops of the Dignity Battalion, President Nachos' loyal Palace Guard. Brian felt he had walked right into the middle of what would soon be a war zone. Sandbagged gun emplacements were being set up at all street corners and he noted snipers on some of the roofs and higher windows. He could hear the roar of tanks a few blocks away in the direction of the palace.

In the afternoon, the sound of gunfire began getting closer, indicating that the fighting was nearing the Old Quarter. The air was busy – crowded and noisy – with US Army helicopters flying low overhead. He assumed some were buzzing the Vatican Embassy and others seeking snipers. By early evening, he noticed Vivien's bodyguards had faded away. It was time for him to move in.

When he knocked on her apartment door, she came to the peephole and was surprised he was there. "Brian, how did you get here?"

"I've been holed up in the fitness club for hours. Did you see all the Presidential Guards on the street? The Americans are two blocks away and fighting door to door. It looks as if fighting will break out any minute here. There are already buildings burning nearby in the Old Quarter. Once those fires get out of control they can create a firestorm. It's very unsafe – you don't want to be a civilian casualty. Come with me. I'm going to make a run for the American lines to get back to the Marriott. That part of town has already been taken over by the American troops."

"Oh shit! It may be too late," Vivien said as she unlatched the door chain and opened the door. "You might be safer here. This building is modern concrete. Come in."

Brian brushed past her as he entered. She felt a sharp pain on her thigh. "Ouch! What was that?"

Brian showed her the hypodermic needle in his hand. "Truth serum. Don't worry, you won't remember anything when you wake up." She collapsed in his arms and carried her to the sofa. He let her lie there for twenty minutes before he was sure the dosage had fully taken. In the meantime, he tossed the apartment looking for papers, a diary and a safe. He found all of them. Again the safe was hidden behind a picture on a wall in her bedroom. He tested the dosage by asking for the combination to the safe which she readily gave up.

He turned on his tape recorder, took out a note pad and pen, then turned back to Vivien and began his interrogation. He began by asking her where President Nachos would take refuge other than the Vatican Embassy. She told him about his vacation retreat in the north, his yacht on the Caribbean coast, and his jet parked at the main airport – all of which Brian had been briefed on, which verified she was deep into the dosage and very truthful.

Brian then asked her about President Nachos' bank accounts and she listed off several she knew of both in Panama and abroad. For some, Vivien knew the account numbers and passwords. She listed and described some of the drug lords she knew who had done business with President Nachos in her presence. She described how Steve Charleston and Jesus Cruz helped move funds to offshore accounts and launder some of it into clean investments in America, Canada, France and the Bahamas.

He opened the safe and found a stack of U.S. dollars, which at quick glance he estimated to be over two hundred thousand. There was also some excellent jewelry and papers pertaining to offshore bank accounts and safety deposit boxes in the president's name. He had hit pay dirt. After pocketing half the U.S. dollars, he continued rummaging through the safe and came up with a Seagram's Crown Royal whiskey blue velvet bag. He opened it and shook out some of the contents into his palm. Diamonds – large, unset, investment grade diamonds. "Probably part of El Presidente's emergency fund –

very portable," he whispered to himself before pocketing the bag of diamonds. He then set about photographing all the papers he found in the safe including the diary.

Brian noticed the gunfire outside was coming closer, getting louder, more rapid, and punctuated with grenade and mortar bursts. He assumed the U.S. troops were pushing the remnants of the Presidential Guard further down the street. Soon, the gunfire diminished on the street below and he could hear it moving farther down the next block.

By the time Brian had finished with Vivien, the gunfire had moved a few blocks away much closer to the palace. After returning the papers and diary to the safe, he left Vivien on the sofa and made his way to the street.

He found a squad of American soldiers walking down the street and asked the sergeant which way he could get to safety and the Marriott hotel. The sergeant pointed and said, "Get your ass that way. We've cleared it but we can't guarantee there won't be any snipers."

After going through multiple roadblocks by showing his Canadian passport, Brian finally made it back to the Marriott. The parking lot had been converted into a command center for the U.S. troops which gave him a sense of security.

Back in his suite, Brian counted the money – close to ninety thousand dollars. He examined the bag of diamonds, counting over five hundred – all one carat, clear and well cut. "Not bad for a day's work – danger pay," he said to himself with a smile.

When he called Bill Mason on the satellite phone and filled him in, Bill was pleased. "Well done, man! I'll pass on these bank account numbers right away. We'll either grab or freeze his assets where we can. I'll sent one of our guys around to pick up your film. As for Vivien Mays, I've got a team on their way now to pick her up. How long do you think she'll be knocked out?"

Brian checked his watch. "She's probably good for a few more hours. With the dose I gave her, she'll remember nothing."

"Great. The team's been given orders to enter but wait until she awakens naturally before they arrest her and bring her in."

"Good! Am I done now?" asked Brian. "I've done all you asked of me."

"Well, the airlines aren't running and there's still fighting. If we had to we can get you out on a military flight. But it would be best if you hung in there until we get President Nachos. We've got a million dollar dead-or-alive wanted poster out on him which could hinder him from leaving the safety of the embassy."

"Is negotiation possible? Like, can you give him some hope that he won't be killed or jailed for life?"

"Possible. Our first objective is to remove him from power and stop his criminal activities."

"You want to bring him to the U.S. for a show trial. What will you charge him with?"

"Racketeering. That's the easiest federal case we can make. The French want him for money laundering but they'll have to wait in line."

Key Largo, Florida

"Manuel Nachos finally surrendered and came out of the Vatican's Embassy in early January," Bill Mason said. "It took a lot of diplomacy to convince him to surrender. Brian had a hand in that."

"How?" asked Pete.

"He convinced Vivien to phone him. She had no knowledge Brian had rifled her safe so she told Manuel all was OK there. Brian got Vivien to convince Manuel to surrender and that was arranged."

"Isn't there some story about Nachos almost going nuts in the embassy when our Army set up loud speakers and bombarded the embassy with loud rock-n-roll music?" Pete said.

"That was true," Bill replied. "We knew he hated rock-n-roll. It played nonstop for days on end."

"What happened to Nachos?" asked Richard Duggan.

"There was a show trial back here in the States and he got forty years for racketeering. He served only seventeen before he was extradited to France and tried for money laundering. They gave him a sentence but he was extradited back to Panama in 2011 charged with murder and other crimes. They jailed him. He died of health problems in 2017."

Bill took a swig of his beer and smiled. "Lucy Nachos changed religions, left Panama and got a divorce. She eventually moved to the Okanagan in Canada and became one of Brian's followers. We didn't get at all of Nachos' bank accounts or valuables he had stashed away in safety deposit boxes – Nachos had some stashes the women weren't aware of. When he was first in custody, he got Lucy to access some to pay his legal fees and such. She filed for divorce in America and claimed way over fifty percent of all the funds she was aware of. The court ruled in her favor. She became pretty well off and contributed a lot to Brian's ministry. She even bought him a car and an apartment."

Laughing, Sanford raised his beer in a salute. "That's our Brian!"

Chapter 49

GORBACHEV

Key Largo, Florida

Sid went over to the ice chest and selected another beer. "I guess Brian's last escapade with the Soviets was when Gorbachev got into trouble and we rescued one of his economic advisors. You remember that one? The Soviet Union was beginning to disintegrate."

Richard leaned back, put his feet up on a bollard and smiled. "Yeah, that was a pretty smooth operation."

"The good thing was the Soviets were in major turmoil, with the old guard fighting the new guard factions. They weren't paying too much attention to airport security."

Moscow, August 1991

Brian made his way through the Canadian Embassy and knocked on the open door to the office of Marie Beauchamp, 3rd Secretary of Cultural Affairs. When she looked up, she smiled and beckoned him to enter. "Hi Brian! Welcome back!"

Brian took a seat across from her desk. "I gather you're living in interesting times here. There's quite a military presence on the streets. What's happened with President Gorbachev?"

"Right now, the hard-liners of the Communist Party have him under arrest. They grabbed him while he was on vacation in the Crimea. Vice President Pavlov turned against him and seems to be deeply involved in the coup. On top of that, Boris Yeltsin appears to be marshaling a different force of his own loyalists. This could be the makings of a civil war."

"Ouch!"

"Anyway, it's led to an interesting problem for us. One of Gorbachev's top economists, his expert advisor on China and one of the senior members of the committee advising on economic restructuring – you know, Perestroika and Glasnost – is here seeking political asylum."

"You're kidding!"

"He's got a legitimate argument. If the coup turns really ugly, his life is likely in peril. He could easily take some of the blame for the failure of Perestroika and Glasnost and the collapse of the Soviet Union. The hard-liners hate him."

"So, what to do about it?"

"You're going to take him to Canada, then maybe on to the United States. Both countries, as well as the U.K., are willing to take him in."

"When?"

"First flight out tomorrow. We've got two First Class seats reserved for you on Air Canada. Of course, you've got to use your excellent resourcefulness to get him safely to North America."

"O.K., let's get started. I want a Canadian diplomatic passport for him after we do a little makeup change. We'll need to find something in his size in a Canadian-tailored suit, shirt, tie, underwear and Canadian-made shoes. Also a wallet with Canadian ID papers, credit cards, etc."

"No problem."

"We should change his hair style as well."

"No problem."

"What about his teeth? Any steel caps? They'd have to be changed."

"No, he's good there."

"Also, I'd like four two-pound cans of ham. They're great for bribing authorities."

"That it?"

"Until I meet him. I'll also need some supporting papers and someone to help coach him on his new identity. Let's make his background simple with few relatives."

Serge Yakodev stood, smiled and warmly shook Brian's hand when he entered the meeting room with Marie. Brian introduced himself in fluent Russian and told him he was assigned to take him to North America in the morning. Serge appeared to be in his late fifties, about five foot ten with a medium frame that was slightly on the thin side. He had a large head with brown eyes, thin Soviet-style steel frame bifocals, and longish wavy white hair.

Brian switched to English and Serge apologized. "My English isn't very good."

"It's not bad," Brian said. "But I wouldn't want you carrying on a long conversation."

Serge switched to French. "My French is a little better. Perhaps that may help?"

Brian replied in French. "Impressive! You have a Parisian accent. Good, we can converse in that when we're travelling. Just follow my lead, whichever one I use at the time. You'll have to be careful around some French Canadians as their accent can be pretty harsh and hard to comprehend. I'll get you fitted with a hearing aid so you can pretend you're hard of hearing if you can't understand."

"I was raised in China until I was sixteen. I'm also fluent in Mandarin and Shanghai dialect."

"Good for you. But don't let on you understand and don't use it when we're on the move," Brian said. "That could blow your cover."

"Let's get started," said Marie. "First the hair stylist and glasses, then the tailor and photo for the passport. I've already arranged an identity that should fit well."

Serge's hair was trimmed to a crew cut and dyed brown. His glasses were replaced with heavy brown frames that made a huge change in appearance in itself. He was fitted for a blue double-breasted suit and provided with a white shirt and navy blue Maple Leaf tie, Canadian Government-issue, and shown how to make a Windsor knot with it. It was well past midnight when they finished the identity change and were satisfied with the identity coaching. Brian and Serge managed to snatch a few hours rest in embassy bedrooms and, after a quick breakfast, were soon on their way to the airport in an embassy car with a specialist driver.

Military and police presence on the route to the airport was intense. They were stopped by three roadblocks but their embassy license plates and diplomatic passports got them through.

Their driver, Johnny Marshall, eventually got them to the airport and parked the car in a no-parking zone close to the main entrance. Johnny, who was also in the security service, turned to face the back seat. "Nobody touches a car with embassy plates. I'll take you in. I've got an arrangement with airport security and the ticket agents. We'll jump any line as you're VIPs."

"I've got four canned Danish hams in my carry-on bag," Brian said. "Would that help?"

Johnny smiled. "It will. Some are getting tired of gold-plated lighters and rubles. Those hams are like gold man!"

Each pulling their own wheeled carry-on luggage bag, with Brian also carrying a diplomatic bag handcuffed to his left wrist, they followed Johnny to an airport security officer at a baggage x-ray machine. Johnny shook the man's hand and gave him an old comrade greeting, which paid off in them passing through after only a quick look at their tickets. The diplomatic bag was ignored. Johnny sided up to Brian and spoke in a low voice. "He likes rubles."

"Yeah, I noticed," Brian said. "Smooth man!"

As they approached the airline check-in counter, Johnny waved to a uniformed woman who turned out to be a supervisor. She smiled warmly and motioned them to a check-in position that had not been opened. She took the tickets, entered info into a computer and handed them boarding passes. "You can go right to boarding." She pointed. "That way." Johnny gave her a big hug and a handshake.

"One more security check, "Johnny said. "Brian, make sure the carry-on bags are unlocked."

"They are."

Brian and Serge followed their driver into a short line reserved for aircrew and up to the security person, who gave Johnny a big smile and friendly hug while Johnny whispered in his ear. He waved Serge through once his bag had been x-rayed, but he detained Brian. "Sir, what have you got in the bag that's metal?"

Brian looked at Johnny, who nodded. "I have four Danish canned hams."

"I'm sorry sir, not allowed."

"I understand."

The man opened the bag, extracted the hams and put them on a shelf out of sight under the counter. He then closed the bag and took a quick look at Brian's ticket before waving him on.

Johnny had a quick word with the boarding agent at the departure gate, which resulted in a hand shake. The agent motioned to Brian and Serge. "You may pre-board now."

They had one more hurdle. “Due to the unrest, the police are checking passenger ID’s after they’re seated,” Johnny said. “I can’t help you there.” He shook their hands. “I’m off. Have a good trip.”

Once everyone had boarded, a stewardess came on the speaker. “Ladies and gentlemen, there’ll be a bit of a delay while the police check your ID’s and, if you are a Soviet national, they want to see your travel permits. Please have them out and ready for them as that will help speed up the process.”

When one of the officer got to Brian and Serge, he scrutinized both passports and noted Brian had the diplomatic bag cuffed to him. He handed Brian his passport. In English, he said, “Thank you, have a good flight.”

“Thank you,” Brian replied in English.

As he handed Serge back his passport, again in English, he said, “Thank you Monsieur La Croix. Have a good flight.”

“Merci beaucoup,” Serge responded.

A few minutes later, the flight was cleared for takeoff and soon airborne.

Serge turned to Brian and whispered in French. “I think I need a drink!”

Brian smiled and nodded. “But not vodka. Stick with your Canadian heritage. You know, wine, cognac, scotch on the rocks, rye and seven, beer, even mimosa.”

Serge replied in a low voice. “What is this rye and seven? Mimosa?”

Chapter 50

When the flight stopped in London to refuel and add passengers, all on-going passengers had to deplane into an in-transit holding area. Those in First Class had a separate luxury lounge which Brian and Serge were ushered into. Once settled there, they were approached by a couple who had been in the seats behind them. The man introduced himself as Nigel Rawlings then introduced his companion, Verna McGreggor. "We're from your U.K. friends. We've got your "6" and will be with you through to Toronto."

"Are there others?" Brian asked.

"Yes, of course. We even have a couple of Americans doing the same thing. We've also got the economy class section covered."

"So this guy's a VIP?" said Brian.

"I gather."

Landing in Toronto, Brian and Serge were met just before Immigration by a woman who called Brian by name. She introduced herself as May Fields and handed him two tickets and boarding passes. "Come with me. We've got you on a connecting flight to Baltimore, where you'll be met by a man identifying himself as Mike O'Riley, and taken to a safe house for debriefing. Mike is six foot, forty years old, fit with a black crew cut and a scar on his right cheek running from nose to ear. Brian, you're assigned to stay with Serge through at least half of the debriefing until he feels comfortable. They'll fill you in more when you get settled in."

Once they were in the air again, Brian, speaking in French, asked Serge, "You say you're a specialist on China, how does that fit into Glasnost and Perestroika?"

Serge sighed. "It's a long story. Basically, we were closely watching China modernize. They made a lot of mistakes moving toward an, ah, shall we say, a controlled but entrepreneurial economy? They would change the rules and then go in one direction to excess, which they could not control and encouraged corruption. Then they would bring in excessive limiting rules and much frustration. This occurred all across the country and was very difficult to control.

"I advised Gorbachev to limit his experimentation in entrepreneurship – call it a controlled market economy, if you will – to a confined region. In our case, we selected Estonia. We allowed anyone, if they formed groups of three or more people, to take over an entity. This worked very well – up to a point. Often, the existing management took over and productivity instantly soared by an average of forty percent within six months. We had some excellent successes such as a committee of workers becoming shareholders in a pharmaceuticals factory and developing a huge export market. It was a model of success. Unfortunately, breakthroughs like that contributed to a nationalist movement where Estonia sought to separate from the Soviet Union. We lost control. Not only did local nationalism bloom, but criminals pushed in to take over many companies. We created some vicious oligarchs. Add to this the near bankruptcy from the arms race with America, and the Soviet Union imploded."

Chapter 51

PERU MINE GRAB

Key Largo, Florida

Richard tossed his empty in the trash bucket and reached for another beer. “Toward the end of the Cold War, he got involved in Peru. It was ‘official’ business but he made some interesting connections that paid off later.”

“Didn’t he see some action there?” asked Sanford.

“He did. That’s how he got a scar on his forehead looking like a thunderbolt.”

Ottawa, Canada, Prime Minister’s Office (PMO), 1991

Brian walked into the outer office of Pierre Pontaine, Special Assistant to the Prime Minister, and greeted the receptionist, Monique, in her native French. She responded cheerfully. “Bonjour, Brian! Ça va?”

“Très bon!” Brian replied, then switched to English. “You said on the phone that Pierre wanted to see me?”

“He’s not busy. He said for you to go right in.”

Brian knocked, then opened the door and walked in. Pierre rose from behind his desk and warmly shook Brian’s hand and offered refreshments.

Brian declined and took the offered seat across a coffee table from Pierre. “Brian, we’ve got a delicate matter that you could help us with.”

Brian smiled. “Go on.”

“As you know, our Prime Minister Jackson and our former Prime Minister, Peter Monroe, are the best of friends.

Since he left office, Peter was appointed to the boards of directors of a number of corporations."

"That's quite normal," commented Brian. "The corporations can often benefit from the contacts or connections developed while someone like Peter was head of state."

"Right! Quite normal," Pierre said. He looked Brian in the eyes, trying to read him. "Peter's asked for a favor and we'll be happy to assist. The situation's partly at the Head of State level anyway."

Brian, a bit cautiously, said, "O.K...."

"From this point on, everything's completely confidential. We're at the deniability level. Understand?"

Brian smiled. "Completely. Go on."

"You probably saw it in the news a while back that Peter Monroe was appointed to the board of directors of Oro Grande Minerals?"

"Yes, the largest gold mining company in North America."

"That's right! Did you notice a few weeks ago that Will Watson, the former President of the United States, was also appointed to the Board of Oro Grande?"

Brian nodded.

"Well, ex-President Will Watson and ex-Prime Minister Peter Monroe were best buddies when they were in office. That's carried over into civilian life as it was Peter who had Will appointed to the board of directors of Oro Grande."

"Understandable."

"Each receives an honorarium for being on the Oro Grande board – well over a million dollars U.S. a year plus stock options."

Brian half laughed. "The perks of having been the head of state!"

Pierre smiled and nodded. "They've got to earn it though. They're expected to bring in some business or run political interference, or both."

"I can see that."

"They've gotten Oro Grande into a mining venture in Peru that could be quite profitable – that is, after a little political situation is straightened out."

Brian leaned forward. "A little political situation?"

"Yeah, there's an old border dispute between Peru and Bolivia which is presenting problems. Both countries claim the land Oro Grande wants to develop."

Brian sat back in his chair. "Ouch!"

"Both Peter and Will are good friends with Peru's President Carlos Mendoza. He's agreed to send in troops and claim the land for Peru."

"Ah! So what's his consideration?"

"Cash. Twenty million in U.S. dollars and high-grade diamonds," Pierre said. "And, of course, some shares in Oro Grande Minerals LLC. Plus, we've learned Mendoza also has a financial interest in the ownership of the mine site."

"Sounds straight forward. Of course, Oro Grande will have a Cover-Your-Ass deal with Bolivia's leader?"

"Wish it was so simple! But Bolivia's leader is about to lose the next election and the future leadership is a bit unpredictable."

"O.K. So, where do I fit in?"

"Bag man to start with. Because Carlos Mendoza is President of Peru, you can get directly to him as a diplomatic courier. You will deliver his payment. We may also need you to eventually do the same with the new leader of Bolivia, but that has yet to develop."

"You're making this sound simple. It's not, is it?"

Pierre smiled. "No. There's a rival mining development company out of Australia that's working with the Bolivians. They want the property and want to push out Oro Grande. President Mendoza's agreed to send in the troops in a couple of days. That is, if he gets a cash advance on his consideration. You're to be on a flight to Peru tomorrow with the diplomatic bag full of you-know-what."

"Easy enough!"

"You're to tranche out payment. After a deposit, you'll need concrete proof that the troops have been sent in and the border re-established to Peru's advantage. You'll make final payment once we agree the Bolivians aren't going to protest too much and the property title transfers to Oro Grande."

"Think they'll have a shooting war?"

"They've done it before."

Chapter 52

Lima, Peru

Brian caught the Canadian Airlines flight from Montreal to Lima, landing at Jorge Chavez International Airport in the early morning. He was picked up by a Canadian Embassy car and driver and taken directly to the embassy, where he deposited the diplomatic bag in the main safe. The 3rd Secretary, Maria Gomez, took him to the guest quarters wing and checked him in. "Brian, you can get a few hours' sleep," she told him. "You've got an appointment with President Mendoza after Siesta at four p.m."

"O.K. I'll have to transfer some of the contents of my diplomatic bag to another before I go. That OK?"

"Orders are to accommodate. Whatever you need."

Brian arrived at the Presidential Palace fifteen minutes before his appointment. He was escorted through the gates and taken to the Office of the President, where he received V.I.P. treatment by the president's assistant and was taken directly in to meet President Mendoza. They shook hands when introduced and Mendoza dismissed his aide. The president spoke in Spanish and motioned Brian to a sofa. "I've been told your Spanish is very good."

Brian answered in Spanish. "You have a Castilian accent. Your Spanish is very clear."

Mendoza smiled. "Excellent!" They made small talk for a few minutes as Mendoza was sizing him up. "Yes, we can converse in Spanish," he said, but then switched to English. "However, I studied in America, at M. I. T. and received a Doctorate in Civil Engineering. So, English is good too! Let's use it around here as it cuts down on prying ears a bit. Now then, down to business. We're ready to go on this end. Where's the consideration?"

Brian pointed to the diplomatic bag at his feet. "There. BUT, there's a BUT. I'm to pay you in tranches – a down payment of one third to get started, another third once the land is secured and transferred to Oro Grande, and the final third when we are assured there will be no retaliation from Bolivia."

Mendoza frowned and thought a moment before replying. "I have expenses up front."

"Agreed. Some of the cash – U.S. dollars – up front. Mixed cash and shares on the second tranche, balance in diamonds."

"Hummm."

Negotiations continued for an hour. A deal was completed on a handshake and a handwritten note of undertaking. Brian demanded the note of undertaking to cover his own ass and prove the first tranche of the money had been transferred.

After the handshake, Mendoza picked up a phone and was put through to General Diaz, head of Peru's army. His conversation was short, giving the orders to commandeer the mine site property and delineate the border as they had previously planned. He hung up and turned to Brian. "We've been building the case in the media for a few weeks now. It's a foregone conclusion that we're going to assert ownership of our version of the boundary and that the mining property is part of Peru." Mendoza looked at his watch. "The morning papers and other media will be announcing our takeover."

Brian smiled. "You were right! You were ready to go."

"Yes! Brian, hand over the cash."

Brian elaborately took the cash out of the bag and placed it on Mendoza's desk. "Report to General Diaz at Army Headquarters tomorrow at ten a.m.," the president said. "He'll have an escort fly you out to the property and the border so you can see the situation first hand. Dress casually."

Next day, army Captain Francisco Sandal, an aide to General Diaz, met Brian at Army Headquarters. He was fitted out with a pair of army boots and a cotton military jumpsuit similar to the one Captain Sandal was wearing. "Best if you look like a soldier," said the captain.

Brian noticed his jump suit had a Lieutenant's insignia on it. "Looks as if you outrank me."

Captain Sandal smiled. "Si, in the field, you will follow my orders."

Once suited up, they went to the airport where they caught a military flight to the city of Puerto Maldonado. While the aircraft was making its landing approach, Brian noted the terrain was quite lush. He remembered it being called tropical savannah when he was being briefed. The land descended from the Andes Mountains into tropical rain forest as part of the vast Amazon Basin. When they landed at a military airfield, they transferred to a helicopter.

After half an hour airborne, Captain Sandal used his headset microphone to inform Brian they were over the proposed mine site. Brian could see a few portable buildings in a cleared area.

"Where's the border from here?" he asked.

Sandal pointed. "We're heading that way. Couple more minutes, we'll see it. Our soldiers have cut a swath in the forest and are laying survey markers. Ah, you can see part of it now."

Brian could see the newly-cut swath and a few personnel on the ground with survey transits and bulldozers. As the helicopter got directly over the swath and began to follow it north, the pilot came over the radio. "Tracers! Tracers at three o'clock! We're taking fire! We're taking fire!" The chopper lurched and the engine started smoking and grinding loudly. "Engine's hit! Brace! Brace! Brace! We're going down."

The pilot managed to guide the chopper down in a dive with the propeller blades giving some lift as they rotated from the wind generated by the falling chopper. He expertly pulled out of the dive at the last minute and flared upright, dropping the landing skids on the ground and hitting hard. They had landed along the border on newly plowed earth which helped soften the impact.

Brian and Captain Sandal, although badly knocked about and bruised, managed to help pull out an unconscious crew member, Sergeant Garcia, who had been manning the machine gun mounted at the side door. When they laid him on the ground and examined him they discovered he had been shot fatally in the chest. The pilot and co-pilot, who had managed to get out unharmed, hurried over.

"We can't stay here," the pilot shouted. "We're exposed. Head for cover!" He and the copilot led the way into the bush, dragging Sergeant Garcia with them.

Brian grabbed Captain Sandal's arm and pointed to the machine gun mounted in the doorway. "We could do with some firepower."

"Good idea!" Together they detached the gun. Captain Sandal ran with it and the attached ammo belt cradled in his arms, following the pilots who had taken cover on the other side of a berm composed of soil, trees and bush that had been plowed to the side when the border path had been cut. Brian took a moment to reach into the cargo area of the helicopter and grabbed two additional cans containing belts of ammo for the machine gun and a first aid kit. He sprinted across the barren ground and dove into the bush pile where Sandal was waiting.

Captain Sandal was well composed, assessing the situation. "Including Sergeant Garcia's, we've got four handguns between us with three clips of ammo for each." He handed Brian the late sergeant's pistol and two spare clips of ammo for it. As Brian checked the gun, Captain Sandal watched and commented. "Looks as if you know how to use one of those." Brian nodded.

"Plus, we've got the machine gun with three belts of ammo. Our troops will have heard the gunfire but we've no way of communicating with them. We need to find a good vantage point for a field of fire. The Bolivians will be coming soon."

"Let's make a smoke signal," Brian suggested. "Who's got a match?"

Captain Sandal looked confused. "What?"

"Shoot holes in the fuel tank of the chopper. Let's set it on fire. The black smoke will lead our people to us."

One of the pilots produced a lighter. Captain Sandal put a few shots in a gas tank of the chopper and fuel began to dribble out onto the earth. The pilot with the lighter ran out and touched off the fire. He got safely back to cover as flames began to engulf the aircraft, producing a thick black smoke.

"That will also attract the enemy," Sandal said. "They'll focus on the crash." He directed the pilots to take a position of cover about thirty feet up from the burning helicopter, which would give them a field of fire around the chopper's tail. He motioned to Brian and they moved to good cover thirty feet in front of the helicopter. They made a crutch out of two tree branches as a makeshift mount for the big gun. Sandal said, "I assume you know how to feed a belt of ammo to one of these?" Brian nodded as he was laying out the belts of ammunition beside the feed side of the gun.

Settled in and waiting, Sandal quietly asked, "Are you a military person? Ex-military? "

"Something like that," Brian said.

They waited. About ten minutes later, Sandal nudged Brian and pointed, whispering, "Two in the bush there." They could see their pilots' position and one of the pilots waving four fingers. Sandal waved back with a "hold it – not yet" signal and motioned that they had two showing at their end.

Cautiously, two Bolivian soldiers nearest Brian and Sandal eased out of the bush and began to come around the nose of the burning chopper. One gave an all-clear signal and two more materialized while the four near the chopper's tail cautiously moved in single file.

Sandal raised an arm to signal the pilots and they all opened fire. The surprise was complete. All eight Bolivians were shot down but not before some fired toward Brian and Sandal's position. Brian jerked backwards and crumpled to the ground, falling on his left side. Once Sandal was sure there was no more movement from the enemy, he turned to look at Brian, who seemed to be recovering consciousness but had a bloody forehead. Sandal held him down and looked at Brian's head, which had a bloody gash across part of his upper right forehead. The captain proceeded to grab the first aid kit, wipe away some of the blood and put a field dressing on Brian's wound. By then, Brian was conscious.

"'Fraid I got hit."

"You're lucky. It's a graze but head wounds bleed a lot. It's stopping now."

Wiping some blood out of his right eye with his sleeve, Brian struggled to a sitting position beside the machine gun and picked up the ammo belt, ready to feed it again. "Any more movement?"

"No. Seems quiet. Either they're laying low and regrouping or they were just a patrol. More will be coming though. Both sides will have heard the gunfire."

They waited. No more movement from the Bolivian side of the new border for ten minutes. They heard helicopters coming and waited. Friend or foe?

One chopper made a pass and Brian could see the Peruvian Army insignia on it. It turned and came in lower, this time raking the bush on the Bolivian side with machine gun fire. The other chopper joined in for a few bursts of gunfire before they both split off, one going north on the boundary and the other going south. They came back a few minutes later and Sandal cleared cover and waved. While one circled above, the other landed near the burning hulk and the crewman on the door gun waved for them to get aboard. Once they had loaded the body of Sergeant Garcia and climbed in themselves, they were quickly airborne and taken to the Peruvian Army Command Post. After Brian was attended to in the First Aid tent, they were escorted into the operations tent and paraded before Lieutenant General Blanco, the officer in charge.

Chapter 53

Although curious who Brian was, General Blanco didn't enquire any deeper into Sandal's explanation that they were observers for General Diaz. That prompted General Blanco to give a lecture on how the takeover of the new border had transpired, where troops were now positioned, and the strength of resistance they had encountered to date. Luckily, the territory was in dense bush with no civilian inhabitants, save for a few Peruvian mining workers at the mine site. Blanco was expecting more retaliation from the Bolivians and was well prepared for it. The fact that the Bolivians shot down a Peruvian Army helicopter and killed one soldier was adequate provocation for a pre-emptive strike on the Bolivian's main army camp. That was currently under way.

He dismissed Sandal and Brian and had them escorted to the airfield to await transport.

When Brian got back to the Canadian Embassy, the officer at the gate looked at Brian's bloodied bandaged head. "What happened to you?"

"Just a graze, they say. But I've got a bit of a headache, though."

"Shit!" He motioned for Brian to sit down and called for the medical emergency team. Then he called Maria Gomez, who arrived just as Brian was being coaxed to lay down on a stretcher.

She looked at the bandage. "What the Hell?"

"It's a bit of a story – but I'll tell you later."

In the infirmary, the embassy doctor removed the bandage, examined the wound and ended up putting in twenty-five stitches and prescribing a mild pain killer. Finishing up, he said, "So, somebody took a shot at you and I can't ask why.

You're a man of mystery for a diplomatic courier – a damn lucky one. Anyway, you're going to have a scar. You may want it removed with cosmetic surgery sometime. You've also got a concussion which we'll keep an eye on for a while. You're grounded until I release you."

News broadcasts the next day lauded the battle at the border, claiming over one hundred twenty Bolivian soldiers killed compared to only fifteen Peruvians. Broadcasters in Peru were adamant that their country was only enforcing what had been the traditional border for centuries, accusing Bolivia of trying to seize land only because of the potential for mining wealth. A few days later, a breaking news bulletin declared that Bolivia had surrendered its challenge and was standing down their armed forces, claiming the dispute was a matter for the World Court to be taken up after the Bolivian elections.

That afternoon, Brian was summoned to the Presidential Palace and met once again in private with President Mendoza. After enquiring about Brian's bullet graze, a pleased President Mendoza said, "Having been to the border, you can certainly verify the actions we've taken. Now that Bolivia has surrendered, I'm looking forward to my payment."

Brian agreed he could verify the new border and that Peruvian troops were protecting it. They placed a conference call to Messieurs Peter Monroe, Will Watson and the president of Oro Grande Minerals, who were all in a boardroom in Montreal.

They congratulated President Mendoza, thanked him for his services and authorized Brian to turn over the next tranche.

"I don't really expect any more conflict with Bolivia," President Mendoza said. "After all, our army is far superior in numbers of troops and equipment. However, the political situation, as you readily know, is unstable in Bolivia. I trust you are handling it from your end?"

Will Watson replied. "The three parties contesting the Bolivian presidency have all been approached. All accepted generous donations. Each presidential candidate has privately accepted shares in Oro Grande Minerals placed in trust accounts in Switzerland. I don't see any problems."

"Good! Good!"

"We want to develop a very positive image for the mine," Will continued. "Not only will we be hiring and training a few hundred Peruvian nationals as laborers and skilled workers, we're also sending you our mobile hospital aircraft and a medical team for a couple of months. It's a Boeing 747 converted into a surgery theater and recovery hospital. We want to position it at the closest airfield to the mine and make advanced medical care available to all civilians in the area. Of course, we'll be working closely with Peruvian medical personnel and inviting them to participate on-site. We'll even offer training in some surgical procedures, such as eye surgery."

"Excellent! I look forward to it."

"Please feel free to promote it as a partnership with your government," Peter said.

"Of course! This will be most welcome."

Will went on. "To smooth the waters in Bolivia, we have offered them the same arrangement and it has been accepted by all parties. They will wait to announce it until after their election."

Chapter 54

Montreal, Canada

Brian was escorted into the Board Room of Oro Grande Minerals where Will Watson and Peter Monroe were seated. They rose to welcome him, shaking his hand and motioning him to a seat. Peter spoke first. "Brian, we're very pleased with what you did in Peru. We're well aware you went beyond your normal governmental role."

"Yeah, Black Ops for the private sector," replied Brian, half in jest.

Will Watson laughed. "I guess you could see it that way! Anyway, in Peru you were dealing with the head of state on behalf of American and Canadian commercial interests, with facilitation by your own head of state."

"That's one way to look at it. But I almost got my ass shot off!"

"Understood," Will declared.

"And appreciated," Peter chimed in. He slid an envelope across the table to Brian. "Please consider this as a token of our appreciation."

Brian opened the envelope and glanced at the bundle of U.S. hundred-dollar bills.

"There's also a letter in there authorizing you an option on a thousand shares of Oro Grande stock," said Will.

"Thank you! Much appreciated."

Chapter 55

OFFSHORE TRUST AND LAUNDRY

Key Largo, Florida

"How did Brian get involved in that trust company?" asked Sanford.

Pete took a swig of his beer and laughed. "He knew some drug dealers and gun runners who had problems investing their profits – especially bringing cash back into America or Europe for legit investments. They had to keep their money in offshore tax havens and many of them were coming under the scrutiny of the U.S. Government, which was trying to stop the flow of drug money. And, as you know, these problems also applied to our own dark money operations. Brian's thoughts coincided with ours so we put him on the development team.

"He helped set up a deal where the operation would invest in a trust company outside America, say in the Bahamas. Trust companies are sort of quasi banks – almost all the functions of a bank but not as heavily scrutinized. In turn, that company would become a major investor in other trust companies or smaller banks in America. Quite a large portion of these trust company dealings were loans made in America guaranteed or underwritten through the offshore trust company. Funds did not have to be transferred into America unless there was a default because the American trust company or bank could borrow at wholesale rates from American banks on the strength of the offshore guarantees.

"Brian became one of the guys fronting the operation. He took some of the credit for conceiving it and attracting many of the investors. Most of his offshore investors hid behind numbered companies but were mainly big drug dealers and gun runners. In addition to taking shares in the business, they made very large deposits."

"Mainly?" Syd asked.

"Well, we provided some capital, expertise, a clean front and incorporation with impeccable credentials. We always maintain controlling interest. You know, a friendly clientele with money movement problems can come in handy in our line of business. Besides, it gave us a way to move some of our black funds too. Surprisingly, the offshore trust operation earned good profits for everybody – and still does."

PMO, Ottawa, Romance Languages Desk, 1986

Brian walked into Pete's office in the sub-basement of the PMO building. "Thanks for giving me a moment."

Pete took his feet off his desk and put his newspaper down, motioning for Brian to take a seat across the desk from him. "You said you had an idea?"

"Well, yeah. You know I'm between marriages and have been dating this woman across the river over in Hull who's an executive with D'Iberville Trust?"

"Yeah, that's Rose LeClerc, isn't it?"

"That's right! We've been going around for a few months. Anyway, she's been telling me a bit about how a trust company operates – at least in Canada. You know, they have similar function to banks but are not so heavily regulated. That got me curious so I've been researching it a bit."

"And?"

"Guys I've met – people in drugs, guns and black market money movement – say it's been getting harder to move funds into or out of America ever since the feds set up the clearing house inspection center in St. Louis that monitors all transactions. I think there's a way to circumvent that and make some money doing so."

Pete sat back in his chair. "Uh-huh."

"Maybe we could set up an offshore trust company or a bank to move and hide funds – even do some money laundering. From what I've seen, we could probably make use of something like that, too."

"Interesting. I can pass it on."

A month later, Brian was asked to join Pete in one of the conference rooms where he was introduced to Roland McIntosh and Dave Jennings, who turned out to be from CIA Langley. "The powers that be here decided your idea may be of more interest to our Langley friends," Pete explained. "It ping-ponged around there and the result is Roland and Dave are here to explore your idea."

"We did a little research on trust companies and the legislation they operate under here in Canada, in America, and in many other countries," Roland said. "We learned most of the eighty British Commonwealth member countries and the United States have similar legislation – all quite relaxed compared to the stringency applied to full-fledged banks."

Dave jumped in. "As you know, Langley has some operations best called 'on the fringe'" as they're outside of approved financial channels."

"Like moving drugs and money, owning business ventures and buying services you don't want people to know about," Brian said.

Roland frowned. "You know that's not to be mentioned. If anything, say 'black or dark' funds."

"Sorry!"

Dave went on. "Anyway, we've been thinking down similar lines – perhaps an offshore bank that we can control. At first glance, your idea of an offshore trust company, bank or near bank is interesting."

"We're digging into this," Roland said. "Brian, since a trust company was your idea, how would you like to be seconded to us for a while as part of a team to think this through? Maybe you can use this connection of yours, a lady friend we understand, to shed some light on the practical details of operating a trust company."

Brian looked at Pete, who nodded. "It can be arranged."

Chapter 56

CIA HQ, Langley, Virginia

A month later, Brian was in a conference room deep in the bowels of CIA HQ. Roland and Dave had amassed a six-person team, all of whom were eager to learn what senior management would say to their proposal. Rick Dunsmuir, a legal advisor, spoke for them. "Roland, you're keeping us in suspense. What's the word?"

"Well, our concept business plan for an offshore trust company has been approved in principle," Roland said. "That includes the tentative budget we proposed."

After some high fives and congratulations all round, he went on. "The fact that a trust company can be privately held was attractive. We are free to proceed with one in the Bahamas as we recommended. They also agree that we should seek to quietly purchase an existing entity with a sterling reputation to avoid attracting attention."

Rick Dunsmuir jumped in. "Since we forwarded our proposal up the line, my legal people have identified five potential candidates. We're currently discretely reviewing their business affairs and human resources."

"The idea of linking into banks or near banks in America and trust companies in Canada spurred quite a discussion at the executive level," Dave said with a smile. "We got a green light on that. Since the banking systems between Canada and America are different, they feel we can easily buy up some small banks in America, but this would be highly difficult in Canada. In Canada, purchasing a smaller-sized trust company would be the best route – as we recommended, I should note."

Caroline Weiss, an expert on international banking, jumped in. "I visited London and met with many of the key players in international finance. We should have no difficulty working with Lloyds for co-insurance deals or any institutions participating as clearing houses. Thanks to Brian, I met with some Swiss bankers in Geneva and made some arrangements for converting hard U.S. cash into gold and gold certificates. Brian feels that will be very important. Brian?"

All eyes turned to him. "Thanks Caroline. As you know, one of our greatest opportunities, and fears, is to be swamped by investors and depositors who bring us hard cash in great quantity. For example, Miguel Garcia, in Bolivia, has surplus U.S. dollars and seeks to deposit them – but many banks are now refusing to do so under pressure from Uncle Sam. He's talking a container load of U.S. dollars that he wants to put to work."

That raised some eyebrows. Barry McRue, a Chartered Accountant from the cash management division, joined the conversation. "From our point of view, we can make do periodically with large sums of hard cash for various projects. That gives us one advantage – for example we can convert Miguel Garcia's deposit of cash into a checking account for him to draw on."

Rob Jones, from the real estate division, smiled. "We'll require a fair-sized property with a huge vault."

"I was comparing notes with Ron Wong on the Asia and S.E. Asia desk back in Ottawa," Brian said. "He says the money market traders in his region have refined a system for physically moving hard currencies between countries. For example, there's a huge number of Filipinos working in Hong Kong and mailing Hong Kong dollars home. The recipients go to money changers to convert into pesos – it's a huge market for the money traders. There's a charter cargo flight out of

Manila once a week returning Hong Kong dollars to Hong Kong. It's all legitimate as a number of governments have signed approval. It's justified as a necessity and they have an association of currency traders operating it.

"He says there's something similar operating between Europe and the Latin Americas. Unfortunately nothing with India or the Communist states. I've got the name of the main contacts for Europe and Caroline and I have an appointment to see them in Geneva next week."

"Unfortunately, Uncle Sam will not go for that type of arrangement – it opens the door for free flow of dirty money," Rick mused.

Roland interjected. "But it's done among the European countries?"

"Yeah, but not with the ones on the other side of the Iron Curtain," Brian said. "Plus they work with all countries in the Americas south of Uncle Sam."

"Bingo!" Roland smiled and clapped his hands. "So our Nassau trust entity could become a member of the system?"

Caroline smiled. "That's why we're going to Geneva."

"Will it work for a Canadian trust company?" asked Dave Jennings.

"We're not sure, but we'll ask," Caroline said. "What, you're thinking of opening another back door?"

Dave nodded. "Yeah. A Canadian route for funds."

Brian smiled. "That'll come in handy."

Chapter 57

A month later, the group was reviewing progress. Rick Dunsmuir was excited. “I’m pleased to announce we closed the deal on Nassau Island Private Bank and Trust Ltd.”

After congratulations went around the table, he continued. “As you know, this has been a smaller operation with ownership tightly held by one family. I am pleased to say we outbid all other contenders in the estate sale and we now own it.”

“Now, we’ve got our work cut out for us,” said Brian. “We’ve got to get a takeover team in place and tie that in with the auditors.”

Roland smiled. “That’s under way but it looks as if we’re all moving to Nassau for at least six months. You’ve all been appointed to the Board of Directors. As the planning team, you won’t be involved in the daily operations. You’ll be steering the expansion.”

Rob Jones, always thinking of real estate, said, “Their premises are a bit small for our expansion plans. We’ll need to build a bigger vault.”

Barry nodded. “What about a separate building just for a vault in the new industrial zone beside the airport?”

“Good idea! Rob said. “It’s a free-trade zone. The local customs authorities won’t look at air cargo if it stays in the zone. I’ll get right on it.”

Caroline was thinking ahead. “What about the idea of picking up a small bank in America as a subsidiary?”

Roland nodded. “We’re cleared on that. You and Rick can start looking for a suitable first candidate.”

He turned to Barry. “It’s time to get some money into the entity’s coffers.”

Barry smiled. "We've paid the estate in full for the entity from one of our grey money accounts – a numbered double-blind account. Our ownership of Nassau Island Private Bank and Trust is hiding behind a numbered company registered in the Channel Islands which, in turn, is owned by a numbered company based in Belize. We need to supplement working capital to tie in with our business plan. I'm pleased to say we have ten million cash waiting to be deposited as supplemental startup capital from our grey operations accounts."

"OK," Roland said, then turned to Brian. "Brian, what about you?"

He looked at his notepad. "As of this morning, I have six people committed both to buy shares and deposit. That's six hundred thousand dollars for shares and six million for deposits. As you'd expect, these people are a bit cautious but are willing to take a fling because we've managed to get Lloyds of London to insure the deposits up to a million per depositor. They're content with the low yield on their deposit because of the insurance. By the way, this is all hard cash. I presume the existing vault has enough room."

"OK. It's a great start," Roland said. "Get the paperwork going. Work with Barry on that. Just try to get them to deposit bigger bills. I shudder at the likely space a million dollars in ones would occupy – probably well soiled and stinky as well."

"One other thing," Brian said. "They're all willing to buy bonds at LIBOR yield to help pay for purchasing the banks in America. Of course, they expect to get priority on loan applications there."

Caroline chimed in. "We've made arrangements in London and Geneva to deposit hard dollars and even buy gold bullion and other hard currencies. Both countries even have arrangements with the U.S. Treasury to return damaged U.S. dollars. That will really come in handy when Uncle Sam comes out with the new currency they've been talking about that will be harder to forge."

Brian looked at his watch and stood up. "I've got a plane to catch. I'm meeting with a Colombian drug lord in Antigua who's interested in moving some cash. Then, I've got a meeting in Trinidad with a Russian flying over from Cuba who needs to talk about moving some hard cash.

"I've met a couple of guys who've been involved in moving funds for some Latin American leaders – I've got a meeting with them arranged in Barbados to see if they're interested in bringing in deposits."

"Go to it!" Roland said.

Chapter 58

Key Largo, Florida

"What about the attempt to revalue the Georgian bonds?" asked Richard Duggan.

Bill laughed. "Yeah! That was a good one. We were watching that."

"Bullshit! I believe you guys engineered it!" Richard said.

Pete raised a silencing finger and looked at Sanford. "That project still needs deniability."

Sanford looked at the others. "I've been cleared on it. You're right that some of it is still classified, but the money trails are so ancient and buried so deep, the origins are impossible to trace. It was really two deals, wasn't it? The offshore trust company – call it laundry – and then the Georgian bond revaluation? The Georgian bonds deal is now history – forgotten history. Mind you, it worked. However, the trust company framework he helped set up is still functioning well."

"Brian deserved a lot of the credit for conceiving it and pulling together both operations," Pete said.

"He had some success with the Georgian bonds?" Sanford asked.

"You could call it that," Syd said. "You've got to remember that the Soviet empire had collapsed and the West was looking for ways to prop up some of the former Soviet countries – the ones that were leaning into western influence, like The Republic of Georgia. Read opportunity. Brian took advantage of that and skimmed a little money from brokering money laundering."

"How did that work?" Richard asked.

"It was pretty clever, yet simple, really. It was smoke and mirrors" Syd said. "And, you've got to give Brian credit for that. It was his brainchild."

"So, what did he do?" Bill asked. "Where did the Georgian bonds come into the equation?"

"That was a few years after the Nassau Island Private Bank and Trust company was well established with numerous branches both in America and many tax havens. Brian concocted the idea of getting the offshore trust company to place a value on the Georgian bonds if used as collateral."

"How'd he do that?"

"Simple," Syd replied. "The Republic of Georgia had defaulted on the bonds way back in 1917. When they went independent at the collapse of the Soviet Union, the International Monetary Fund was putting some pressure on Georgia to clean up old debts and improve their credit rating. Russia had done so by declaring its intention to pay so many cents on the dollar to buy up Czarist bonds from 1915. Brian copied the idea with a twist. He got the Georgian government to declare that they would honor the bonds if some were presented to them. Of course, they could only be surrendered to the Nassau Island Private Bank and Trust company for redemption."

"That could have been a problem. Did the Georgian government have funds to do that?" Sanford asked.

"No. Not for a large quantity. But before they stated they would honor them, Brian led a team that bought up the old bonds cheaply for the trust company. That in itself started to build the value of them. Anyway, he did a smoke and mirrors thing with a few of his drug dealer friends to buy some of the bonds from the trust company. They bought the bonds at face value plus accrued interest BUT they only paid a ten percent down payment. The rest was on a promissory note. In turn, the trust company placed the full value on their books to inflate their asset base. They then accepted them as collateral in Nassau against the drug dealers borrowing funds from the American subsidiary. That created a demand for the bonds from drug dealers looking for clean money. If ever there was a call by the trust company for full payment on the bonds, the trust company would accept hard cash."

Sanford looked at his empty beer bottle contemplating if he should reach for another. "Pretty neat!"

Pete continued. "Part of the deal was that the buyers could not try to cash them in with the Georgian government. The bonds had to stay with the trust company as collateral. That gave the trust company more funds on the books to invest and use as collateral and it gave the drug dealers a way to launder their money. It was truly just smoke and mirrors. The trust company used the funds to invest in their American banks and Canadian trust companies, which in turn gave preferential loans to the drug dealer/investors."

"And so, the Georgian government won brownie points with the International Monetary Fund and boosted their credit rating," Sanford said.

"Right! Brian made good bucks setting up the trust company and Georgian bonds deals. However, he got screwed on the next deal."

As Sanford helped himself to another beer, he asked, "I read a bit about that. I gather we weren't involved?"

"We weren't," replied Pete. "In fact we felt he was getting a little too rogue and needed to be taught a lesson."

"I don't remember that one," Syd commented. "What was it?"

"Well, he discovered some people were having trouble financing the working capital for exporting goods. You know, some countries, like Canada, have government agencies that will provide export credit insurance guarantees to get banks to finance the transactions. However, there are many countries that do not and, of course, there are some goods that don't qualify."

Sanford laughed. "Like illegal arms?"

"Yes. Well, Brian got the notion to create a monetary instrument as a guarantee to banks for financing. Of course, this was sold to the big drug and arms dealers as a way to make money by, quote, 'renting' the guarantee. These guys had huge funds and it was another way to launder them."

"So, what happened?" asked Sanford.

"Let's just say someone stepped in and convinced the world money markets not to recognize the financial instruments when some failed to pay off on a guarantee. We figure Brian lost quite a few million and had his reputation blackened with his drug dealer friends. He got thrown off the board of directors of the trust company."

Chapter 59

THE GOLD BUG

Key Largo, Florida

Pete ducked into the cabin and emerged with a bucket of Kentucky fried chicken. He helped himself to a leg and a paper plate to put it on. “Anyone else hungry? Help yourselves.”

Bill took another sip of his beer. “In the early eighties, he got pulled into a gold deal in the Philippines. Remember that one?”

“President Santos’ gold? That one?” asked Sanford. “There’s always been a lot of rumors circulating about that.”

Bill laughed. “Oh yeah! I guess we trained him well as he made a lot of acquaintances in the Swiss banks when he worked for us. It paid off for him.”

“He got pulled into it by a ‘gold bug’ on the west coast who claimed he helped President Santos of the Philippines find stashes of gold and gems the Japanese left behind,” Syd said.

Sanford asked, “Was this gold bug for real?”

“Oh, yeah. He loves to go by the nickname ‘Goldie’. He’s quite wealthy from his share of the discoveries – so is Emily Santos and the Santos family. Santos and our President Stewart were good friends. Goldie had been one of our guys so he had backup if he needed it – with the approval of our head of state, of course.

“Brian helped move some of the gold as it was more than a little complicated. People had to turn a blind eye to the point of origin of the gold because there are ways of tracing where it was mined and smelted. That’s where Brian came in.”

Chapter 60

GOLDIE IN LUZON
(Goldie Smithrite)

Caraballo Mountains, Central Luzon, Philippines, 1980

He thought, *it's a great way to stay in shape and it's still better than a long winter in Utah arguing with my ex-wife's lawyer and kids that hate me.* Even with a ten-man crew, it was hard slogging cutting a path in the tropical heat. They were barely carving three thousand feet of trail a day out of the jungle and they had two miles to go. Still, Goldie was happy he was taking advantage of the December to April weather window of Luzon's relatively short dry season. He would have hated to be struggling through heavy rain and knee-deep mud as well. Right now, he was just one of the crew with a machete chopping and hacking a trail through the dense brush and, in a way, enjoying the sweat and the slogging. The men were great – all hard-working ex-Army Rangers and members of his church. They were tough and loyal and knew how to keep a secret. He had managed to keep the team together through eight successful hunts over the past decade as he rewarded them well for their loyalty.

Goldie had flown over the region with the Aerial Ground Penetrating Radar (GPR) Mark III he had "borrowed for field testing" from his technology transfer company in Salt Lake City, Utah. Analysis of the GPR imagery revealed a long abandoned road reclaimed by the jungle – a path leading to his target. Now, he just had to follow that path – albeit overgrown – to the target zone.

The imagery mapping showed the road clearly beneath the overgrowth but in the years since the Japanese abandoned it in 1945, the vegetation had really taken hold. Bamboo, ever spreading and thriving in rich soil with heat and moisture, was embedded everywhere along with mahogany, dipterocarp and even a few oak and laurel trees signaling the transition to higher elevation.

They were following the overgrown remains of the roadbed winding its way up a box canyon, leading to a landing about two thousand feet higher up the steep mountain below an eroded volcanic cinder cone. Volcanic activity that had created the cinder cone had ceased millennia ago. Now, everything was covered in lush overgrowth.

Japanese photos and construction documents from WW II clearly showed the road, the landing, and a large building nestled below the cinder cone with fortified anti-aircraft and artillery gun emplacements embedded in and around the cone. That had spiked his interest and brought him here.

Goldie had parlayed his military-funded research at the university into a successful technology transfer company with advanced equipment capable of identifying and seeing through vegetation. Basically, he had only one customer for his GPR – Uncle Sam – since much of the technology was still evolving and highly classified. He had reduced the electronics to a compact package that was now on many satellites – both spy and commercial. For the commercial satellites, he was in a partnership with Uncle Sam that permitted the sale of some forms of imagery to select customers.

His gold hunting started as a hobby well after he had discovered how to “tweak” GPR resolution into identifying various types of vegetation and mineralization. With Uncle Sam, he had spun off a separate entity that sold crop analysis from his satellite radar imagery. It had proven profitable to commodity traders trying to predict crop yields and to government departments like the Drug Enforcement Administration (DEA) watching poppy production and postharvest movement in the Golden Triangle and Afghanistan – among other crops. His latest research was directed toward geotechnical analysis predicting oil and mineral deposits.

Between himself and the university where he was a senior professor, he co-owned over one hundred patents and was highly respected in the advanced imaging technologies field, which resulted in Uncle Sam allowing him some free reign.

Goldie was smart enough to recognize he was more inventor than durable businessman and had elected early on to assemble a professional management team to manage the businesses. That left him time to profess and time to invent. "Find a need and fill it" was a motto hanging on his office wall.

He caught the "gold bug", as he called it, when his marriage broke up. With the grinding divorce action depressing him, he wanted to get far away from Salt Lake City – to retire from academia and business and search for new adventure. Besides, his patents and the businesses had already made him a multi-millionaire – but his soon-to-be-ex wanted a huge chunk of that. Maybe a midlife crisis from turning forty added fuel to his wanderlust.

His latest imagery "tweaking" was enabling him to identify mineral deposits beneath an overburden. One experiment in the Nevada desert had confirmed he could find gold and silver with the new technique. That brought him today to the Caraballo Mountains on the island of Luzon in the Philippines, searching for yet another cache of Japanese gold.

He had been intrigued when Fred Deely approached him on a cold, snowy morning in Salt Lake City. The morning had started poorly with a demanding telephone call from his pending ex. She was really getting nasty, turning the children and her family against him. He was getting frustrated – and the overcast cold snowy weather didn't help his mood.

Fred, one of his contacts with the U.S. military who was responsible for overseeing the delivery of GPR units and software, brought up the proposition over coffee in Goldie's office. They had been discussing Goldie's success in finding gold in Nevada and selling the claim to a large mining company.

"One of my superiors was wondering if you could apply your technology to searching for caches of gold stashed away during World War II," Fred said.

Goldie thought for a moment. "Probably – but we'd have to know roughly where to hunt. We're well on our way to adapting the GPR to a portable version we can use on the ground instead of high overhead. It won't be capable of quickly covering large areas the way we can by flying over. It'll be slow but will penetrate deeper with more definition."

"It might be a good test for your equipment."

Goldie was pragmatic. "Yeah, but what's in it for me? I don't feel like hunting for gold for a lousy salary. Mind you, I'd like to clear the hell out of Salt Lake City – even America – right now."

"Well, there's a guy in the Philippines who can help make this happen that we can introduce you to. As far as we're concerned, whatever you do would be freelance – however, we'd benefit from you field testing the equipment and using that knowledge to improve or modify it. Anyway, you'd have to work out an agreement with this guy – probably looking at costs plus a percentage of the findings."

"Does this guy have any credibility?"

"He's already found over a thousand tons."

Goldie, just taking a sip of his coffee, choked a bit. "Say again? How much?"

Fred tried to keep a straight face. "Over a thousand tons."

Goldie leaned forward in his chair. "OK…"

"Plus, he's got some influence in the region."

"Tell me more…"

"Well, he's a Filipino national who led a rebel group – the Hukbalahap, or Anti-Japanese Army, fighting the Japanese in World War II. He was quite a diplomat who merged various splinter groups of rebels – left, center and right wing – into an effective resistance movement – with our help of course. He got a reputation as a real hands on fighter – a genuine leader."

"I heard a little about the Resistance Movement," Goldie said.

"Anyway, toward the end of WW II he led an attack ambushing a Japanese convoy and seizing a huge amount of gold the Japanese were transporting to a hiding place in the interior of Luzon Island.

"Since then, he's kept up searching for other gold deposits and even found some more. He's convinced there's lots more to find. He claims he's come across Japanese records identifying well over nine thousand tons of gold hidden on land and some on ships sunk in transit. Right now, he can't do it himself as he's pretty busy. He's looking for some help."

Goldie was hooked. "When can I meet him?"

"Oh, I should mention he's currently the President of the Philippines."

"Is this hunt going to be on behalf of the people of the Philippines or for his own personal fortune?"

"He's kept all he's found so far. But he has a reputation for looking after those who are loyal to him. He especially takes care of his old comrades-in-arms from WW II."

Chapter 61

Luzon, Philippines

They resumed cutting the trail shortly after dawn the next day. The crew had spent the night camped out in tents in a makeshift staging area they had cut out of the jungle, out of sight a few hundred yards in from the main road. Goldie thought it best not to attract too much attention from people traveling by, even though he had spread the word that they were a mining survey crew looking for a copper deposit.

At least the camp food was quite passable. He had a great cook, Len Jones, from New Orleans, renowned for his stews and home-baked bread. Goldie provided a sizable food budget as he didn't want any grousing over food. Overall, the camp was comfortable – as best could be expected in the conditions. They'd break camp and set up right at their target zone eventually.

Right now, the trail was following a fast-flowing creek leading them up a box canyon, one of many on the steep volcanic mountain. For now, until they had positive results from their search, the trail would be sufficient to bring equipment in by mules. Then, if things looked good, they'd bring in the heavy equipment to bulldoze the road and excavate.

He was thankful for the leads provided by some of the elderly men and women he had interviewed. He always made an effort first to casually meet the locals in the area and build a positive rapport before moving the crew in. Wherever possible, he sought out the chief of a village for his approval to interview the elders. Over the years he had learned Tagalog, the local Philippine language, and had also picked up some of the variant dialects, such as Ilocano and Bikol, which were found on other islands. He had also learned to read and write Japanese – both Katagana/Hiragana script and the Kanji characters adopted from the Chinese.

He found the elderly were most helpful for filling him in on local history. Relying on his presence being approved by the chief, he liked to drop in to a village's social gathering spot during the day when the able men and women were in the fields. Usually it was a bar or informal bar where elderly men would gather during the day to play cards, drink and pass the time. Most of the men loved to recount some of their wartime experiences and Goldie was a welcoming listener willing to buy drinks for stories.

Word of his presence usually spread quickly, drawing many of the elderly women as a white visitor was a novelty. Often their memories were clearer than those of the men. This had paid off many times with information helping to narrow his search.

This search had been no exception. Many of the elderly had stories of the Japanese building a road into the canyon – in fact, two had been enslaved to work on it and were fortunate to have survived as many from the village had paid with their lives.

The villagers were able to verify where the road to the target branched off from the main road but had never learned why the road was built in the first place. However, they knew the Japanese had secretly built something up toward the end of the box canyon which some assumed were anti-aircraft emplacements. The Japanese had demolished everything with explosives just before the end of the war. One man said there were volcanic caverns – lava tubes – near the end of the box canyon that his father had played in as a boy before the war, but for some unknown reason the Japanese had destroyed the entrances.

This day, great progress on the trail was being made. The dense bamboo-filled brush was starting to give way to large oak and laurel trees with less dense underbrush and a higher dark boreal canopy as they climbed in elevation. In spots, they could still make out traces of the original road.

Goldie had worked up a heavy sweat by midmorning when the crew took a break. As he crouched sipping from a canteen of water, he reflected on his first visit to Manila:

He had settled in to the Intercontinental Hotel in Makati District and managed to catch up on his sleep before he was contacted. A uniformed Army Colonel knocked on his door and introduced himself as Colonel Enrico Robles of the Presidential Guard. He had been ordered to collect Goldie and take him to the Presidential Palace.

After passing through security at the Presidential Palace, Goldie was ushered into a parlor within the presidential quarters and left to wait. After a few minutes a man entered from a side door and introduced himself a Leyland Santos, President of the Philippines. Santos was of average height and weight with a charming smile, good manners and an ability to make others comfortable. He was wearing a light blue elaborately designed Barong shirt of raw silk fabric interspersed with lace motif, loosely fitting and layered over a white tee shirt. The Barong served as a traditional formal garment, which he wore with dark blue suit pants and black penny loafers. Goldie knew Leyland was about fifty-five years old, married to a younger woman and they had three children.

After shaking hands, Leyland poured Goldie a rum and coke with ice into a cut crystal glass from the bar credenza, then motioned to take a comfortable seat on a vintage couch. He took a seat opposite and leaned forward holding his drink (Black Label Scotch neat in a cut crystal glass). He held up his glass for of toast before taking a sip. "Cheers!"

Goldie returned the gesture.

He looked Goldie in the eyes and smiled. "Goldie – do you mind if I call you that?"

Goldie shrugged.

Santos went on. "I like that nickname for a gold hunter. How'd you get it?"

Goldie took a sip of his iced rum and coke and smiled. "It partly goes with the blond hair of my youth and I was pretty bright in my university years, which earned me the nickname of 'Golden Boy' for my ability to get government research grants and patents."

"Interesting! Yes, I've heard about some of your work. I understand one of your companies has been trying to sell my government on crop yield analysis."

"I'm a little removed from that now, though."

"I understand you've been informed that I'm a gold bullion hunter chasing WW II Japanese gold?"

"And you're wondering if some of my technology can improve the odds of finding stashes of gold."

"Quite so! I have resources that can contribute to a partnership – such as access to archives and protection."

"And financing?"

"Of course!"

"On a fifty-fifty partnership?"

"No! But I can guarantee you would not have a chance to try looking on your own in this country. From the other side of the equation, my research suggests there's at least nine thousand tons of gold out there either buried in my Philippines or sunk in Philippine waters."

"That is certainly attractive. I understand you have already found some?"

"I have found over one hundred tons now in addition to what I obtained during the war. I know there is more – much more."

"Let's get back to the basics. What's in it for me?"

"All expenses, basic salary for you and your people. Fair rental fee for your special equipment and a performance bonus on what you find."

"A fifty percent bonus after expenses."

Leyland smiled and sipped his drink before looking Goldie in the eyes. "Five percent."

Negotiations finally settled at twenty percent. Goldie insisted on a legal contract enforceable in both the Philippines and America. Although Goldie insisted he would provide the exploration crew, Leyland was adamant he would supply a security detail from his Presidential Guard for both transport security and safely moving the findings. The president conceded that he would keep them at a distance yet vigilant and available.

Goldie's first hunt went smoothly. Within two months, he found a cache of three tons of gold bullion on the island of Iloilo. Since then, more gold was found in Bicol and Luzon – sixty tons to date. All was brought to the Presidential Palace and stored in vaults in the basement of the presidential quarters prior to dividing it up. Goldie often accepted equivalent value of his share in U.S dollars as Leyland cherished gold bullion and was prepared to buy from Goldie in dollars at the current market price. That enabled Goldie to pay off his men with cash bonuses and keep money on deposit in a tax haven. Leyland settled his accounts quickly, which boosted Goldie's confidence in him.

From his analysis of Japanese records, Goldie's current target was sizeable. The Japanese apparently had established a series of large vaults in one of the lava tubes in a box canyon complete with a hardened entrance portal and concrete defensive bunkers. He had even found the blueprints, material requisitions and delivery records for the construction. This made him feel he was really onto something this time. He had found no record of the Japanese moving cargo out of the area toward the end of the war.

A flyover with a GPR pinpointed remains of the cave entrance and defensive bunkers, revealing all had been destroyed. The cave entrance seemed to be well buried in rubble. However, his instrumentation identified gold about sixty feet below the overburden and he figured it would take a lot of gold to register. That got him excited.

Goldie's reminiscing was interrupted with a call on his portable radio. Len, the cook at the base camp, had a message for him. "Company coming your way. Probably ten minutes out. They're armed. Six of them. Young guys. Maoist headbands. I've served coffee and two are still with me. Don't think they're hostile. The leader asked to talk with you."

"Ten-four," replied Goldie.

He waved the crew over to gather round. "Company coming," Goldie announced. "Likely armed Maoists."

He motioned to Bill and Rod. "Fade into the bush with your rifles but don't do anything unless we get into trouble." They nodded and took off into the dense brush. Get back to work or at least look busy when they get here," he told the rest of them. "We've got nothing to hide. I want to see what they want."

A few minutes later, six men, all with vintage M-1 Garand WW II rifles slung over their shoulders, appeared on the trail. Goldie had placed himself at the rear of the bushwhacking team so that he would be the first to greet them. When they came into view, he paused with a machete in his hand and waved with the other. The greeting was returned by the first man whom Goldie immediately assumed was the leader.

When the men got closer, Goldie greeted the leader with a welcome in Tagalog, which pleased the leader who replied in kind. "I was told you speak our language."

"It has been a pleasure to learn it. My name is Goldie."

The leader nodded. "I am Sebastian. You are looking for something?"

"We're with a mining company searching for deposits of copper. Who do you represent?"

Sebastian pointed to his headband. "We are with the New People's Army."

"The NPA. I've met and worked with some of your people on the islands of Iloilo and Bicol," Goldie replied. "Are you from the taxation department?"

Sebastian laughed. "Indeed you have worked with our people before!"

"And, I know you are widespread, with most of the people in the countryside supporting you and the ideology of Chairman Mao. I want to co-operate with you and help support your movement – in return for your protection, of course."

"That is what we seek. How long will you be here?"

"Our work will likely take less than a month. After us, if others come, that's another deal."

"I see. There are eleven of you?"

Goldie nodded. “Eleven of us here plus the cook.”

“Then I want a head tax of a thousand pesos per man.”

Goldie smiled. “I paid only two hundred pesos per man in Bicol.”

The bargaining had begun. Eventually a deal was sealed with the leader telling Goldie he could be contacted through his father, who was the village chief.

Chapter 62

They had cut and slashed their way to a fairly high elevation when the roadbed leveled and turned a corner, then widened out at the end of the narrow canyon. After they cut some trees down to get a clear view of the mountainside, Goldie took his bearings off three points of land and referred to both his satellite imagery map and the topographical map he had copied from Japanese wartime archives. He figured they had reached the landing in front of what had been the entrance to the cave. Using machetes to clear some of the brush, they cleared the way to the base of the hillside of huge broken rocks which Goldie assumed were the residuals of a landslide created when the Japanese demolished everything. The Japanese had done a good job obliterating their work, but they found scattered remnants such as twisted rebar imbedded in concrete.

He set three of the men to clearing the brush from the landing area and sent the others back to base camp. Their instructions were to help Len break camp and bring everything up to the landing, where they would set up camp again. Luckily, they had six pack mules to move everything.

Over the space of a couple of long days, all underbrush in the former landing area was cleared away, revealing more landslide rubble at the base of the mountain. Referring to the Japanese topological map and construction drawings, they identified two bluffs above them that probably had held antiaircraft gun emplacements before being obliterated. Goldie used the bluffs as reference points to get a feel for where the main entrance likely had been.

Sitting around the campfire that night, Goldie held a strategy session. "Guys, we've got the landing pretty well cleared. Although I doubt there's anything directly below it, I'd like to set up the GPR first thing in the morning and run it over the level ground just to make sure everything is working well. Bob and Bill, you can handle that."

They nodded.

Fred Jones spoke up. "Goldie, it's more likely the cave runs deep laterally into the mountain rather than down. You know that from all our other work around lava tubes."

Bill Bellson jumped in. "Yeah, normally. But remember that test we did on the Big Island in Hawaii? The cave went straight down for sixty or seventy feet first before it turned lateral."

"Oh, yeah," Fred said. "I forgot about that."

"The aerial telemetry indicated metal behind the biggest rock-fall," Goldie said. "But it wasn't clear. There was a lot of steel showing though. We may be looking at a spot where the Japanese buried their heavy guns."

"It's going to be difficult but we can scan into that rock-fall," Bill said.

Fred thought for a moment. "We'd have to haul the machine up the rock-fall face with ropes. We can rig something."

"The Japanese destroyed everything," Len said. "They probably didn't have time to haul out the guns and ammo from the antiaircraft emplacements and artillery batteries. I'd bet it's all buried in the avalanche rubble. If so, the machine should pick it up."

Goldie agreed. "As old as it may be, there's always the possibility of touching off some munitions when we try to move debris. Everyone be careful."

The GPR was a bit cumbersome. The current model weighed over three hundred pounds and looked like a tin box, four feet wide by six long and two deep suspended on four big wheels. It had to be disassembled and transported on four mules to get it to the landing. In order to operate, it had to be placed and secured before the men could take positions twenty or more feet away while the GPR "zapped" the ground and produced a paper readout. It was also slow and quickly drained its batteries. As Goldie worked with it in field conditions, he began to mull over what he could do to improve it (he loved problems like that).

As expected, the survey of the landing showed nothing. Next step was to rig the machine with ropes and pulleys to move along the rock and rubble face of the mountain. The third day working along the wall of rubble produced some results. When Goldie looked at the printout of the latest sounding, he figured he had found the cave entrance. Now they had to remove the overburden – a huge task – but the GPR was indicating gold about a hundred feet in. He got some of the crew to start removing the overburden while he repositioned the GPR father along the cliff face at another rock-fall zone. He was partly playing a hunch – the Japanese blueprints he had obtained showed two entrances and several ventilation shafts.

The hunch paid off next morning when the GPR read-out showed a small tunnel, a ventilation shaft perhaps, buried under only a few feet of overburden. He called Fred over and together they began to remove the debris. Luck was with them as a big boulder had blocked the tunnel which prevented smaller, looser rubble from filling the hole. They managed to pry the boulder out and exposed the shaft. It was big enough, roughly three feet around, for a man to easily crawl into. Goldie grabbed a flashlight and entered with Fred following. After only about a hundred feet, the shaft ended in a cavern.

Goldie eased himself out, got to his feet and helped Fred emerge. They shone their lights around and revealed a large cavern, more likely a lava tube, running left and right of them into darkness and about fifteen feet high.

Goldie had a good sense of navigation and figured it best to go right first, which led them a couple of hundred feet toward what Goldie felt was the main entrance. They found a cave branching off to their right, advanced into its entrance, and shone their lights in.

Fred gasped as Goldie took a step backward. "Oh shit!" They were facing a huge gold Buddha looming out of the darkness, bright and eerie in its golden glow.

Fred took a moment to run his light around the effigy before checking out the entire chamber. "That took my breath away!" he exclaimed. "Is it gold or just gold plated?"

Goldie focused his light back on the statue. "I doubt the Japanese would have hidden a low-value Buddha." He went up to it, pulled out his knife and dug the point into one knee of the idol. It only scratched the surface, so he knocked it with the shank of his knife and got a solid sound. "I think it's all gold."

They moved further into the room, cautiously exploring. Behind the idol were stacks of wooden ammunition cases. Goldie gingerly tried to lift one, finding it very heavy. With Fred's help, he pried the lid and revealed a case full of gold jewelry. "Looks like Japanese loot," Goldie quipped.

Eventually, they made their way into another chamber filled with wooden ammunition boxes containing gold ingots. They glimpsed at three more chambers, all storing ammunition boxes, before their lights began to dim and they had to exit back through the ventilation shaft,

The rest of the crew gathered around when they emerged. Len was the first with the question everyone had on their tongues. "Well, did you find the mother lode?"

Goldie smiled. Fred laughed and said, "I guess you could say that. Anyone got a good idea how to move what looked like a twenty ton gold Buda?"

Chapter 63

Goldie left the men working on clearing the entrance, made his way back to Manila and booked into a suite on his favorite floor at the Intercontinental Hotel. As soon as he got into his room, he placed a call to Leyland and told the switchboard operator at the Presidential Palace that his call was Priority Four – a code he and Leyland had to indicate success.

Leyland quickly came on the line. "Welcome back! When can you get here?"

"I'm going to have a shower and change, I can make it in an hour and a half."

"I'll clear a half hour for you. See you soon."

They met in the president's music room. Leyland spoke first while he was pouring drinks. "I gather you found something?"

"Yeah. We estimate about a thousand tons of mixed bullion and jewelry – plus an idol."

"A thousand tons? You're almost equaling my record haul during WW II. Congratulations!" Leyland saluted with his glass and took a sip. "What's this idol?"

"A large Buddha which I estimate is about twenty tons of solid gold. It'll be quite an effort to move it whole."

"Not my religion. I've never heard of a big gold Buddha in the Philippines. It must have come from Malaysia or Indonesia."

"So, it's OK if we cut it up to move it?"

"No problem with me. Just keep quiet about it as my people of Chinese and Japanese ancestry could take offense."

"Of course! We'll cut it up and conceal the pieces from prying eyes. In addition to reporting to you, the main reason I'm here is that I need to bring in some heavy equipment to cut a road to the site for removing the gold. I'll also need security and trucks to haul out the treasure. But then again, I don't want to attract attention or incite conflict between the local Maoists and your forces."

"Go ahead and get whatever equipment you need. I'll ask General Mak from my personal guards to work with you – he will provide the security, trucks and troops for transport. I'm sure he can keep a distance from the Maoists yet ensure you are well protected without the locals becoming aware."

Goldie met with General Mak to work out a plan. Goldie would tell the village chief he had found a large quantity of munitions left behind by the Japanese. As the munitions were extremely sensitive because they were so old, he had called in the military to safely dispose of it. However, before that could take place, they needed to bulldoze a road. Goldie would suggest to the chief that the NPA members should lie low for the duration.

This worked well. An Army construction and demolitions contingent established a camp at the entrance to the box canyon and quickly completed the road. In the meantime, Goldie and his crew opened the entrance. Under the cover of darkness, General Mak supervised the transport of the treasure. As a parting note, the villagers were warned there would be a series of large explosions – ostensibly destroying ancient munitions – which would once again obliterate any trace of excavation and access to the lava tube.

Chapter 64

BRIAN

Manila, the Philippines, 1980

Goldie was waiting for Brian when he emerged from Customs and Immigration at Manila International Airport. Goldie was bald, in his fifties, ruddy-faced, stocky and muscular but short at five foot six. After a hug and a handshake, they made their way to the parking lot. "Glad you're here," Goldie said. "I need your help."

Brian, towing his suitcase, said, "The problem sounded pretty interesting on the phone. I stopped over in Geneva and made some tentative arrangements. Technically, I'm on leave but your three-letter friends back home told me to say they have your back."

"Good. Good! We'll get you settled in a suite at the Makati Intercontinental and you can tell me more then. Meantime, I don't talk in front of my driver."

"Understood."

"I've got you a suite on the VIP floor near mine. You'll even have butler service and all club privileges."

Goldie helped himself to rum and coke with ice from the bar fridge in the suite and settled into a comfortable chair. "When I mentioned on the phone that I need to move some gold with discretion, we don't have a small problem."

"So, what's the big problem?"

"President Santos hired me to do some treasure hunting for gold and valuables the Japanese seized during their occupation. There had been lots of stories floating about the

Japanese stashing gold and gems in the Philippines. I brought in a research team who searched Japanese records and confirmed their validity. The Allies executed a General Tomoyuki Yamashita here in the Philippines at the end of the war but he left behind records of seizing gold and jewelry not only here, but even in Malaysia and Burma. He was nicknamed 'The Tiger of Malaya' for being very harsh with the Malaysians. Apparently, a lot of gold and valuable jewelry seized here and from other countries was not moved to Japan during the occupation and wound up here for safe-keeping."

"And you and your team were able to track this down?"

"It took a while. Thankfully, I speak and read Japanese and Tagalog, the local Philippine dialect. We got ahold of Japanese documents from the war relating to the gold and jewelry and worked from there. It helped that we were able to schmooze with elderly Filipinos to get their oral history. Then the search had to be localized. That's where schmoozing with the locals really helped. Eventually, we narrowed in on a few general locations."

"You mean, like finding caves in the jungle? Maybe buried? Underwater? Lots of jungle and shipwrecks in the Philippines."

"Yeah. But you know me. I have a few tricks up my sleeve that I developed – let's say, perfected."

"Like what?"

"GPR for one – that's short for Ground Penetrating Radar. When I was a professor at Utah State, I had a contract with Uncle Sam that led to some patents on certain equipment."

"And you've now adapted something for civilian use?"

"Yeah. But, right now, I'm keeping it a secret. It's worked well for locating select metals underground."

"Select, as in gold?"

"Yeah."

"Congratulations!"

"Keep it quiet."

Brian helped himself to a beer from the fridge. "My lips are sealed."

"Well, to shorten the story, we narrowed down some potential locations and I brought in my machinery. We were pretty successful but we still have more to track down."

"How successful?"

"That's the problem. How can you move eleven hundred tons of gold bullion, some of it bearing Japanese, Malay, Burmese or Philippine markings from here in the Philippines to a Swiss bank and sell it on the world gold market without raising questions?"

Brian did a double take. "Excuse me. I don't think I heard right. How many tons?"

"Roughly eleven hundred. And, I shit you not. A good portion of this was a huge gold Buddha that we had to chop into pieces to transport."

"Ah! Add to that the ability to trace the gold's source with spectrographic analysis."

"Yeah, and the Santos family does not want it traced."

"They're going to keep it all to themselves and not return it to the people?"

"Got it!

"So, how're you covering your ass?" Brian asked.

"You mean, making sure I get paid and stay alive?"

"Exactly!"

"For one thing, there's more to find – there will always be more to find. I take a percentage of what we find plus they cover all expenses, including the wages of my people and a basic wage for me. Expenses I invoice monthly and they pay within ten days. So far, they've been great paying the finder's bonus. I can get it in bullion or U.S. dollars. I tend to take the U.S. bucks – it's easier to pay bonuses to my crew that way."

"Can you trust the Santos family?"

"About as far as I can throw them or as long as I'm valuable. They've got a lot of friends here and life is cheap if they want it to be."

"Not surprising." Brian went to the bar fridge and took out another San Miguel beer.

Goldie took a sip of his drink. "This isn't the first time Santos has been involved in finding Japanese gold. He was a guerilla in the resistance when the Japanese held the Philippines in WWII. There's a story that he hijacked a Japanese convoy transporting gold and got away with it. The rumors abound that he's a billionaire because of it. That may have whetted his appetite to search for more."

"Makes some sense."

"Yeah. He told me a little about it. I gather it was close to five thousand tons. And it seems he's got that safely stashed away in Singapore as it was moved out of here in the early 1950s and converted to gold certificates."

"Interesting," Brian mused. "Nowadays, that would be hard to do as the United Nations established a repatriation convention ruling that gold identified as conflict-related has to be returned to its rightful pre-war owners. And, pure gold ingots bear hallmarks of their countries and foundries of origin. Banks and dealers can face prosecution if caught with gold from conflict zones that is unreported. As well, technology has advanced to the point where analysis can identify a region and even the mine the gold came from. The authorities have really tightened up the movement of bullion."

Goldie nodded, sipped his drink and went on. "Santos has been in power quite a while. He's become autocratic and has been stifling unrest with an iron hand. He implemented martial law and is pretty tight with some of the generals."

Brian took a sip of beer. "How long can he last?"

"Good question. They – the family – recognize the problem and have been making contingency plans to get out of Dodge when the time comes. Our President Stewart is a good buddy with Santos and has offered exile in Hawaii if Santos leaves the Philippines cleanly – that is, with little or no bloodshed. Uncle Sam does not want to see a civil war or a Communist takeover."

Brian was skeptical. "Communists?"

"Yeah. It's been kept quiet but they're big in the countryside throughout the islands. It's quite a guerilla movement. Right now, it's estimated there are more than ten thousand under arms – and that's not counting the Muslim anti-government movement in the south on Mindanao."

"With your treasure hunting, surely you've met some of these guys?"

"Oh yeah! So far, I've been able to buy them off since they need money and arms."

"OK, now for the big question. What am I to do and what's in it for me?"

"We need you to move the gold to a Swiss bank and make it difficult to trace the origins of it."

"You want me to change the chemistry? Like, re-refine it with other gold to mix it up?"

"Yeah. Whatever. Just so long as it can't be traced back to the Philippines."

"I want expenses and daily wage plus a percentage of the gold value – either in gold or hard currency."

"Expenses are OK if pre-approved. A thousand U.S. dollars a day wages. Percentage? What percentage? I can't see more than a quarter of one percent." He rose and went to the bar fridge. "Let me get another drink before we get annoyed with each other."

"Two percent! Also wages on a 7-day week."

He thought for a moment before sitting down. "You're really driving me to drink." He took a big swallow. "Half a percent!"

The bargaining took a while. Brian had to call room service to have the bar fridge replenished and send up food. Eventually, they settled on a percentage and a plan of action.

Although not apprised in detail of the full extent of Goldie's problem, Brian had stopped over in Geneva to confer with one of his accommodating bankers. He learned the bank had a client who smelted precious metals and could discretely re-refine the gold. Brian had tentatively prearranged with the banker to trade some ingots of gold the bank held in its vaults for some of the Santos gold to mix in with the re-smelt to help obscure the source.

When he told Goldie about it he said, "They'll do that for you?"

"I've built up a good relationship. Besides, they take a fee for it. Looks like they've done it before."

"And I'll bet the gold seldom leaves their vault."

"Yeah, mostly they just move it around in the vault between customers. This bank is big in the worldwide gold trading market. The banker showed me one huge vault where gold is stored under various customers' accounts. It was awesome. When a client sells gold, most often it's simply moved to the buyer's storage locker from the vendor's locker in the vault. Very rarely does it leave the bank's premises."

"Good to know. The Santos family doesn't want the gold traced back to the Philippines. I'm sure they'll go for re-refining and the bank's fees for it. Now the next problem is getting the gold to Geneva."

"Yeah, who can we trust?"

Goldie looked at his near empty drink. "Air freight is the best bet but we can't put all the eggs in one basket. It would have to be multiple trips."

"And we provide our own security. No problem getting an armored car service from the bank at the Geneva end, but what about here in the Philippines?"

Goldie thought for a moment. "Good point. I've got my own guys, of course, and we can bring in some other mercenaries we know we can trust if we need to – but local Filipinos are a problem"

"What about military loyal to Santos?"

"A possibility. We can always ask Santos. It would be good if we could access an airfield without drawing any attention. He's got a following of generals who seem absolutely loyal to him. We also have the advantage that he's declared a state of martial law. Mind you, we can't trust his people to look out for us."

"Who do you have in mind for air cargo?"

"Well, a regular cargo line won't work too well. Maybe a tramp. You know, somebody like Ashok Gopal. You know, Cashmere Air? I hear he's flying 727s out of London now."

"I've never heard of him having a problem – at least concerning what I was involved in," Brian said. "By the way, where have you stashed the gold you've found?"

"Someplace safe." He laughed. "Quite safe. I'll show you tomorrow. Oh, by the way, we're meeting Leyland and Emily and a couple of their kids tomorrow at the Presidential Palace. They want to size you up. I'll pick you up about ten. Wear a suit and tie."

Chapter 65

The Presidential Palace was a sprawling compound of various buildings situated majestically on the Pasig River. It was a short distance from the Intercontinental Hotel in Makati but traffic had slowed travel to a crawl. They received preferential treatment and were allowed to park inside the fence near the palace proper.

A butler escorted Goldie and Brian to the Music Room. It was large and tastefully painted in mint green with white trim that Emily had selected. They stood and waited a few minutes before Leyland and Emily Santos made an entrance from their private quarters.

Leyland and Goldie shook hands while Emily fixed her attention on Brian. She wore a gold traditional Chinese ankle-length dress (called a Cheongsam) made of raw silk with an intricate dragon pattern on the fringes. Brian couldn't miss the slit up the side of the skirt seductively revealing her nylon-covered leg and a gold high-heeled shoe. Holding out her hand, she said, "Welcome to Malacanang Palace, Mr. West. Goldie has told us a lot about you."

Brian caught a whiff of her perfume, a light fragrance of Lily of the Valley. "Thank you, Lady Santos. I hope I may be of some service to you."

She looked at him appraisingly as they shook hands. "Indeed."

Leyland turned and shook Brian's hand. "Welcome, Brian. It's a pleasure to meet you."

"Thank you."

Leyland moved to sit on one of the armchairs that formed a cozy circle by the grand piano. "Please, please be seated." As they were sitting down, a young adult man and two young women joined them and were introduced as Tommy, Alma and Amy. Once everyone was seated, Santos went on. "Now, you and Goldie may fill us in on your ideas for moving our bounty."

Goldie sat forward in his chair. "We've discussed this at length. Brian has tentative arrangements to have the gold blended with bullion sourced from other parts of the world in order to make scientific identification of the source more difficult."

Tommy asked, "Where would this take place?"

"Switzerland," Brian replied. "There's a bank in Geneva that deals heavily in gold and will have it re-refined and blended with great discretion. You may also open an account with them to store your gold in their vault. With their trading activities, when and if you chose to sell some or all of it, the gold would likely only transfer to another locker within the vault and never see scrutiny."

"Excellent!" Leyland said as he looked over to Emily, who smiled. "Excellent! I presume for a fee, of course."

Brian nodded. "I'm sure you will find it quite modest."

Goldie interjected. "Sir, the bigger problem is logistics. We feel it too risky to place all eggs in one basket and ship everything at once. Better to have a number of shipments."

Tommy nodded. "Agreed."

Goldie continued. "My people, and maybe some others you trust, can accompany the shipments. We feel air freight is best and we suggest a charter company called Cashmere Air Cargo. We've worked with them before in similar circumstances. It's owned and operated by a Punjabi out of London."

"Reliable?" asked Emily.

"For our needs, yes," Goldie answered. "Also very discrete."

Brian chipped in. "The only thing we can't cover is logistics at this end. We need secrecy to move the gold and get it airborne – much of that requires your input."

"We will use a military airfield and my elite troops," Leyland said. "That can be handled."

Brian couldn't help but ask. "Where is the gold now?"

Goldie smiled and put a hand to his forehead.

Emily laughed. "Goldie didn't tell you?"

"I thought it would be fun to keep him in suspense," Goldie said.

Emily stood. "Come Brian, let me show you my shoe collection. I have over three thousand six hundred pairs."

A little confused, Brian stood and let Emily lead him through a door to the private quarters. They walked through a massive, ornately furnished bedroom and into a huge room lined wall-to-wall and floor-to-ceiling with racks of ladies' shoes.

Brian was dazzled. "Wow! Quite a collection!"

"Few people know that I own the largest department store chain in the Philippines," joked Emily. "It's one of my hobbies to collect them. I get them as samples or wholesale, unless I go shopping abroad and see something I like."

She led the way through an aisle of racks toward a door at the other end of the room. Entering the next room, Brian encountered a massive safe with a floor-to-ceiling door that seemed to take up one full wall. She led him into the open safe and pointed to a pile of hundred-kilo gold ingots stacked neatly in front of a pile of ammunition boxes that reached the ceiling. "There's what bullion we have so far. Those ammunition boxes are full of it. Goldie assures us there is much more to find."

Brian tried to throw out a joke. "I guess you can call this secure."

Emily laughed. "There is an active legend that Malacanang Palace has ghosts. One in particular, the butler of a president in the 1800s, seems to appear frequently. We've made a point of mentioning he has been seen often in the vault. Our people are quite superstitious, which helps with security." She laughed again. "We have a ghost on our side."

Brian looked at a few of the ingots. "I see your problem. The ingots have Japanese characters stamped in them."

"Yes. Some others molded with the stamp of the Bank of the Philippines, Burma or Malaysia."

When they joined the others in the Music Room, Leyland looked up. "Ah, we were just discussing the jewelry."

"Goldie didn't mention that," Brian said.

"Well, you see, there's also a large quantity of jewelry the Japanese seized during their occupation. We have it in another vault."

"Oh!"

Tommy interjected. "We've decided it's impossible to track down the rightful owners from so long ago. It's ours now."

Brian and Goldie remained silent.

Leyland turned to Brian and Emily. "Before you came back in, Goldie suggested it may be best to disassemble the pieces – take out the jewels and melt down the gold."

Brian nodded. "Unset gems and re-refined gold would be impossible to trace. Goldie has a good point."

Amy said, "I agree, but some of it is so pretty."

"Better to remove the gems and melt the gold," Tommy said.

Brian weighed in. "It would be best to dissemble the jewelry here before shipping. The bank we're using specializes in the gold market. Mind you, you can acquire personal safety deposit boxes where you could put gems and jewelry. In order to trade gold, the bank requires ingots for trading to be certified 99.95% fine. Crude ingots from melted-down jewelry – which is probably 22 Karat gold at best – would only be about 91% fine and 18 Karat is only 75% fine.

"The bank commonly accepts crude ingots of gold for re-refining. But I'm afraid they might raise an eyebrow if you sent them jewelry to dissemble for the gold. Best we do that here. We can always melt and cast the gold here into impure ingots for re-refining."

Brian could see he had their undivided attention. "Unset gemstones are no real problem. They're very compact to transport. Real colored gemstones like emeralds, sapphires and rubies – that is, not synthetic – have soared in value, making them very easy to sell. On the other hand, diamond cutting has changed over the years, increasing facets to make the gems more reflective. Old diamonds need to be re-faceted – but it can be done if you want to get a high price or really obscure them. Surratt, in India, is a good place for that. You must accept the fact that disposal will be at a base wholesale level – subject to negotiation – certainly not retail, which would be at least four times higher than wholesale."

Leyland looked at Goldie. "Can you handle this?"

Goldie nodded. "Yes, disposal is no real problem. However, you may wish to have your own people separating gems from the gold and recasting ingots locally. It's mainly labor and a little smelting knowledge which any goldsmith has."

Leyland said, "I will get someone, a local jeweler or goldsmith, to separate the stones and smelt the gold into impure ingots."

"There's another problem," Brian said. "I looked at some of the ingots. Nice that they have 99.5 percent purity stamped into them. BUT they all have either Japanese, Burmese, Philippine or Malay markings of origin stamped into them as well. The bank would be obligated to inform the UN if they showed up. I would recommend they be melted down here and mixed with the gold from the jewelry and we ship it all to the bank as impure ingots for refining."

"A bigger job," Goldie said. "Requires more people."

"I can get the people," replied Leyland. "I'll discuss it with General Mak and get back to you when we have made some arrangements."

Chapter 66

Goldie and Brian were seated in the main restaurant of the hotel having a late lunch. Brian looked at two men who had just been seated at a table nearby and remarked to Goldie, "I notice a lot of men here carry purses. To me that's a bit unusual."

Goldie laughed. "Notice each guy over there has their purse strapped to their wrists?"

Brian looked closer and nodded. "Uh-huh."

"They call them 'quick draw' purses here. They're armed. It's quite common. This country is like the old American Wild West. Guns and shootings are common. It's sort of good etiquette to keep your purse on the table where it's visible rather than on your lap. There's also a preference for large-caliber pistols – it's a macho thing."

Once they placed their order and the drinks arrived, Goldie leaned across the table. "What did you think of our meeting this morning?"

"First of all, who's this General Mac?"

"Oh, he's the head of the Philippine Army and head of the Presidential Guard. Highly trusted by Leyland. Likely, he'll supply the troops to do the job. I've worked with him. He seems totally loyal to the family and seems to have benefited from it."

"Do you trust him?"

"Not me. But Leyland does and of course…"

Brian cut in. "We don't trust Leyland."

"Right!" Goldie looked over at the two men with purses and frowned. "I'll get you a gun. We've always got to watch our backs out in the field. Would a Glock 40 do?"

"Adequate. Shoulder and belt holsters too please. I don't want to be obvious carrying a purse."

"I presume you still carry a dagger or switchblade."

"Yeah, a commando dagger – courtesy of Canada's Special Forces."

"Me too! An Uncle Sam issue though. With these guys, keep it handy."

Chapter 67

Brian was woken by the phone next morning. It was Goldie. "I'll pick you up at ten. We're meeting with Leyland and General Mak at the palace."

Leyland, Emily and Tommy were seated with a man in uniform. They stood when Goldie and Brian entered and Leyland introduced Brian to General Mak. Once all were seated, the president began. "We have resolved most issues. General Mak will provide the location and the people we need. He has also found a goldsmith who will direct the gem recovery and smelting."

He motioned to General Mak. "We feel it best to locate at a military base close to the palace," Mak said. "We have decided on a remote hangar on the military side of Manila's international airport. That way, your cargo plane can be brought right to the hangar for loading. It will be secure – guarded by my men. I understand you will provide security on each flight?"

Goldie nodded. "When can we start?"

"Tonight, during curfew we'll move some of the jewelry," General Mak answered. "We'll begin separating the gold from the gems in the morning. Tomorrow night we will move the ingots and begin smelting to blend the gold. Moving the cargo with army vehicles and an escort during curfew hours should go relatively unnoticed."

"Good!" said Brian. "We have spoken with Cashmere Air Cargo and they can have the first flight arrive in six days."

Leyland spoke up. "Confirm it then."

"They should plan on arrival and departure during curfew hours," General Mak said. "I will arrange special clearance for them when you give me further details."

"Once we get the flight arrival and departure worked out, I'll make tentative arrangements with the Swiss bank to have an armored car service meet the flight and take the gold for purification," said Brian. "Leyland, perhaps we can spend a few minutes for you to open an account or accounts with the Swiss bank? I'll help you on that. Then we have to settle a contract with the bank for re-refining and we must have that buttoned down before the cargo is in the air." Brian looked at his watch. "Allowing for time zones, the bank opens for business late this afternoon, so we should contact them then."

"Thank you. I suspect the cost of their discretion may be expensive. Do you think it's negotiable?"

"I'm sure they expect that but I can advise you a bit there. I've done similar deals with them before."

"You are becoming valuable, my friend."

Chapter 68

General Mak arranged passes for Brian and Goldie to get on the military base. He had the hangar well-guarded when they arrived in the morning and were escorted into the building. Inside, General Mak greeted them with a salute and handshakes. "Did you have any problems getting the cargo transferred here?" asked Goldie.

"Not at all. With the curfew, no one really cared about army vehicles on the streets. Here, let me show you around."

As they walked through the hanger, General Mak pointed out five men sitting at crude workbenches busily engaged in separating stones from the gold settings in jewelry. Beside them was a tall pile of ammo boxes which General Mak said contained some of the jewelry. Four well-armed soldiers stood nearby watching the workers. "The soldiers are here to keep an eye on the workers to ensure nothing is taken," the general said. "They have no knowledge of the quality of the stones. We've trained them only how to extract them from the mountings without too much damage. The goldsmith collects and sorts the extracted stones."

They watched the workers for a few minutes. "As you can see, there is lots to do," General Mak said. "We have more to transfer tonight. It will be a while to get through all of it."

Brian noticed some bunks and tables in a corner near a door labeled as a washroom. "Do the workers sleep here?"

General Mak smiled. "As we want high security, the workers here are all sworn to secrecy and are sequestered – confined – to this building until the job is done. As an added precaution, they are all uneducated farm workers brought in from a remote province and have been selected because they have no relatives or contacts in Manila. They will live, eat and sleep here with absolutely no outside contact. "

"Have you started smelting the ingots?" asked Brian.

"That process is at the far end of the hangar, where we've built ventilation for the ovens. Let's go over there."

They found a crude smelting system had been organized, with sand on the floors, a few crucible-type propane fired ovens made from bricks, and exhaust pipes running through the building's ceiling. "We found a goldsmith who set this up," General Mak said. "That's him over there." He pointed to a small, elderly man standing with four younger men – three soldiers, one a corporal, all standing guard. "He's waiting for you to show him how much gold from the jewelry he should mix with the ingots. He's already made some molds for pouring and we have a carpenter and blacksmith making more."

Brian and Goldie supervised the smelting and pouring of the first three batches of gold. Once Brian was confident the workers knew exactly how to mix the fine ingots with the jewelry-grade gold, they left.

A few days later, Brian, Goldie, Tommy, Leyland, Emily and General Mak were seated in the Music Room reviewing their progress. Goldie was speaking. "The men have the smelting and pouring of the ingots down pretty well. Right now, it looks as if we can produce close to forty tons a week of the re-cast ingots. We're only slowed down by the time it takes for the workers to extract the gems from the gold settings and sort the settings by Karat quality. The goldsmith was spending a lot of time sorting and appraising the gems but I told him to lay off that until after the gold is smelted. It can always be done later. However, they are separating what looks like diamonds into a separate pile. They can grade that later as well."

General Mak chimed in. "We're working the men twelve hours a day and that's about all we can get out of them. We could add more men and do another shift if you wish."

"How much jewelry do you have to process?" asked Emily.

"At the rate we're going, it will take about twenty more weeks," Brian replied

Leyland leaned forward in his chair. "Then add some more men. Let's speed this up. Are you still on time with the first shipment?"

"Yeah," said Brian. "Five nights from now."

"Good! I want Tommy to go with you. He can be one of the guards. He'll sign the papers with the bank on my behalf to set up the accounts and sign the re-refining contract."

Chapter 69

The Cashmere Air Cargo 727 freighter touched down a little after midnight. Air traffic control had it wait in the farthest taxiway for a few minutes until a military vehicle arrived with an illuminated "Follow Me" sign and guided it to a large hangar on the military side of the field. Once the engines were shut down and a stairway in place, a turbaned, uniformed East Indian emerged and descended to the tarmac. The white silk turban made him look taller than his athletic six foot two frame, and complimented his impeccably tailored uniform of tan dress slacks and powder blue silk shirt adorned with the Cashmere Air logo and captain's rank insignia. His black beard was neatly trimmed, which signaled to Brian that this man was not an extreme devotee to his religion's prohibition against cutting hair.

Ashok Gopal spotted Brian and Goldie and saluted crisply. "Brian, Goldie, my friends! So good to see you again!"

They shook hands and exchanged hugs. Ashok carried on. "Brian, I think the last time we were together was London, wasn't it?"

"Yeah. Great to see you again! I certainly enjoyed family dinner at your home. Is the family well?"

"Oh, yes. Rannie sends her best wishes. Both of the boys are doing very well in the RAF. They're both flying transports now. And Goldie, last time I saw you was here in the Philippines when I delivered some of your equipment."

"Right! Great to see you!" Goldie said. "Who's on your crew?"

"I'm lead pilot on the run to Geneva. The crew that brought us will hole up in a hotel here for the next flight. I've also positioned a relief crew in Geneva. The plane will turn around quickly but my crews need adequate rest. My brother Kamal is co-pilot and Jas Gupta is engineer and third pilot on this run. "

"Great! Well as mentioned, you won't be maxing out on cargo weight – just thirty tons but high value," Goldie said. "I'm coming with you plus three more for security. We have to do some banking in Geneva so three of us will stay over for a few days. We'll return on your next flight."

"Good! Our max is thirty-eight metric tons. This way, we can carry more fuel. Let's get refueled and loaded. May I ask what the cargo is this time?"

Brian spoke up. "You probably already guessed because our destination is Geneva."

Ashok smiled. "Cocaine and blue jeans like last time?"

"Nope! Gold. We'll be keeping you busy for at least thirty-five flights."

"That's fine. We frequently fly into Geneva. Never had a problem. We maintain our airworthiness certification with IATA and Switzerland recognizes it. Will we have legit cargo manifests stating gold as the true cargo?"

"Yes, as far as you want to know it's jewelry grade gold going to a smelter to be re-refined."

Ashok smiled knowingly. "Excellent! Let's get you squared away on board and you can introduce everyone accompanying us. As you know, we have recliner seats for four plus two fold-down bunks just behind the cockpit. We've got enough provisions in the galley for ten people for the flight.

"We've been cleared for a route to Dubai then into Europe. Weather looks good all the way to Geneva. We'll be stopping to refuel in Dubai.

"Also, I have a discount for you. As you booked us for thirty-five flights, I managed to get backhaul loads off the

Baltic Exchange for most of the runs. Most of the time we'll be bringing a cargo of Swiss cheeses back on the return leg."

Brian laughed. "Sounds good! Both Goldie and I will be coming along on the first run, as well as Tommy Santos and Fred Jones, one of Goldie's men who will be taking turns as security on the flights. Fred, Goldie and I will be alternating runs heading up security."

"Tommy Santos? The president's son? I spoke with him when we were negotiating the airfreight. He prepaid for the first six return flights."

"Yeah, he's got to do some banking and he's volunteered to help out on security."

"Are you bringing arms aboard?"

"Why, we've done it before with you?" Brian asked cautiously.

"No problem! As you know, we can hide the weapons in one of our secret compartments when we get to Geneva. You can have them again in Manila."

"Sounds good! We certainly won't need them in Geneva. Although I have to follow the cargo straight to the smelter and sign it in. We have the bank's armored car service and a limo meeting us at the plane."

"Although we've got three pilots who will take turns flying, we can't turn around as quickly as the aircraft. We need some rest. As I mentioned, another crew will fly back from Geneva while we rest up for the next flight. We can lay over in Geneva and fly you back here when the plane brings in the next load. The crew that flew us here will remain in Manila to rest up for another flight."

"Good! We'll get some banking done and return with you. I booked you guys at the same hotel as us. You got a favorite Punjabi restaurant or two in mind?"

"Of course!"

Brian smiled and slapped Ashok on the shoulder. "Good! I'm looking forward to helping you search for the world's best papadam cook!"

"Don't forget curry. I'm still searching for the world's best chicken curry."

The flight was uneventful. Brian, Tommy, Fred and Goldie managed to get some good sleep and arrived fresh in Geneva, where armored cars and a car and driver from the bank were waiting for them. The transfer went smoothly. With the car and driver provided by the bank, Brian, Goldie, Fred and Tommy followed the armored cars and oversaw the transfer of the bullion to the smelting company. Once Brian accepted a receipt, Fred, who was now familiar with the route and routine, took a taxi back to the aircraft for the return to Manila in order to supervise security on the next flight. The rest checked in at their hotel to freshen up and change while the car and driver waited to take them to the bank. They all dressed tastefully in suits and ties to visit the banker and follow through on details.

Although Brian and Goldie were well known to Claus Schmidt, the banker, Tommy was new. Brian introduced Tommy and got down to business. "Herr Schmidt, further to our discussions by telephone where I introduced you to the members of the Santos family, who opened an account for cash banking, gold trading and safety deposit boxes, Mr. Santos has completed the paperwork you sent. You will note the authorized signatures, his Power of Attorney and code words."

Tommy handed the paperwork across the desk to Herr Schmidt who took a few minutes to carefully read everything over. "It is in order. While my assistant is making copies, permit me to show you the vault with the safety-deposit boxes and explain how to gain access."

"Herr Schmidt, if possible, I would also like a tour of one of your gold vaults," Tommy said. "Brian has told me about your system and I would love to see it in person."

"Of course!"

He pressed a button on his desk to summon his assistant, who brought in a set of papers. "But first, we need to sign off on the contract for re-refining the gold." He handed each a copy of the contract for review. "You will notice the contract requires three parties, plus the bank to sign. You will also note that the distribution of the net proceeds in the form of re-refined bullion is to be divided among your three parties. That is, nineteen percent to Mr. Goldie, one percent to Mr. West and eighty percent to the Santos family."

"Net proceeds?" asked Tommy.

"Yes. You will have our various fees itemized such as armored car and limousine service, actual smelting, refining and certification, safe storage fee, transport from refinery to safe storage and, of course, the substitution of gold from other sources to change the chemical composition of the trace elements."

Brian chipped in. "We agreed to all this over the phone. I see no problem."

"Will you provide us with before and after assays?" Goldie asked.

Herr Schmidt responded. "Do you see a need for that?"

"I do. But not that I distrust the refining process here and your impeccable paperwork. We have an idea of what grade the ingots poured in the Philippines should be but we need a way to ensure someone is not substituting copper for gold."

"I see. No problem. We can also give you a quick turnaround on that. Perhaps a daily summary cabled when processing is underway?"

"Excellent!

Goldie opted to sell some of his gold for credit to his U.S. dollar account as he wanted to pay the crew a portion of their bonuses as soon as possible.

Back in Manila a few days after the first shipment, Brian and Goldie were in the hotel's bar having a nightcap. Goldie pulled out a telegram and handed it to Brian. "This just came in."

"Assay results on our first delivery. Interesting!"

"Your idea of getting the goldsmith to sort the jewelry by the karat markings and then proportioning in a ratio seems to work well," Goldie said. "There isn't much inconsistency to what you were estimating."

"There were mainly 22 and 18 Karat gold settings and the ratio I recommended with the pure ingots mixed in should get us near ninety percent purity. This says we're running eighty-seven percent. I'd say that's pretty good for such a crude operation."

Chapter 70

The next six deliveries went very smoothly. Brian, Goldie and Fred took turns accompanying the flights to supervise security and delivery. Goldie pulled in some more of his men to help, insisting that at least three of his men, all ex-US Army Rangers, always went with the cargo for security.

Goldie got tired of the routine after a few flights and turned security over to Fred and Brian to organize. Goldie elected to stay behind, saying he had another lead on a Japanese gold stash on Palawan Island and wanted time to follow up on it.

When Brian met him in the hotel bar for a nightcap after he returned from the seventh delivery, Goldie was sour-faced. "We may have a problem." He summoned the waitress. "Let's order first. I need a drink." After the waitress left, he passed a telegram to Brian and waited for him to read it.

"Sixty three-percent? Only sixty-three percent? What the hell? Somebody's sneaking copper and lead into the smelt. And not just one ingot or two, but twenty?"

Goldie said, "I'll call Tommy and arrange to meet with him and General Mak tomorrow morning."

Tommy was furious when he heard the news. General Mak looked shocked. Tommy angrily looked at General Mak. "Get to the bottom of this."

"Right away!" He stood up and left.

Reflecting a bit, Tommy said, "I've watched them putting the pure ingots and gold settings into the smelt many times. I guess someone could substitute copper or lead when nobody's looking."

"It would be hard to do with so many supposedly watching," Goldie said. "Maybe more than one involved."

"General Mak will take care of it," Tommy said in a near whisper.

A day later General Mak was waiting for Goldie and Brian when they arrived at the hangar. "I have news for you but I'd best wait for Tommy to arrive before I tell you."

Brian noticed the workers were very quiet, heads down and fearful. Some had facial bruises and black eyes. A few moments later, Tommy arrived and joined them.

General Mak greeted Tommy with a quick, respectful salute. "Sir, we have found the problem. After observing the workers all day yesterday, we caught the goldsmith substituting lead and copper for gold jewelry settings."

"Good work, General!"

"Under interrogation, he revealed a large stash of gold settings, mainly 22 Karat, hidden in his bed and in a toilet tank. He also had a bag of colored gems stashed in his pillow."

"Did he reveal where he sourced the copper and lead he used to substitute?" asked Brian.

"He did. I'm afraid he had four accomplices – two of whom were soldiers on the cooking crew who brought in the meals. They were bribed to bring in copper and lead."

"What have you done about it?" Tommy asked.

"I was waiting for you to arrive before I completed disciplining them."

Tommy nodded and General Mak motioned to a sergeant of the guards. In a few minutes, the elderly goldsmith and the two workers were brought in and made to stand before the men. All showed signs of severe beatings and were held up by Presidential Guard soldiers.

General Mak told the sergeant to assemble the rest of the workers and guards in front of the thieves. Once they were gathered, he shouted, "These men have confessed to stealing some of the gold and jewels. You will now watch their punishment."

As General Mak went up to the first prisoner, he pulled out his side arm, an M1911 Browning .45-caliber army issue pistol. He made a ritual of slowly slipping off the safety and chambering a round, then held the muzzle to the man's forehead and pulled the trigger. The guards let him collapse to the floor as they stepped aside and stood at attention. The second worker was writhing and pleading for his life but General Mak ignored his entreaties. With the man pinned between two guards, General Mak once again slowly brought the gun to bear at point-blank range and fired an executioner's bullet through the forehead.

He then slowly moved to face the goldsmith, who squared his shoulders, jutted out his chin and tried to stand tall while being held tightly by the guards. Through a bloodied and toothless mouth he managed to spit on General Mak, shouting, "Get it over with, you monster! You'll find your way to Hell." As he spit again, General Mak shot him through the left eye.

General Mak turned and faced the men. "This is a lesson to you all. This is the punishment for theft. You will also keep what has gone on here secret or you will die. Now, get back to work." He turned to the sergeant of the guards. "You will effectively dispose of the bodies. No trace, understand?"

"Yes, Sir!"

Brian looked at Goldie, raised his eyebrows and slightly shook his head.

"What happened with the soldiers who supplied the copper and lead?" asked Brian.

"They were disposed of last night. They were officially killed fighting Maoists in the jungle on the island of Iloilo. There will be an official memorial service for them at the army base in Iloilo."

"Did you see the look on Tommy's face when General Mak was doing his thing?" Goldie asked Brian over dinner at the hotel that evening.

"Yeah, looked like he was enjoying it."

Goldie nodded and took a sip of his drink. "Good that you're now supervising the blending of the settings with the pure ingots. I'll do that while you make the next delivery. Best to make ourselves necessary."

Brian, a little concerned, asked, "So how're you going to cover your ass when the job's done? Obviously the family and General Mak don't like loose ends and dead men tell no tales."

"Good point! I've got a lead on another treasure hunt. There may be a big stash of Japanese gold on the island of Palawan. I'm starting to play that up."

"Good! Play on their greed."

Goldie was serious. "General Mak's the one to worry about. He's sure to have his own agenda."

Brian nodded in agreement. "And he's their enforcer. Convenient to be able to blame a death on insurgents."

Chapter 71

The final flight went off without a hitch with Brian and Tommy accompanying the cargo. When they returned to their Geneva hotel after supervising the delivery of the gold, the front desk clerk had an urgent message for Tommy to call home. He took the message and went to his room. Brian was only in his own room a few minutes when Tommy knocked on his door.

"I've got problems. Dad has kidney failure and he's been hospitalized. Looks as if he needs a kidney. On top of that, there's been rioting against us that's getting stronger every day. The churches are supporting the rebellion. I've got to get home – Mom says to charter a private jet and hurry. I'm booked out with you on a commercial flight the day after tomorrow but mom says to get home sooner if I can."

Brian put a sympathetic hand on Tommy's shoulder. "I understand. I'll help you charter a jet. Ashok is booked to fly a run to Thailand tomorrow but I'll talk to him and see what he can do."

Brian tracked down Ashok and explained the situation. "Well, we're here and the aircraft is at the airport," the pilot said. "Only two problems: legally, we need another twenty-four hours crew rest or a new crew; and I've got to pick up the load in Bangkok. However, Manila isn't too far away from Bangkok. I can take you there on my way. It's not much to backtrack to Bangkok. I'll make my ETA in Bangkok if we leave during the crew rest period."

"It'd be great if you could do it," Brian said. "I'm sure Tommy will pay well."

"I'll fudge the crew's rest log somehow. But I want to be paid in advance with a bonus for all pilots. We can be underway in a few hours. Are you coming along?"

"May as well. You've got room and I've gotten used to your old bird."

Tommy quickly made a bank transfer to Ashok's account and everyone left for the airport.

They arrived in Manila just after midnight. General Mak was waiting for them on the tarmac as the back stairs were lowered and they descended. He saluted Tommy. "Sir, it's good that you're back! Your mother has been quite upset. Your father is in the base hospital here and your mother and sisters are with him."

"Thank you General, please take me to him."

General Mak had a car and driver take Brian to his hotel. He got a little sleep before he tracked Goldie down. Goldie had left a forwarding number with the concierge, who was helpful. "That's a number on Palawan, sir. He said for me to pass it on to you if you showed up."

Back in his room, Brian connected with Goldie. "Brian, you caught me at breakfast. Where are you?"

"In Manila at the InterContinental. I flew in with Tommy. He had to rush home because Leyland's sick."

"Yeah, and there's rioting in the streets. I'll meet you at the hotel this evening. We need to talk."

A little after seven p.m., Goldie knocked on Brian's door. As Goldie helped himself to a rum and coke with ice from the mini-bar, he began. "The unrest has been building. It's even pretty strong on Palawan. I hear there's a huge rally and march planned here for this evening. I passed a lot of people heading up EDSA Boulevard on my way here. The rallying point is the Bonifacio Monument at the Galleria shopping center about two miles from here.

"The Catholic Church is supporting it and making it a 'People Power' event. They want lots of people turning out and they want it peaceful."

"Best we hole up in the hotel for the evening then," said Brian.

"Yeah. I can't see Leyland remaining in power."

Brian helped himself to a beer. "I talked with Tommy this afternoon. Leyland's in pretty bad shape. He needs a kidney transplant – major surgery. He says President Stewart has offered the family asylum and there's a team of doctors on standby in Honolulu to operate on Leyland. I think they'll bug out tonight. However, the deal with President Stewart is that the revolution must be peaceful – no bloodshed."

"Speaking of that, where's General Mak in all this?" Goldie asked.

"Right now, I think he's leading his troops on EDSA Boulevard and trying to push the demonstrators back. He's pissed that Leyland has forbidden him to order the troops to shoot anyone or get aggressive in any way. He's claiming he can't turn the horde back unless he does."

"Typical!"

The phone rang and Brian answered. "Tommy! What's up? Wait a sec. Goldie's here. Can I put you on speaker phone?"

"We're leaving tonight," Tommy said. Two generals have declared they're with the people. It looks as if more will do so. So far, General Mak and the Presidential Guard are loyal and the Air Force general on this base is too. General Mak's going with us. We've got two C-130 cargo aircraft loaded with our stuff from the palace. We'll be leaving within the hour – while the attention is drawn to the rally at the monument."

They wished Tommy good luck and asked to be remembered to Leyland, Emily and his sisters. Tommy promised to send a check to pay for the outstanding expenses.

Once they rang off, Goldie tried the TV but found that everything was blacked out. They went to the hotel bar and found people listening to a radio station that had been commandeered by the revolutionaries, who were calling it "Radio Bandito". The commentators were good, so Brian and Goldie ordered dinner in the bar where they could listen.

They were nursing an after-dinner drink in the bar when the radio announcer said two generals had sided with the revolutionaries and brought their troops with them. At that point, soldiers were withdrawn from opposing the revolutionaries. The patrons in the bar were excited. Jubilant. People Power had won!

Next day, Brian and Goldie met for breakfast. "I see Leyland and family got off safely," Brian said.

"Yeah. Early this morning I talked with someone high up in the Catholic Church who said it's likely Corazon Aquino will be a very quick shoo-in to replace Leyland – you know, the martyr's wife. He's arranging for me to meet her but it'll be a few days after she's sworn in."

"Why do you want to meet her?"

"To carry on business. There's still treasure to find."

"You have any luck on Palawan?"

"Yeah! But it can wait."

Colonel Munoz found his way to their table. When they invited him to have a coffee or breakfast, he declined. "Thank you, but I've been up all night and would rather go home and find some rest." He put a bulky manila envelope on the table and produced a piece of paper. "Sirs, I was ordered by Tommy to deliver this and send him a receipt." He produced a pen and

Goldie and Brian both signed the paper acknowledging receipt of the envelope. He quickly left.

Goldie opened the envelope and peeked inside, then closed it. "I think we better examine this in one of our rooms. Your suite or mine?"

Once in Goldie's suite, he emptied the contents of the envelope, a letter and a bulky smaller envelope, onto the coffee table. Goldie picked up the letter and read while Brian tore the top off the inner envelope and spilled the contents – unset diamonds – onto the coffee table. Goldie handed the letter to Brian while he examined the stones.

Brian read out loud. "Dear Brian and Goldie, you both have been most valuable to us. Please accept the stones as a bonus for work well done. Signed by Tommy on behalf of the family."

Brian picked up a larger stone and examined it carefully. "Old-fashioned cut. I bet they figured it was too much work to get them recut."

"Maybe. But we know the pile of diamonds was much larger than this."

Thinking a bit while admiring some of the stones, Brian said, "Looks like about five hundred grams in weight. Most of the stones are between a quarter and one-half carat, but looks like maybe two hundred or so between one and two carats. I know a gem dealer in Surratt, India who would recut these, no questions asked."

"How'd you like to go to Surratt?"

Key Largo, Florida

"What ever happened with this Goldie?" Sanford asked.

"Goldie went on to serve two more Philippine presidents. He found a lot more gold. He's retired now and living the good life in Washington State." Pete said.

Chapter 72

PERU GOLD BONDS SCAM

Key Largo, Florida

Bill Mason looked at his empty beer bottle, tossed it into the trash bucket, and stood up to reach into the ice chest for a replacement. "Remember when he got sanctioned by the SEC?"

"That was in the mid-nineties wasn't it?" said Pete.

Syd reflected a bit. "Yeah, he was running with that Peruvian gold bond scam for a few years before the SEC caught up to him. Of course, he was the Teflon man and not too much stuck to him – probably because he was hiding in Canada. But he fouled up some of his friends."

"Did our agencies have anything to do with the Peruvian bonds?" Sanford asked.

Syd shook his head. "No. That was purely Brian and some of his fringe friends in the underworld. Mind you, we encouraged the SEC to shut it down as we were nurturing good relations with Peru at the time."

"How did Brian latch on to the bond deal?" asked Bill.

"He was friendly with an elderly woman in his church. She had recently become a widow when she came across a few of the bonds in her late husband's desk and asked Brian what she should do with them. He said he'd help her try to put a value on them."

Seattle, Washington, 1995

Brian was seated in his favorite Seattle restaurant at a window overlooking one of the many marinas on Lake Union. His luncheon mate was Nick Stephens, a tall, slim and trim ex-USAF fighter pilot in his fifties, now running his own boutique investment firm catering exclusively to select high roller clients.

Nick took a sip of his glass of water. "I did a little research after you told me about the bonds."

"Interesting?"

"Yeah, there seems to be about fifty of them still outstanding. Probably most got buried deep in personal safety deposit boxes or framed on walls and considered worthless. Apparently, even the Smithsonian has one. I was able to get a photocopy of the bond from them."

"Did you find the covenants of the bond?"

"Yeah, and you were right. There's a promise to pay the face value principal and interest in ounces of gold if the bond defaulted. You know, gold was selling for about twenty-two dollars an ounce way back in 1876 when they defaulted."

"The promise to pay in gold tells you how desperate the Peruvian government was for U.S. dollars when they issued it in 1875. They had defaulted on U.S. investors previously and they've done so many times since. They really had to step up to get a bond issued and sold in America back then."

Nick smiled. "Right now, Peru enjoys a very good credit rating on their sovereign debt – and they want to keep it that way. Someone claiming payment on these old bonds could be a bombshell."

"If we can verify the bonds are real, we could lay a claim in U.S. courts against the Government of Peru. After all, the bonds were printed and issued in New York and their face value is in U.S. dollars. Interest on that debt is significant when calculated over one hundred and fourteen-plus years."

"Ah, but you're missing something."

"What?" Brian asked.

"Remember, the promise to pay in gold if they default was specified in ounces of gold, set at the market price of gold at time of default. So, what's the price of gold today? It's been running around three hundred eighty dollars an ounce."

"Three hundred eighty-three dollars and forty-three cents this morning. I checked before I came here."

"If you calculate seven percent annual interest compounded on one thousand U.S. dollars over – right now – one hundred nineteen years, that's huge."

"After lunch, let's go back to the office and use a calculator," Brian suggested.

"No need. I worked it out before I came. One thousand dollars at seven percent interest compounded annually over one hundred nineteen years is just over three million – three million, one hundred thirty-eight thousand, one hundred nineteen dollars and ninety-eight cents."

Brian took a sip of water. "Significant in its own right. But payment upon default is in ounces of gold – the guarantee – so, what's that worth today?"

"Well, taking the price of gold on the date of default in 1876, which was twenty-two dollars and thirty cents, that's forty-four point eight-four ounces of gold. Today, that's worth seventeen thousand one hundred eighty-four dollars."

"But that's not counting interest. One could argue in the courts that the value of the gold should be compounded at seven percent for one hundred nineteen years as well."

"That's dependent on how you interpret the wording in the default section of the bond covenants. I'd say the chances of winning that argument are better than fifty-fifty," Nick mused.

Brian leaned forward in his chair. "Even if Peru repudiated the debt, there's still cause for a lawsuit in America as the bonds were printed, issued and sold in America to American citizens. That could embarrass the current government in Peru and probably hurt their credit rating."

"They could settle out of court just to keep it quiet."

"If we were to take an interest in playing with this, say embarrassing the Government of Peru into making a settlement to pay off the bonds, would it be worth the effort?" asked Brian. "Lawsuits like this can be very costly if they go to trial."

"Well, it starts by verifying the bond you've seen and, maybe in parallel, quietly trying to find out how many more still exist. Can you get me a photocopy of what your elderly lady friend has?"

"Sure. Would someone at the Smithsonian be able to tell us how many bonds were sold, and possibly to whom, way back in 1875?"

"It's worth a try. We'll also have to research correspondence between the Government of Peru and claimants to see if anyone has attempted to claim the gold value before. Maybe some were successful while others were ignorant of it. It's also possible a subsequent Peruvian government repudiated the debt. You never know."

"If it starts to look interesting, we would be best off trying to track down other bonds and buying them up before word gets around."

"We'd need a bankroll," Nick said. "We'd need money to grab some bonds. Then, there's the cost of certifying authenticity – that's not cheap, yet necessary for the courts. Mind you, the payoff can be huge."

"We can create a syndicate. We both know some high rollers."

"Will this old lady be willing to sell the bonds?" Nick asked.

"She's in my church and we're close friends. I don't want to get a bad reputation for cheating her."

"What about a formal contract bringing her into the venture? Pay her so much now – a token amount, say one hundred dollars, as if they're only worth selling to collectors as wall art – with a promise of say, ten percent on any net proceeds above the token value?"

"I'm sure she'd go for that."

Nick and Brian met a week later in Nick's office. He took a sip of his coffee before speaking. "I've been talking this up quietly among some of my high roller clients. So far, I have six interested to throw a few dollars into the pot to cover initial expenses."

"My friend who owns the bonds is quite willing to accept a thousand bucks for all five, but we signed a contract entitling her to ten percent of the net proceeds if we make any additional money on them. I've paid her and now have the bonds in my safety deposit box."

"There's a company in New York that authenticates old bonds but they won't value them. I contacted them and the fee for authentication would be twenty thousand dollars per bond."

"Ouch!"

"We must get one authenticated before we go any further."

"Who wants to put up the cash?"

"We should form a limited company – call it an investors' syndicate – to hold the ownership of the bonds, then sell shares."

"We can do that."

Brian took a sip of his coffee, thinking. "I wonder if we should approach the Peruvian government to see if they'll honor the debt. I know President Mendoza from a project I was on a few years ago. He's not my favorite character. He'd want a piece of the action if any were to materialize, but maybe we could accommodate that."

"Not yet, let's see if we can round up some more bonds on the cheap first."

Chapter 73

Seattle, Washington

Nick's business operated out of an old but well maintained house in an industrial/commercial quarter of Ballard. Eight members of the investors' syndicate plus Brian and Nick were gathered around a boardroom table in what was once the dining room. They were focusing on the speakerphone in the center of the table, listening to an authenticity specialist they had commissioned in Washington D.C. named Stanley Fellows. "Nick, since you called the other day, I've done a little research. The original bonds were signed by Manuel Frevre, who was Peru's ambassador to the USA at the time. He presented documents of authority from the Peruvian government and the documents are still on file. We'll have no problem verifying his signature on a bond since there are lots of reference samples."

Bill (Wild Willie) Goldman, a multimillionaire currency trader, leaned into the speakerphone. "Mr. Fellows, Bill Goldman here – who printed the bonds and how many were printed and sold?"

"Good questions. The bonds were printed by the American Bank Note Company of New York. That company still exists. In fact, they still have the original print plates and paperwork sitting in a vault. As far as quantity produced and issued, one thousand were issued – sold, that is – and six printer proofs were produced and are accounted for. A sample of the paper used was retained and there is also a record of who the bonds were sold to."

Brian jumped in with a question. "Stanley, have you got a handle on how many bonds are still in existence and the face values of them?"

"Difficult to say. Very difficult. Some went to merchant banks and it is possible to confirm if some of them were written off or destroyed for tax purposes. However, many will be sitting in safety-deposit boxes, as was the case for your friend, or as framed novelty pieces on somebody's wall. Others may have simply been destroyed by heirs who thought them to be worthless. From what I've seen so far, there's likely not more than two hundred or so around – if that. That's including the one in the Smithsonian. You'll probably be able to purchase a copy of the list of original subscribers, which may lead you to tracking down some of the current owners."

Nick interjected. "We now own twenty-three of them with ten thousand-dollar face values and we know of eight hundred that were written off and destroyed."

Stanley responded. "The next step for you will be to get them authenticated."

"Right!" Nick said. "We've formed a limited liability company for this syndicate. From what you've said, verification of the bonds should be straightforward. What are we looking at for cost?"

"Figure on what I quoted, twenty thousand dollars per bond. That gets you a guaranteed Certificate of Authenticity. When you go to court, all bonds presented to the court will have to be authenticated."

Heads were shaking around the table. Arnold Hare, a high roller who owned a large insurance company, jumped in. "We've agreed to have one authenticated. Then, if it's good, we can go further."

Stanley sounded a note of caution. "You must also bear in mind, our company only rules on authenticity. We will not assign or estimate a value."

Chapter 74

Lima, Peru

Seated around a coffee table in his luxurious office, President Mendoza was meeting with Juan Mendel, his Minister of Finance. Both were sipping coffee and passing the time with some idle chat while waiting for the butler to vacate the room. When he left, Mendoza got to the point. "Juan, I've had an interesting conversation with a fellow I met a few years ago. He's a Canadian who worked in their diplomatic courier service and was also linked to their secret services and the CIA."

"An interesting conversation?"

"Yes. This person took retirement when the cold war ended and seems to have become a financial opportunist. He approached me to enquire about our views on honoring some defaulted 1875 bonds that our government issued in America. He claims they were backed by a guarantee to pay equivalent value in gold bullion in case of default."

Juan leaned forward in his seat. "Such bonds were issued in America about that time, yes. But subsequent Peruvian governments repudiated the debt."

"I see. I know over the years we've struggled with federal solvency and there have been many other instances since then where we have simply defaulted on debt."

"We did, and that earned us a very poor credit rating that has taken us years to overcome. Right now, our country is considered well-managed financially and our credit rating is high – thus the cost of borrowing is low. Previous defaults are long forgotten."

"This man claims he has some of the old bonds in his possession and is seeking redemption – in gold or U.S. dollars for both the face value and accrued interest," Mendoza said.

Juan laughed and sat back in his chair. "How ridiculous!"

"He's threatening that a lawsuit in an American court will pull down our current credit rating and urging us to make a settlement."

Juan frowned and leaned forward in his chair. "A court in America, if they are willing to look at the case – and that in itself is a big question – may well side with the claim. However, the claim would only be enforceable in America."

"Would it hinder our ability to borrow on the American currency exchanges?"

"It could." Juan reflected for a moment. "Yes. And it would jeopardize our cost of borrowing on other world markets."

"Nuts! I guess we'll have to resolve this somehow."

"There are some precedents and options. The Republic of Georgia recognized some of their Czarist debt and boosted their credit rating by doing so. So did Russia – albeit a token value which they settled. On the other hand, we can simply say that's old history – we repudiated the debt long ago and it is a closed chapter of our history. "

"Do we know how many bonds that are outstanding?" asked Mendoza.

"I'll check."

Chapter 75

Three weeks later, President Mendoza was on the phone with Brian. "This line is secure, but I will have you on speaker phone so that my minister of finance can participate."

"I'm sorry I cannot provide a scrambler at this end but the line is secure," Brian said.

"We have discussed this matter. How many of these bonds do you possess?"

Brian bluffed. "Fifty-three. Plus, we will soon have options on another twenty."

"And what value do you place on these?"

"We calculated for a ten-thousand-dollar face value bond that, with outstanding interest, the value would be thirty one million, three hundred eighty-one thousand, one hundred ninety-nine dollars and eighty-four cents."

Mendoza took a deep breath. "I see. So this is what you want?"

"No. The covenants on the bond promise to pay in ounces of gold bullion – principal and outstanding interest. With the current price of gold today, that is fifty three million, nine hundred twenty-five thousand, four hundred fifty-three dollars and eighty-one cents. I remind you that this is for each ten-thousand-dollar face value bond."

Mendoza shook his head and looked at Juan, who did the same. "I see. So, you will take us to court in America to get a judgment that forces us, the Government of Peru, to pay such a huge amount to redeem the bonds?"

"That is correct. I'm afraid a settlement in our favor would upset the credit rating of the Peruvian government and make it more expensive to borrow on the international markets."

"The cost of a trial can be very expensive," Mendoza said.

"We have a syndicate of investors with very deep pockets," Brian replied. "We're prepared to go to trial."

"I see. Thank you for calling. We'll discuss the matter."

When he disconnected, Mendoza was livid. "I think that son-of-a-bitch is trying to get revenge for almost getting killed on our frontier."

"You said he got a scar on his forehead from a bullet graze," Juan said.

"Too bad he survived. That bastard!"

Juan got back to the problem. "There's no way we can pay off those bonds at face value plus interest – let alone at bullion value."

"I'm sure they know that. I assume they're willing to negotiate a value."

"But do we want to play that game? We're not sure how many bonds will surface."

"True. Let's step back a bit and research our adversaries. Let's get our people at our embassies in Washington and Ottawa to identify and profile everyone participating in this so-called syndicate."

Three weeks later Mendoza and Juan met with Thomas Houston, the U.S. Ambassador to Peru. He had brought along Meir Simons, his 2nd Secretary. After coffee was served and a little small talk, Mendoza got to the matter at hand. "Thomas, you must admit that relations between Peru and America have been excellent for quite a while."

"Yes, Mr. President. That is so."

"We have encountered a delicate problem that I hope you can help resolve. Deep in our history, back in 1876, the Government of Peru was encountering financial difficulties, so we sold bonds backed by gold in New York and ended up defaulting on them. We have been approached by a person representing an investor's syndicate in America demanding we honor our debt or they will sue us in an American court. The compounded value of the bonds would break our treasury if we were to honor them. As well, a judgment to honor them would be prejudicial to our ability to raise funds on the international markets."

"As you know, we currently enjoy a very good international credit rating built up over many years of fiscal responsibility," said Juan.

"Yes," Ambassador Houston replied. "In many respects, you have been a role model for fiscal responsibility in South America."

Mendoza picked up a file folder from the coffee table and handed it to Houston. "We have researched the parties in this syndicate. You will see there are two Canadians. One, the gentleman, is a former diplomatic courier who is now holding forth as a church minister in a New Age version of Christianity. The other Canadian is an elderly woman who is a member of his congregation."

Thomas Houston took a quick look at the file before passing it on to Meir Simons. "And the rest are Americans?"

"Yes – the leader of the syndicate is a stockbroker, Nick Stevens, with his own business based in Seattle catering to a select clientele," Juan said. "The rest are high roller clients of Mr. Stevens. You'll notice many of them have questionable backgrounds."

President Mendoza interjected. "On the surface, it looks as if this Nick Stevens is the leader, but I have encountered this Brian West, the Canadian, in the past. He's slippery. I think he's the brains behind the syndicate."

Ambassador Houston ended the conversation. “Mr. President, we understand your problem. I’ll see what we can do about it.”

Chapter 76

American Embassy, Peru

Thomas Houston and Meir Simons sat in the ambassador's office nursing coffees. "Meir, I discussed this with the powers-that-be in Washington," Houston said. "The Secretary of State says we are to help our Peruvian friends in any way we can. We will have the fullest cooperation from the FBI, SEC and your people to put the matter to rest. You're to go to Langley and brief the inter-agency task force that's been put together."

When Meir got to Langley, he was introduced to Gordon McKay, a CIA veteran assigned to lead the joint task force. As they settled with their coffees at a table in the cafeteria, Gordon spoke first. "We've been busy researching the backgrounds of all the members of that investors' syndicate."

"Anything interesting?" asked Meir.

"Did you know this Brian West is one of our retirees from the Cold War and still on call?"

"One of our guys?"

"He was mainly in deep cover for us as a diplomatic courier with the Canadians but also did some work, including wet stuff, with us in Central America and other places."

"Oh shit!" exclaimed Meir. "No, I didn't know."

"He got to know President Mendoza while doing some work as a diplomatic courier."

"Yeah, we gathered as much."

Gordon went on. "He got into, let's say, 'wheeling and dealing' in high finance while employed with us. He's quite a bright guy – very creative with money movement."

“And the others?” Meir asked.

“The only syndicate member who isn’t a high roller is an elderly widow up in Canada who wound up with some of these Peruvian gold bonds when her husband passed away. The rest have interesting histories.”

Chapter 77

Kelowna, Canada

Brian took a call from Nick. "Hey, Nick, it's four a.m., what's got you up so early?"

"Last night, the FBI knocked on my door and presented me with search warrants for my home, my office, my bank accounts and safety deposit box. They went through my house with a fine-tooth comb, same for my office. They took all my files and computers."

"Wow!"

"Then they took me downtown and grilled me. There were two guys from the Securities and Exchange Commission there as well. I got raked over the coals. They say I'll be charged with securities fraud – at the least, I've lost my broker's license."

"What for? What's it all about?"

"The Peru gold bonds. They're claiming what we've been doing is fraudulent."

"Ah, shit!"

"What's worse, they released it to the media as a warning to the public. It's national news – they're depicting it as a scam run by me, a licensed broker. They also named the other members of the syndicate and are alluding that they'll soon be charged."

"Have you seen a lawyer?"

"Oh yeah! He's of the opinion they may drop the fraud charges if I give the investors back their money. Some of them have been interviewed already by the FBI and SEC. A few are playing dumb, claiming they were duped and want their money back."

"But you've spent the money on making sure the bonds are legitimate, buying up bonds and incorporation and legal fees."

"Yeah, it sucks. Hey, what happened to 'WE'? You got me into this. They'll be after you too. They've got your name. You spent a lot of the money running around the country chasing down bonds and living high on the hog while doing it."

Chapter 78

Seattle

For stock brokers on the West Coast, their day is tied to the opening and closing times of the New York markets. Nick arrived at his office about six a.m. – nine in New York – prepared to make a few early trades. Since the SEC stepped in, his license had been suspended but he was making trades through another broker. He was shocked to find two men dressed in blue suits standing on his doorstep at that hour – he seldom saw clients at the office and tended to do so only after the trading day ended at two p.m. Nick pulled the office key out of his pocket as he approached the two men. “Gentlemen, what can I do for you?”

The tallest one, who seemed to be in his mid-fifties, spoke first. “Mr. Nick Stevens?”

“Yes. What’s this about?”

The younger one, who appeared in his mid-thirties, presented Nick with a business card. “I’m Bill Schroeder and this is Sam Renton. We’re from the Internal Revenue Service.” Sam also handed Nick a business card.

Nick did a double take. “The IRS? What’s this about?”

Sam Renton produced a document from his breast pocket and handed it to Nick. “This is notification that you have been selected for a tax audit. We’re following up on a complaint filed jointly by the SEC and FBI. As you are probably aware, we will review all your accounting and tax records for the past five years, for both your personal and business affairs.”

Nick stammered a bit, eventually saying, “My administrative assistant isn’t due in for at least an hour. I’m not sure where all the records are.”

"We'll wait in your office" Sam Renton replied. "You may want to phone her to come in earlier than usual, if you want."

"This stems from the Peru bonds situation, where the SEC sanctioned me?" Nick asked.

Bill Schroeder kept a stern face. "Yeah, let's say that drew our attention. By the way, the IRS takes poorly to people who try to hide money offshore. If you've been into that, you'd best declare it now instead of have us hunt for it and find it – the penalties will be much higher."

<u>Kelowna, Canada</u>

A week later, Brian took a call from Nick. "All of the bond syndicate members have been hit with IRS audits – to some, that really hurts. Goldman really got hammered, so far they're claiming he owes the IRS thirty million and they're still working on him. Norm Jones is in real trouble as they found he was laundering money through three numbered accounts offshore. They're after him for over a hundred million and also have a criminal case. They say he'll be lucky to get only ten years jail time."

Brian could only say, "My Gawd! That's awful!"

"They seem unable to come after you – probably because you're living in Canada. But one of them told me there's a warrant out for you. Any time you try to cross into the United States, they'll get you."

"But you, what about you?" Brian asked. "I would think because you were a licensed broker, you're likely to be squeaky clean anyway."

"You're right! I was just highly inconvenienced. They even reviewed my wife's tax records and she's pissed with me for that. Oh yeah, add in all of that negative press over the audit and my reputation is even muddier. I'm out of business, man. I've lost all my clients and I can't get brokers to trade for me. I'm not even allowed to invest my own money. I've gotta find something else to do."

Chapter 79

Seattle, two months later

Nick and Doris, his wife of thirty years, had lived in the prestigious Blue Ridge neighborhood of North Seattle for over twenty years. The kids had grown, graduated and started their own families – one in Portland, another in Dallas and the last in Memphis. The home was feeling a bit large and empty but Nick and Doris were well entrenched in the community, rubbing shoulders with Boeing executives and other corporate CEOs at the country club and church. The community could best be described as upscale, trendy and attractive.

They lived on a tree-lined street that was made up of half-acre lots. Their mid-century modern, two-story house was set back from the street with a double carport attached to the house and a seventy-five foot driveway from the street. Both property lines were planted with ten-foot-tall cedar hedges that provided privacy from their neighbors.

It was a fairly mild mid-afternoon in Seattle, with cloud remaining from an earlier rainstorm but a hint of sun peeking through. Nick parked his Mercedes in the carport and was closing the door when a pretty, middle-aged woman called him from the sidewalk, waved and approached. "Mr. Nick Stevens?"

Nick turned toward the woman. "Yes?"

She smiled as she walked closer. "Oh, Hi! I'm glad I caught you."

"Are you from the media?" Nick asked. "I don't know if I have anything to say to you."

They were a few feet apart now, almost face-to-face. "No, I'm not from the media." She raised a silenced pistol and shot him point-blank twice in the chest, then turned and calmly walked away while pocketing the pistol in her large purse.

Key Largo, Florida

"So, this Nick Stevens got nailed and hung out to dry by the SEC. Sort of a warning to others not to try the same thing?" asked Bill.

"Yeah!" Syd said. "It worked. The IRS even seized quite a few million from some of the players. Trouble is there are still some of those bonds out there. Maybe someday someone else will try to get a payoff."

"Didn't this Nick Stevens get killed a little later?" said Pete.

"Yeah. A hired hit. We're pretty sure it was a present from President Mendoza – and a warning to Brian.

Sanford asked, "What happened to all the bonds they collected?"

Syd took a swig of his beer. "Good question! You'll find one listed for sale on the internet. The vender has a certificate of authentication. He's been asking a hundred thousand dollars for it but there haven't been any takers in over seven years. And the SEC still has an active fraud warning published about the bonds – that's quite a deterrent."

Chapter 80

Langley, Virginia

Sanford was on the phone with Hayden Whitley, who was calling from London, U.K. "So our people had a look at Brian's safety deposit box in his Channel Islands bank," Hayden said "We used a court order and swore the bankers to secrecy on the grounds that it was a security issue. We examined and photographed the contents before locking it back up."

Sanford asked, "Was there anything significant?"

"Well, we found no secret documents, which leaves us to conclude that he was loyal in terms of not betraying secrets or using information for blackmail."

"That's good!"

"However, he amassed substantial wealth."

"Go on."

"The safe deposit box contained a quantity of very fine grade, unset one carat diamonds – we estimate their value at over five million dollars wholesale."

Sanford whistled. "Wow!"

Hayden laughed lightly. "That's what you Americans would say. Yes, a significant surprise. But that's not all. There were also six U.S. dollar-denominated bearer bonds of significant value and ten thousand shares of Oro Grande Minerals."

"How much, as you say, significant value?" Sanford asked.

"Three million face value plus accrued interest – approximately five million dollars. Plus Oro Grande Minerals stock valued today at two million."

"Oh!"

Hayden continued. "His bank account has seven hundred fifty thousand U.S. dollars in it. Our people sat down with the bankers and reviewed Brian's transactions. It looks as if he cashed one bond in the mid-1980s for a little over a million U.S. dollars and put it in an account from which he made modest withdrawals over the years. We also found a statement that he has two hundred ounces of gold on deposit in Geneva."

"Interesting! I bet I know where the gold came from. I'd appreciate a photo copy of the bonds you found. I'd like to check their serial numbers against some we acquired in the early 1980s, as Brian did some work for us back then that dealt with similar bonds. We always wondered if some things were never inventoried."

"Was this significant to your operation?" Hayden asked.

"I'd have to say insignificant compared to the huge sums involved. We'd see it as just a little leakage."

"May be best to let it rest. His bank account had some periodic new injections of cash in the late 1980s through 2010, then nothing since."

Sanford thought for a moment. "That sort of makes sense. He was retired from the diplomatic courier service and intelligence when the Cold War ended. We know that he was into some questionable dealings afterwards. However, he slowed down around 2010 when he had triple bypass surgery. Since then, he stayed relatively close to home in Canada in British Columbia's Okanagan region."

"Save for his annual trips to the Channel Islands to do some banking."

"Ah, yes."

"May I ask who inherits his estate?"

"Except for a token amount of a thousand dollars to his surviving son, it all goes to a charitable trust that purchases land and restores it to wilderness."

"I guess he didn't think too much of his kids or ex-wives."

"Looks that way."

Shirley called Sanford from Bellingham. After a few minutes commiserating on the weather in Bellingham and DC, Sanford filled Shirley in on what he had learned from Hayden Whitley. "That explains why none of his family stayed around for the Celebration of Life," Shirley said. "His surviving brother and two sisters showed up for the reading of the will but left right after. I don't think anybody was able to contact the one surviving son. We traced him from Victoria to Powell Street in the Skid Row district of Vancouver. His mind's pretty well fried. He wasn't with it."

"Such a shame," Sanford said. "His dad was a genius in some respects but it doesn't look as if that DNA was passed on."

"Bob went to the Celebration of Life. Brian's congregation put it on at a retreat property they have outside of Salmon Arm. It's a nice place, about a hundred acres on a hillside, treed and tranquil, with a conference center and accommodations for a couple of hundred. The event was well attended – overflowing with a real cross-section of people. The *Devil's Brew* motorcycle gang showed up in force with their Capo, Donny Fortunato, and his wife. The Midlake First Nations also showed up in force with Chief Hazel and Joseph Branson. As did the Chief and her people from the Salmon Arm tribe. Plus a dozen or so of the Vietnam War draft dodgers he brought in who settled in the area. Three shamans from the local indigenous tribes, who were close to Brian, attended along with two from the Navajo Nation. His core congregation, mainly women, was surprisingly sizable."

"All good intel, I guess," noted Sanford.

"Bob had a ball! He said the event started at two p.m., going through the night and into breakfast for many. Drugs, psychedelic herbs and booze flowed freely. The event started with a 'Talking Circle' where everyone held hands in a huge circle and took turns recounting some of their memories with Brian.

"They set up one small room as a prayer room, where the ritual involved people taking turns for the duration of the celebration continuously praying to honor Brian.

"Some dropped out and went home after the barbeque dinner but many, including Bobby, elected to spend the night in the dorms.

"In late evening everyone was invited for a 'Psychic Sauna' in the sweat lodge. Bob said they sprinkled moistened psychedelic herbs from the Navajo Indian Nation on the hot rocks. Bathing suits were optional. By that time, Bob had paired up with one of Brian's lady followers for the sauna and afterward. He said she gave a good massage and was very knowledgeable."

Sanford snickered. "That's our Bob, all in the line of duty!"

About the Author

C. Edgar North is a pen name for Glen Witter, who resides in the sunny Okanagan of British Columbia, Canada.

Glen retired from an eclectic career as a "workforce development" consultant that led him to work in over 30 countries. He is writing fiction under the pen name of C. Edgar North to maintain a separation from his many non-fiction publications.

Contact: cedgarnorth@gmail.com

Facebook: C. Edgar North

Books are available worldwide in e-book, hard copy and audio formats through major distributors such as: Amazon; Barnes & Noble; Indigo; Kindle; iTunes/Apple Bookstore; Amazon; Audible.com; Audible.ca; Copia; Baker & Taylor; eSentral; Scribid; Flipkart; Ciando and EBSCO.

Fiction to date:

Nighthawk Crossing
Blood, Fire and Ice
Nighthawk: African Ice
Nighthawk: Chief Hazel
Nighthawk: The Deacon

Look for C. Edgar North's next book coming soon:

LYNDA: THE ART FLOGGER

Lynda DuPont has a successful career as a Fine Art Auctioneer on the cruise ships until she marries the love of her life and settles on the island of Cozumel, Mexico. There she partners with her husband successfully growing a tourist diving operation, boosting local artists and raising three children. Tragedy strikes when her husband, Dan dies. She sells the business and moves to Bellingham, Washington to be close to family.

Eventually, she establishes as a famous art auctioneer in demand across America. She is approached by a Texan billionaire to help sell some of his art collection unaware he is a king pin in a Colombian drug cartel. As the DEA begins to investigate art sales linked to cocaine dealers, she is eliminated as a loose end.

The book is written with audio book production in mind with a series of short stories following events in her life.